SECRETS WE KEEP

NOLON KING

STERLING & STONE

SECRETS WE KEEP

Chapter One

"You'd be surprised what women will do — you're famous, and surrounded by book nerds. One of them just might want to ride the man who writes their fantasies."

John laughed, not buying a word his wife said. "You can google 'Harriet Noble' and see how slim my pickings are. She's the closest thing I've had to a groupie so far."

"You're going to the banquet? And you're signing copies at the publisher's booth?"

"Yes and yes. I'm doing everything in my power to find us another Harriet Noble." That got him the laugh he'd been hoping for. He knew Vicky couldn't help it, she got into a loop and couldn't turn her thoughts off. She was "working on it" with her therapist, but even the meds didn't always help. So it was up to him to bring things back to an even keel.

"I'm sorry, it's just that I know we can do better. But I also know that we can't get there unless you *want* to, so I need you to want it a little more."

"I'll do my best to want it more."

"Thank you, John. I love you. Now go have fun!"

Fun. Right. John hung up, wishing it was an option to say what he actually felt. That all he wanted was to hole up in his hotel room eating takeout instead of spending the night trying to be witty and charming to strangers. But despite Vicky's "groupie" comment — her way of saying sorry for what happened before he left — telling her the truth didn't feel safe. Not when she needed him to be the strong one.

He would go back downstairs and be charming to their fans. He wasn't breaking his promise if he took a little nap, was he?

When the piano notes started to tinkle forty minutes later, John got up, killed the alarm, and dropped the phone in his pocket. Then he went back to the conference, zipping up his jacket to hide his badge after a moment of indecision. Yes, he needed to mingle. But only *after* a drink first.

An hour later, John felt like a coward, sipping his second French martini in a pub called The White Lion while everyone else sucked down free drinks and made small talk at the end-of-fair mixer.

Small talk was the *Candy Crush* of conversation. So many people seemed addicted, and he would be thrilled to never play again. People thought it was a social lubricant. It wasn't. Small talk built a wall of triviality between people. You learned more by watching them from the edges of a crowded room than you did listening to them chatter about minutiae.

He was about to leave when the man two stools down started talking.

And talking.

And talking.

"But that's only on Tuesdays and Thursdays," he said to John. "On Monday, Wednesday, and Friday, I need to get there at least ten minutes early. Otherwise the class is full and I get fat!"

The old man guffawed, though this was no more humorous than any of the other absurdly mundane things that had already fallen out of his drunken mouth, seemingly without any filter for value. There was no way for John to enjoy the exchange, but he could keep himself from feeling suicidal if he turned it into a game. But it still felt easier than heading to the mixer and waiting for someone to recognize him. Every time the old man paused for a response, John answered him with exactly one sentence consisting of precisely five words.

He said, "I walk an awful lot."

"I can't walk for more than nine blocks because . . ."

If John was being completely honest with himself, the real reason he was still sitting there listening to this man blather, despite the dull knives of anxiety digging into the base of his skull, was the adorable blonde at the end of the bar who seemed to be . . . batting her lashes at him?

But no. That wasn't possible. Because John was a rumpled, middle-aged writer, and this was a woman in her prime.

She flashed him a smile. He blinked.

Me?

She smiled again.

The old man paused.

John guessed that walking was still the topic of discussion, so he said, "I trade out my shoes."

"Exactly! That's why . . ."

He pictured himself back at home, in his office, writing. Not one of the *Worse Than Murder* books with Vicky, but something of his own, where the characters had time to steep and he cared enough to dig sufficiently deep into the story to scratch the surface of his soul. A story about a man in the pub, wondering if the girl at the end of the bar was checking him out.

That fictional man would hold the girl's gaze deliberately, letting her know that he'd noticed. Then he'd grant her a quirk of the lips, to let her know he appreciated the attention.

John did the same. Research for the story, he told himself.

The blonde flashed what might have been the widest smile John had ever seen . . . aimed in his direction, anyway. She took the final swallow of her drink, set her empty glass down, then came over to sit between him and the old man.

The old man didn't seem to notice. Or maybe he thought his enthralling tale of family drama on Facebook had lured the blonde.

"I posted right back, told Mum to stay outta my business. Gave her a piece of my mind about a few other things she needed to hear. This was two days ago. Today, I log on and Facebook has removed my post due to 'bullying.' Can you believe that shite? *She's* the bully. I deactivated my account and am planning to file a lawsuit against Facebook for slander."

John looked from the old man to the blonde, who winked at him.

The man kept talking. "I don't understand why *I'm* the target here. Do you have any idea how many times I've reported violent videos? But according to Facebook that's not a violation of their standards . . ."

"Can I have a turn?" she asked John, in the same accent as the old man's, but on her, it sounded delicious.

"A turn?" John repeated.

The old man blinked. He actually stopped talking.

And the blonde said, "So I say, fuck Facebook!"

4

Then the old man slapped the table appreciatively and snorted.

John snorted too, but probably not for the same reason. He couldn't believe that this girl had caught on to the game he'd been playing.

She turned her back to the old man, leaning closer to John. "That was the worst. I was dying for you. Traffic, the weather, workout schedules, and Facebook. Those are the four worst topics, and he covered them in order."

"Hey lady —" the old man cut in.

"Don't 'hey lady' me, like *I've* done something wrong. This poor man has been stuck here for a half hour. Say something interesting, or get lost."

The old man grunted, emptied his glass, and left the bar.

John turned to her, laughing. "Thank you . . . I guess."

"Definitely thank you." Her accent was crisp, her eyes blue and inviting. "I had to help. I couldn't watch you suffer another second. Though I did like your game."

"I love that you noticed." And that she smiled at him like he was the sexiest thing she'd ever seen. It had been years since Vicky looked at him that way.

He shouldn't have been enjoying it, but he'd forgotten how good it felt . . . and if he was going to write that novel, he needed to remember life before marriage, didn't he?

The blonde tapped the top of John's conference badge, the edge barely visible above his jacket zipper, then opened her purse and showed him the corner of a similar badge.

"So, are you a writer? A publisher?" She laughed. "A wannabe?"

Good. If his name wasn't visible, then John could stay in character. "It's my first time at the fair."

"Mine too!"

"So, what did you think?"

"Of the conference? I liked it, I guess. I'm just trying to figure all of this out. I never would've gone if I wasn't in London. Did you hear Yardley Ross's presentation?"

John rolled his eyes. That Ross woman's presentation had driven him back to his room.

"Oh, so you're not a fan?"

"I'm not *not* a fan. But I'll admit to being sad if that's where the industry is headed. Algorithms. Ad stats. Staying *relevant* on social media, whatever that means."

"Well, I'm glad, because otherwise a girl like me would never have a chance."

She raised her hand and the bartender scooted toward them. "Yes, love?"

"I'd like another vodka tonic." She pointed to John's glass. "I see he's empty, but I'm not sure what the hater is having."

"I'm not a hater," John said. "But I'll have a French martini."

The bartender nodded and started pouring.

"A French martini?" She winked again. "That's not girly at all."

John was about to say *my wife likes them*, but then realized that this woman surely wouldn't want to know about his wife. Besides, the man in his possible novel wasn't married.

Didn't want to mess up his research.

"So why do you hate Yardley?"

"I don't *hate* Yardley," he said, "but did you know that her name isn't even Yardley?"

"Of course it's not. Who writes under their own name anymore?"

"Yes, but Yardley only picked her name because the first letters are —"

"YA, which is what her ideal reader is searching for on Amazon. You don't think that's smart?"

"Well, sure, it's *smart*. But is that what we're going for here, crafty naming tricks? As storytellers, shouldn't we be committed to telling the best possible stories, instead of trying to manipulate search results?"

She shrugged. "Everyone's trying to crack the code in the post-Amazon apocalypse, aren't they?"

"I remember when an author became successful because an editor loved their work."

"I've had editors love my book, but *still* not touch it. Because everything right now is a gamble. A girl like me deserves a chance, don't you think?"

"Just because everyone *can* publish doesn't mean that everyone *should*. If you keep writing great books, someone will eventually publish you."

"Spoken like a traditionally published author."

"I'm not a traditionally published author," John lied.

"Oh?" She raised one eyebrow. "I've been wrong before, I just wasn't expecting it today. Help me adjust, darling. What is it you do?"

She touched his chest again, not tapping this time, but pressing the flat of her hand over his heart just long enough for him to feel the heat from her palm. He wondered if her accent would have made him want to kiss her, even without the two drinks. Or maybe it was the fact that she'd smiled at him more in the past ten minutes than Vicky had in the past ten years.

This is research, he reminded himself.

What would the man in my story say?

"I write for TV. I produce occasionally, too."

"TV? Wow, that's impressive. Network or cable?"

"Streaming."

"Anything I know?"

"Well, right now we're working on getting the rights to Felix Blanchard's last book, *The Crimson Keep*. Netflix wants to turn it into a serial." It felt good to be someone else, if only for a moment. John held out his hand. "Grayson James."

She laughed like his name was a punchline and held out her hand. He took it and the opening line of that story popped into his head, a gift from his muse. No, from *her*.

He felt electric when she touched him, as though a circuit inside him had finally closed.

"I'm Lottie," she said. "And it's really great to meet you, Grayson James, even if you don't know shit about self-publishing."

She laughed to let him know she was joking, leaning in to rub her hand on his shoulder.

Something inside him sparked. Lit up with megawatt intensity.

The bartender set new drinks in front of them. Lottie downed hers. John sipped the fire to its finish.

They ordered another round.

Then another.

"So, Grayson James," Lottie said, looking down at his ring. "Is Mrs. James waiting in your room?"

Grayson's next words were trapped in his throat. Was this gorgeous creature really hitting on him? Of course she was. Because everyone loves a producer.

How far was he going to allow himself to fall into this flirtation?

For research, of course.

"Mrs. James and I aren't exactly getting along right now."

The corners of her mouth turned playful. "Do you want to talk about it?"

"Not even a teeny, tiny bit." John smiled. "How about you? Ever been married?"

"No way, it's too much fun being single. Have you ever Tindered?"

"I've heard the word, but it scares me." Another laugh. "Tell me about it."

"Thanks to Tinder, Millennials no longer have to suffer the endless game of going to bars and getting rejected in person. Now we can craft virtual profiles with surgical precision, and post selfies taken at the perfect angle. That's how all those dating apps work, but Tinder does one better with the swiping. Now when you're looking for someone to date" — her delicious accent fell to a whisper — "or let's be real . . . to *fuck* . . . you swipe through a bunch of selfies until you see one that makes you wet. Well, not you. Me." Her laugh was like music. "You reject or like someone with a swipe, then send messages to the people you like."

"That sounds terrible." John gestured at the space between them. "What's wrong with this?"

"This is . . . wonderful. You're right. Much better than Tinder."

"Is that where you're hoping to find Mr. Right?"

"Oh *God*, no!" Lottie slapped the bar. "Tinder's all about hooking up. That's what your twenties are for. Sex is currency. You want to earn and spend as much as possible while you're young. Otherwise, the rest of your life you're likely to feel trapped." She glanced down at his ring. "No offense."

"None taken," John said.

"You have to remember, at any given time on Tinder there are tens of thousands of girls who are all DTF."

"DTF?"

"Down to fuck."

"*Oh.*" The way she said *fuck*, like it was her favorite word, softened and hardened him.

"If you're a good-looking girl, you're going to have a

ton of guys messaging you, so getting good dick is easy. Tinder's the most superficial app out there, which is also what makes it the best."

"For getting the good dick?"

Lottie laughed, the musical sound sweeter each time. "Like I said, my twenties."

He didn't want to leave, even for a second, but the pounding in his bladder insisted. "I'll be back."

Lottie looked down at their empty glasses. "Shall I refill us while you're gone?"

That would be a terrible idea.

"Maybe one more?"

"One more sounds great," she said. "*If* I can order you a man's drink."

John laughed. "I'll be right back. Order me whatever you want."

In the men's room, reeking urinal cakes dragged him back to reality while he pissed.

What the fuck am I doing?

Fishing for attention. Pretending to be Grayson James not because he needed to research a novel he'd been longing to write, but because something inside him was dying.

He wasn't imagining it — Lottie was into him. And her attention felt good. It had been rough with Vicky for too long. He wasn't sick of the ups and downs so much as the flatlining attention. He was jerking off more now than he had as a *teenager*. Before marrying, they'd had sex almost every day. Then a few times a week after Dakota was born. After Evie, it'd stagnated to one or two begrudging times a month if he was lucky. It had been a long six weeks without his wife's most intimate warmth when John — quite reasonably, he thought — requested a blowjob before leaving for London.

But Vicky got offended that he had the nerve to ask. Then he'd exploded, unleashing everything he'd kept bottled inside for years. His furious resentment at Vicky for all the things she wouldn't do anymore, for all the excuses she made when he wanted some physical affection, for how distant she kept herself. Vicky cried and told him that he wasn't being fair — he didn't understand what it was like to be a woman, and he was clearly watching too much porn.

But all John really wanted was to be wanted. And as he'd stood in a long line waiting to board his plane to London, John had wondered if Vicky cared about his needs at all. These days, everything was about her. She needed quiet. She needed pills to quiet the chaos inside her head. She needed him to deal with people and money and paperwork and all the normal, everyday things that somehow had become too overwhelming for her to deal with.

It wasn't fair. He'd given his wife everything, and she couldn't even give him a quick blowjob.

And now here was this woman — laughing at all his jokes, touching his shoulder when she wasn't touching his knee, and seeming to hang on every word he said.

He tried not to think about her teasing the top of her blouse, then shimmying out of it, her breasts tumbling into view as she laughed.

That laugh.

He tried not to think about her licking her lips and falling to her knees.

"I wonder," she would say in that delicious accent, *"do Americans taste different?"*

He tried not to think of her crawling on all fours, looking back at him, her silken hair spilling over her face.

Do you want to put it in my arse, John?

And that brought him back.

Because he wasn't John to her. He was Grayson James.

John shook the final few drops onto the cake and squeezed the erect tip, his dick now firmly on the launch pad and awaiting a countdown.

Put it away, asshole. That's only trouble.

After staring at himself in the mirror, and splashing ample cold water onto his face, John got his gut and his heart to agree. He wouldn't be sleeping with Lottie tonight, even though she was making it clear that she would be "DTF." He just wasn't —

Do you want to put it in my arse, John?

John swallowed. Then he took out his phone and scrolled through some photos. Dakota on her last Halloween trick-or-treating, and Evie on her first. Last Christmas, everyone in their Santa hats, Evie chewing on wrapping paper. The four of them saying goodbye at the airport. His family. He wasn't going to mess that up, no matter how good it felt to flirt with Lottie.

He dropped the phone in his pocket and headed toward the door.

No, he wouldn't be leaving with Lottie. But he would be finishing his drink. Because it felt good to know that he *could* sleep with her if he wanted to, and that he was making a choice in remaining faithful to Vicky.

John just had to stay long enough to prove that this wasn't just idle flirting, and that it could go all the way if he made a *different* choice.

He sat next to Lottie at the bar and looked down at his drink. "So, what did I get?"

"An old-fashioned."

That was the last thing he remembered.

Chapter Two

John blinked.

The world was refusing to reveal where he was, and last night wouldn't come into focus.

He looked around. This wasn't his room.

It wasn't even a hotel room. The comforter was caramel-colored and the walls a dusty blush, hungry for fresh paint. A cheap dresser beneath the window held a jumble of feminine items, and the window revealed an impressive view of a filthy alley. It looked and felt in every way like a working-class girl's London flat.

Despite the empty bed beside him, John had little doubt as to that girl's identity.

But he still didn't remember how he got there, or what he might have done. The last thing John could clearly recall was walking back to the bar from the bathroom, having made a clear choice.

But somehow, he'd made the wrong decision despite himself. And now, here he was.

Vicky. Oh hell. I'm such an asshole.

Bladder near to bursting, he sat up and grabbed the

edge of the blanket. First the bathroom, then he'd figure out what happened to his clothes.

"I thought I heard you stirring in here!" Lottie said, practically skipping into the room, wearing nothing but pink panties and a matching cami.

"Good morning." Because what else could he say? *Thanks for what will undoubtedly be my life's biggest regret?*

"Good morning!" She scrambled onto the bed and planted a wet kiss on his dry mouth, and he struggled not to recoil. She didn't deserve his condemnation — it wasn't her fault he was feeling horribly guilty.

"I didn't wake you," she said, "but I was starting to wonder if I should. In case you had a plane to catch."

A moment of panic. "What time is it?"

"Almost noon."

"Noon? Shit. Yeah. I gotta go." His plane didn't leave for another twelve hours — red-eyes were half the price. "Must be London, or all the alcohol. I've never slept this late in my life. I'm more of a 'no later than seven' kind of guy."

John flipped the covers off and swung a leg onto the floor. Oops, he was naked.

"There he is!" Lottie laughed and leaned down to kiss his flaccid cock.

John blanched, pulling back and then away, blushing. Vicky had never been so playful. "Sorry, I—"

"You sure didn't mind it last night." Lottie laughed again. A conspiratorial chuckle. As if they'd shared some sort of grand secret, in addition to sharing their bodies with each other.

"So we . . . ?"

"Are you kidding?" Another laugh, back to loud. "Three times — and I was sore after two. You definitely know how to drill a girl."

It was ridiculous, but some part of him had been hoping that they hadn't, that he'd stayed faithful to Vicky. *Right, who doesn't go home with a gorgeous stranger for an innocent, drunken snuggle every so often? His wife would totally understand.*

"Drill a girl?"

"Yeah, love, you just kept on going. Or, coming, I should say. And just so you know, your dick is perfect. I'm not into really big cocks. Too much and it hurts. I was with a guy once, his dick was like a baby's arm. He couldn't fuck my mouth without making me want to throw up. But yours . . . I got the whole thing in there, and swallowed every drop, just like you asked me."

Lottie licked her lips and winked.

And his flagging cock began to stir.

Vicky never talked like this, no matter how many times John had asked her to.

Begged her to.

Guilt grated against his arousal, making him sick to his stomach. Or maybe that was the hangover. "I must have been really drunk."

"Oh yeah, you were drunk. But no whiskey-dick for Mr. Grayson James! You kept saying you were going to 'take advantage of London . . . just like Chandler and Monica.' Then you told me all about *Friends*, since I'm apparently the only one in the world who hasn't seen every episode twice. Even though I've only seen a few, I'm *sure* that Chandler never did *that* to Monica."

Another laugh, the loudest so far. John didn't want to know what "that" was.

Except that he kind of did.

And even without knowing, he was sure that he'd like to do it again.

Except that he couldn't. Not now, not ever.

I am such *an asshole.*

But in a way, it seemed a fair punishment for having cheated on Vicky: getting to do everything he'd ever wanted in bed with Lottie, but not being able to remember a single moment.

"I'll be back," John said. Then he planted both feet on the floor and walked to the bathroom naked.

He peed for what felt like fifteen minutes, then gave himself the stink-eye while washing his face.

He needed to get out of there *now*.

But when he walked back into the bedroom, Lottie was on the bed, naked, her legs an open "V" of invitation. "One more for the road?"

His body responded even as his brain demanded flight. He'd been dreaming about this exact scenario for months. Fantasized about meeting a groupie in London, someone in love with his work, impressed by him, willing to not only listen but to hear every word. But that was only a fantasy.

Besides, Lottie didn't know who he was. She was admiring something he'd only made up.

She could *never* discover the truth.

"I'm sorry," he said. "I'm glad that we got together last night, but . . . I'm married. I really shouldn't have done this, and I really can't do it again."

"Are you kidding?" She grinned, her legs not closing, but spreading wide as she arched her lower back. "You weren't concerned with Mrs. Grayson last night. You kept telling me all the things she won't do. She's never let you in her arse. 'Not even once!' you kept saying. And she won't let you lick her twat, except you called it a pussy — and you also said that she hated that word."

John wanted to get back into that bathroom. This time to throw up. Somehow, *I am such an asshole* didn't quite seem to cover his self-evaluation.

He swallowed bile and guilt, then drew a deep breath.

He reminded himself that he was thousands of miles from home, and tomorrow there'd be an ocean between him and this lone indiscretion. As long as Lottie didn't know his true identity, he would be safe. His marriage would be safe.

His family would be safe.

"I was obviously very drunk. And you're very beautiful. You made me laugh harder than I have in a long time. And I'm sure we had an even better time when we got back here to your place. But —"

"You don't remember any of it?"

"No, I'm sorry. I wish I did. Believe me."

"You don't have to wish . . ." Lottie spread her legs. "You could stuff your cock inside me right now."

"Lottie . . ."

"I want you, Grayson. We connected last night — not just our bodies, but our minds. I've had a lot of men. But never anyone like you." Her expression strobed from seductive to pouty. "If you're going back to America and back to your wife, then I guess I just have to face that reality. But please, can't we just have one more time for the memory banks?"

He'd already fucked her. Three times, apparently. What was the difference if he gave in now and did it once more?

The difference was that last night, he'd been drunk and not quite aware of what he was doing. At least not enough to stop. He hadn't meant to cheat with Lottie, he'd only meant to enjoy a brief flirtation before heading back to his room.

If he gave in to temptation this morning, he'd be making a deliberate, cold-blooded choice to betray his wife.

Okay, maybe not cold-blooded. But if he couldn't

claim that sleeping with Lottie was a drunken mistake, what kind of husband did that make him?

She traced one nipple with the tip of her finger as he hesitated, then did the same to the other. "Pretty please . . . with sugar on top?"

John spotted his khakis, draped over the back of an armchair. He grabbed them and put them on, tucking his growing hard-on to one side to keep it from getting caught in the zipper.

Wanting Lottie wasn't wrong, but having her was.

"Really? You're going?" Her pout got sexier as she looked up at him, trailing a hand down from her nipple to . . . John looked away.

"You *can't* go. You told me that I was special last night. That I was the kind of girl you could start over with."

John could never have said anything even remotely close to that. "I never should have done this. I'm *married*."

"I know you're married, Grayson. Do you know *how* I know?" Now she was pouting for real. She waited a beat, though the question was clearly rhetorical. "I know you're married because you wouldn't shut the fuck up about it. At the bar you told me you were married, on the way here you told me you were married, and when we got back to the flat you told me you were fucking married. Do you know when else you told me you were married, Grayson?"

The question sounded like a threat. And every *Grayson* was a slap to his ear, a reminder that he hadn't just cheated on his wife, he'd also lied to the woman he'd cheated with. There was no way he wanted to hear the answer.

But Lottie gave it to him anyway.

"When I was bent over the armchair and your face was buried in my pussy. When I was looking back at you over my shoulder while you were fucking me from behind. And do you know when else you said it? When you told me that your wife wouldn't let you come in her mouth. *Well, I let you come in my mouth, Grayson!*"

Lottie was practically screaming.

And then she was back, her voice silky and soft like some sort of sexy switch had been flipped. "And you can do it again if you want to. My mouth, my back, my face . . . wherever you want. Give me one more time before you go. I want you. I need you. Please —"

"No, Lottie. I can't. I . . . I have to go home."

The words were painful to say with so little blood in his head, but they still felt right on his tongue. Lottie was one of the sexiest girls he'd ever seen, certainly the hottest to ever give him the time of day. And here he was, rejecting her, refusing her, slamming the door on fantasies he'd been having for months.

Because he couldn't do that to Vicky.

No, he couldn't do that to himself. This was not the person he wanted to be.

Lottie jumped off the bed and started dressing, panties first. Her eyes were dancing and she seemed seconds away from letting him have it. He almost wanted her to. Almost.

"Look," he said, walking over and taking her hands, looking into her eyes, softening his voice. "It isn't you, I promise. You're right. My wife doesn't do a lot of the things that I wish she did, and you are obviously good at all of those things." He smiled. "But I can't be dishonest with her, or with you."

He only felt a twinge of guilt, pretending that he'd been honest with her from the start.

He felt a lot worse about what he was about to do.

"I'll be back in London for business next month. What if I sort things at home, then we can get together when I return? I'll even block an extra day or two on the trip just for us. But I need to go right now. I have a plane to catch, and if I stay here any longer," he said, sending his gaze deeper into hers, "I'll never want to leave again."

It worked. Something inside her visibly melted. He told himself it was okay, because once out of sight, he'd be right out of mind. Then it would be easier to forget her. Easier for Lottie to forget him, too.

For all he knew, this was a game she played all the time; she'd find another married man to screw while he endured a sleepless eight-hour flight back home.

"Okay." She gave his hands a gentle squeeze. "Do you promise?"

He squeezed back. "I promise."

"Can I have one of your cards?"

"One of my cards?"

"One of your business cards . . . you know, something to remember you by."

But John didn't have any cards — at least none that said *Grayson James*.

"Believe it or not, I don't even carry them. I only take meetings with people I already know, so there's no need for glad-handing."

Playfully she said, "How am I supposed to remember last night?"

"Seems like you remember it just fine." John laughed. "I wish I remembered it half as well as you do."

Something changed on Lottie's face. She withdrew her hands and stepped back.

"I didn't mean it like that," John said, trying to recover. "But you *know* how drunk I was. We've been talking about it since I woke up."

"I know." She looked at the floor and then at the door. Anywhere but at him. "I guess I'm not ready to say good-bye. And . . . it hurts to know that this means so much more to me than it does to you."

What the hell was with this girl? Why did she care? She was younger, more attractive, and out of his league in every way. What was so special about him that she'd already gotten attached?

Not that he'd thought he was bad in bed, but the way Vicky responded to his efforts, he had a hard time believing his drunken performance in bed was so good that he'd spoiled Lottie for anyone else. Flattering as that thought might be.

"Lottie —"

"Please . . ." Her blue eyes were pleading. "I just met this wonderful American television producer and I'm living a fantasy. Just . . . play with me for a few more minutes."

Looking into Lottie's eyes, moist with tears that seemed desperate to fall, John did want to play. But this was too dangerous a game to resist.

So he kissed her long and deep, on the mouth and then on the neck before moving to each of her earlobes. And damn . . . he should be acting his ass off right now, but he wasn't. This was exactly what he'd craved from his wife all this time. It killed him that he had to leave it in London. He moved back to her lips and she panted against his.

"Can't you feel it? Our destiny?" she breathed.

Was that what she thought?

He had to get out of that room, back home, away from this mistake and on with the rest of his life. "I promise that when I'm back in London next month, I'll show you the time of your life."

But even as John pulled away, he vowed to never, *ever* visit London again.

He scribbled ten random digits on a piece of stationery — he wasn't even sure of the area code, it might have been Vegas — then got dressed, gave Lottie one last kiss, and went downstairs to wait in the filthy alley for his Fastr.

Chapter Three

When John was a child, he thought traveling was magical.

His family had taken exactly three vacations before he eventually moved out. All of them included endless days on the road, crammed into an old Chevy station wagon with his brother Barry on his left, his sister Sherrie on his right, and his parents in the front seat, bickering. Wasn't a vacation without their bickering. Didn't matter about what.

Growing up, John imagined the joy of traveling as it should be: planes and trains, and driving on the wrong side of the road, and magical new territory to explore. But as an adult, he hated to travel. The schedules, the packing, the feeling like he was carrying a loaded weapon or a balloon of drugs somewhere unmentionable whenever he went through security — even though he'd only smoked pot and taken mushrooms that once, and he'd never so much as *held* a gun.

The biggest disillusionment of all? If you really thought about it, everywhere looked the same.

John was dying to get home, and terrified of what might happen once he got there. Guilt chewed his insides.

He rarely sweated, yet his undershirt was soaked through. He took the first flight delay personally. The second one was worse, an hour and a half spent with his life decaying on the runway, stuck in the back of the cabin, hating himself and sweating profusely.

Eight hours to New York felt like a hundred. John was exhausted, but that was fine. His family could see the fatigue on his face — so long as they didn't see anything else.

Especially Vicky.

This was his first marriage. The third for her. Both of her previous husbands were cheaters. And — as she was fond of saying, both in the best of her moods and the worst — the second time nearly destroyed her.

For some women, that would be hyperbole. Not so much for Vicky, with her anxiety and her manic episodes. When she was up, she was amazing, full of ideas and fun to be around. But when she was down, she was either unable to function or terrifyingly angry. Even paranoid. The worst part was that even after so many years of marriage, she'd yet to ever tell John exactly *what* she'd been diagnosed with, because her second husband, Jacob, had used that diagnosis to manipulate her. All he knew for certain was that she took meds to stabilize, and that things got ugly when she missed them.

Vicky made a lot more excuses for her first husband, Jason. He was her high school sweetheart. The first man she'd let inside her body, with fingers or anything else. She'd been a sweet girl, naïve enough to believe that she and Jason would be together forever. They were long-distance throughout their freshman year of college, and tied the knot that first summer.

Two months later, she found out that Jason had been sleeping with half the girls on his dorm floor. It was hard for him to deny when Vicky went to visit him on campus one weekend and all the girls called him "Freckles," on account of the trio of beauty marks on his shaft.

Three years later, Vicky made the same mistake with Jacob, who she said was "perfect enough to deserve a ladder to Heaven . . . or so I thought, before he proved to me he deserved an escalator to Hell instead."

Vicky told Jacob about her failed marriage on their first date. Jacob agreed that men were pigs, much more interested in satisfying their carnal desires than in building anything genuine or long-lasting. But this was only true for young men, he added, those who had not yet learned what it meant to truly love. He was thirteen years older than Vicky, and made her feel safe.

They married six months later. She was over the moon, past Mars, and onto Jupiter.

Jacob was successful, with a small restaurant and an impressive house. Just three months into their marriage, Vicky found out that he was sleeping with several members of his female serving staff. She waited for his confession, desperate to understand. But he lied, and then lied again, and then lied some more. She had to get a divorce. Again.

So Vicky had been suspicious of John from day one. Took him more than a year to earn her trust.

He immediately saw that she was broken. But also beautiful. And smart.

He'd been waiting at his favorite restaurant for a blind date when he overheard her arguing with the hostess about her lost reservation. John told the waitress, "She can have my table." Then he listened as Vicky gave her number, so the hostess could call her when the table was ready. John stepped outside and called her first.

It was the boldest thing he'd ever done, and easily the most stalkerish. But somehow, it charmed her.

She told him her whole story on their first date, for context and as a warning. Because she wouldn't be so easily fooled. Not ever again.

And she hadn't been. Until now.

If she found out now, it would destroy her. And it'd be his fault.

His family was just a few minutes away. Soon, John would have to look them all in the eyes and pretend that he wasn't an asshole, a liar, a cheater. That he was still the same good husband and father he'd always been.

The wheels kissed the runway and he texted:

I'm home.

Chapter Four

As John shuffled out of the airplane, he avoided all eye contact with anyone, as if they might spot the lie hiding inside him.

Keeping his eyes to himself was foreign to John. He may have hated small talk, but he had the hungry eyes of a people-watcher. "Sorry, I'm a writer. It's part of the job," he'd say whenever someone caught him staring, or looking somewhere that perhaps he shouldn't have been. Because a writer was supposed to constantly observe the world around them, then use those observations to make people feel and think and wonder and live through the spaces in his words. So what if he used some of that observation time to also look at beautiful women?

But he couldn't do that now, not with guilt souring his stomach. He turned away from a gorgeous brunette with doe eyes and perfect breasts, beautifully displayed with the strap of her travel bag pressed between them, and felt the guilt dig deeper.

And then, of course, he thought of Lottie.

Lottie with her legs splayed in invitation, touching herself through thin pink panties.

Lottie leaning forward to kiss his cock as he'd practically jumped sideways in flight.

Lottie laughing and talking about how he'd *drilled* her until she'd been almost too sore to keep going.

John hated himself. He hated Lottie, for giving him a reason to hate himself.

When I was bent over the armchair and your face was buried in my pussy. When I was looking back at you over my shoulder while you were fucking me from behind.

He stepped through the terminal doors and saw Vicky's blue Honda Odyssey approaching from two sections away. Perfect timing. Even from a hundred yards or so, he could see that everything was as he'd expected: Vicky frowning, Dakota smiling.

The Odyssey pulled up to the curb and the door slid open.

"Dad!" Dakota scrambled out of the passenger seat.

He gave her a quick hug. As Dakota buckled herself back in, John loaded his bags in the back, climbed into the car, reached back to kiss a squealing Evie on her forehead, then ended the round with a soft kiss on Vicky's lips.

"I missed you."

She smiled, wide and genuine, her frown melting away. "I missed you, too."

And then they were off.

Before they were even on the highway, Dakota said, "We're going to eat at Antonio's."

"Oh?" John looked back at his daughter, eyebrows raised. "What's the occasion?"

"You're home," Vicky said, still smiling. "This was the longest you've ever been away, and it was the first time we've ever had an ocean between us. Besides, we can catch up on the way."

This was the Vicky he loved so much. He felt ten times guiltier than if he'd been picked up by the other Vicky, the annoyed, anxious one.

Right now, John wanted to open his door and roll out onto the highway. Cracking his head open like a melon would be easier than suffering through whatever Vicky would hurl his way if she ever discovered the truth.

Fortunately, the truth was more than three thousand miles away.

Almost an hour of agonizing small talk later, they pulled up to Antonio's, their go-to for family celebrations. Evie looked up from her car seat, recognized the giant neon sign, and giggled.

The hostess was happy to see them. So was Fausto, their favorite waiter. He was from Ecuador and had a thick accent. He was also short and round and hilariously awkward. But he'd apparently worked at Antonio's since the Cretaceous period, and he knew all the secret dishes that weren't on the menu, the ones the chefs made for themselves when they were homesick or feeling especially creative.

"There's a special manicotti tonight," he told them with a gleam in his eyes. "You're going to *love* it."

"What's in it?" Dakota asked, because the chef liked to change the stuffing.

Fausto beamed. "Broccoli rabe, creamy ricotta, and fresh mozzarella, in marinara with extra garlic. The ricotta is herbed, oregano and a hint of rosemary." He pronounced the *H* in *herb*, and like a punch in the dick, John thought of Lottie.

"I promise, you will love them," Fausto added.

"You've never been wrong before," Vicky said.

Evie started crying when her gurgles had gone ignored too long. Fausto produced a lolly from a pocket in his apron and handed it to her — just like he'd done for Dakota a decade before. And then he disappeared.

John was on his second breadstick before he finally realized that there was something off about Dakota.

"What's wrong?" he asked. "You seem bothered about something. Did Cartoon Network cancel something or other?"

A small chuckle, probably a pity laugh for her less-than-funny dad. Then, "It's nothing."

When she was younger, she ran to him first, told him everything, looked to him for advice. He got that teenagers were different, but he still missed the way she used to gallop toward him.

"It's never been nothing." He turned to Vicky. "Isn't it always something when she says nothing?"

Vicky nodded.

Still looking at Vicky, John said, "Do *you* know what this is about?"

Vicky nodded. Evie giggled around her lolly.

Dakota rolled her eyes. "Fine. Brittany's being a big B-word. She's acting like she's better than the rest of us all of a sudden. She's always busy and she never wants to hang out. And she never wants to hear what anyone else has to say. Except Amanda. She's *always* got time for Amanda."

John waited to see if there was any more coming. After a moment of silence, he said, "Hasn't Brittany been a pain in the ass since, I don't know, forever?"

"She's one of my oldest friends, Dad."

"Yeah, but remember that fight you had in sixth grade? And that other time in eighth grade when she totally screwed you over?"

"That was forever ago. She's my oldest friend," Dakota reiterated.

"Well," John said, "*oldest* doesn't mean *best*. Life's too short to spend it around people who irk you more than they make you happy. Does Brittany make you sad more than she makes you happy?"

Dakota looked thoughtful. She shrugged. "Probably."

John gave her a look: *And there you have it.*

Vicky's hand on his knee, squeezing. *Thank you.*

He wished the warmth of her fingers bleeding into his skin didn't make him think of Lottie.

"So," Vicky said, "how was London?"

John started his story with a plane crash in the middle of the Atlantic, and a rescue from Jamaican pirates, which of course led to an eventual trade — a handsome ransom in exchange for the passengers' lives. When Dakota asked why she hadn't heard anything on the news, John said, "Because *they* don't want you to know."

It was a family tradition, making up the most ridiculous story, to see if he could get them to laugh. Or even better, to believe in the silliness, at least for a moment. But this time he did it because he didn't want to tell them the truth. If Vicky sensed his guilt, she wouldn't stop picking at it until he told her everything.

The point of his trip was to find ways of promoting their older books, and figure out if self-publishing might be right for them, now that they were nearly finished with the final books in their contract. He had learned a few things that would help: that's what he'd talk about, until Vicky was sick of hearing it. Make it sound like he'd been obsessed with finding a way to revitalize their careers.

See what a good husband I've been?

He'd also come home with a prize find that was sure to become a family heirloom: the most delicate little music box. It was an English cottage that opened to a simple ballerina and played the simpler but no less elegant "Für Elise." The music box was ostensibly for Evie, but John bought it for everyone.

When he'd cheated on his wife, he'd cheated on his entire family.

By the time Fausto was placing their manicotti on the table, John had half-convinced himself that he'd spent that last night in London drinking with some Japanese businessmen who were at the fair to promote their company's manga imprints. And his family gobbled up the list of things he'd learned about publishing trends faster than their pasta.

Or at least Vicky did. Not because she was interested in the details, but because she'd wanted him to figure it out for her. The nicest gift he could give her right now was the assurance that he'd brought home the secrets to moving their mysteries en masse.

By the time, they were sharing an oversized bowl of spumoni, John felt welcome. Appreciated. Adored.

It felt good to be home, and though part of him felt like a monster, it was easier to ignore that feeling in the glow of Vicky's smile.

He would do his best to forget he'd ever met Lottie.

On the way home, John was surprised to find himself smiling. He couldn't remember the last time he'd seen Dakota and Vicky getting along so well. The two of them were constantly at each other, and had been since Evie was born. And it was usually worse when he traveled.

Back at home, as he prepared for bed, the guilt returned.

He tried to banish it by focusing on the routine of settling the children for bed. He said goodnight to Dakota first — like always, since she preferred total privacy once her door was closed for the day — then told Evie a story while her music box plinked out *Für Elise*, over and over. She loved the ballerina and insisted on practicing a twirl before he turned out the light.

Once the girls were tucked in, there was nothing to distract John from his wife.

He lingered outside Evie's door, afraid that as soon as Vicky looked into his eyes, she would know. Then, all hell would break loose. How many times had he suffered through one of her tirades?

It started with a drink, then turned into three. Her anger was rarely directed at John, but he was most often the rod for her lightning.

Only cowards cheat. If someone is that unhappy in their relationship, then they need to act like an adult and have a serious conversation with their partner. Discussion diffuses the dynamite. But without it, BOOM! If one person is dissatisfied with the relationship, and doesn't bring it to their partner's attention, then things are going to blow up. Cowards live in the shadows. So do cheaters. And that's where they stay, because that's where it's easiest to be selfish. So if you need excitement, John, tell me. If I'm not doing something you want, tell me. But don't ever cheat, or so help me God I will cut off your dick and kill you with it. You can do anything else to me, but not that. I just can't take it. Promise me, John.

He always promised. Then she always offered her codicil: *I'll know if you do.*

And now he was about to find out if their relationship was going to go BOOM.

Because Vicky had promised to *take care of him* when he got home, and put that awful goodbye behind them.

What if she could smell Lottie on him? He'd been in such a rush to leave her place, he hadn't even showered. How could he not have wanted to scrub that memory off of himself? Maybe he could shower before she noticed.

He'd been sweating his ass off on that plane, and it was reasonable that he'd want to clean up after being in a giant metal tube full of germs.

His phone buzzed. A voicemail. It was after nine, so that probably meant Sam. He stopped unpacking and went to answer.

But it wasn't Sam. The number read *Private*.

He listened to the voicemail, his heart racing as ice water erupted from his pores and the room began to spin all about.

Lottie.

He could barely understand what she was saying, because he could only think one thing, over and over.

How? How did she get my number?

She finally finished, "So anyway, yeah, I really miss you, Grayson. I hope you call back soon. I'm really excited for next month."

Grayson. So she somehow got his number, but still didn't know his real name. Maybe he gave it to her when he was drunk? *Thank God you don't say "John Treadwell" in your outgoing message.*

John wanted to die. Any minute now —

"John!"

He turned around. Vicky, smiling . . . in her tiniest nighty.

She lowered the strap with a giggle and blew him a kiss. "I really did miss you."

Then her lips were on his, and he couldn't help thinking of Lottie.

I am the world's biggest asshole.

Chapter Five

Sunday afternoon, John and Vicky were outlining their final book in the *Worse Than Murder* series, with Evie sleeping in her second crib in the corner of their shared office. Their golden retriever Valentine — so named because they'd adopted her on Valentine's Day five years ago — snoozed next to the crib, keeping watch over the baby like she didn't quite trust John or Vicky to do it right.

Somehow, Vicky had completely failed to notice the stain on his soul, and Lottie hadn't tried to call him back. John was thankful that things seemed to be settling back to normal, and he'd been doing everything he could think of to keep Happy Vicky around. Including taking their brainstorming in a ridiculous direction.

"No." Vicky laughed. "We can't kill Marcus."

"Why not?" John pressed, even though he had no intention of killing Marcus. "Aren't you sick of writing the same stuff all the time? Let's mess with our readers and kill everyone off. It's the end of the series. What's stopping us?"

"How about reader loyalty? They'll never buy another book!"

Was that mock outrage or the real thing? Another joke, to keep her laughing.

"You're always saying we should just start another pen name, no matter how much Sam will hate the idea." He gave her a look of faux-seduction. "Let's commit career seppuku and start over. A lovers' suicide pact. It'll be so romantic."

"You know that's not what I mean," she said, still laughing. "We've spent the entire morning coming up with nothing. I want to finish this book, so we can finally get to whatever is next. So, again, what's our main trope?"

"Have we done the one where the writer really hates the shit he's writing?"

"John . . ."

"Fine. Enemies-to-lovers."

"We've done it before."

"*Everyone's* done it before, Vicky. Because it works." He couldn't help sighing. "I hate this trope-first shit, but . . . opposites attract, and readers love seeing the sparks. It's an evergreen trope and it will make this last story faster to outline and write. Even if —"

"Sold," Vicky said, planting a kiss on his cheek. "Enemies-to-lovers it is. I love you and your beautiful brain. Can we start talking plot?"

"You know how much I *love* plot."

John had never really outlined anything before working with Vicky. When he wrote solo, he preferred to just start writing and see what the muse would bring him. He liked finding the story in the writing process.

But Vicky needed the structure.

She was a big fan of extensive pre-writing, and the planning phase grew more detailed by the book. Because that was one place she could shine, Vicky was determined to shine as brightly as possible. Outlines, character sketches . . . she even liked to scout locations before the first paragraph was ever written. She liked to know everything she might need to know before writing.

Which was silly, he would argue, because it was *impossible* to know *everything* you needed to know before writing.

Besides, he ended up writing ninety percent of the words, anyway.

He had to admit, the books they'd written together from a detailed outline came together faster than anything he'd ever written alone. But they also felt the most hollow.

Of his six published novels before Vicky, all were literary, and most earned solid reviews from *Publisher's Weekly*. *Behind the Curtain* was even nominated for a Man Booker Prize. But there wasn't much money in literary fiction unless you were one of the giants, so after flagging sales on the sixth book in his contract, Vicky suggested that they team up to write romantic thrillers.

He couldn't argue with the money, nor with her process. Vicky's outlining kept them churning out novels, and the *Worse Than Murder* series was earning more than John's entire back catalog ever would.

He also couldn't help resenting that writing mind candy paid so much more than stories that made you think.

Outlining wasn't the only thing they'd argued about, either. Vicky wrote the mushy parts to spare him the agony. Her sex scenes were excellent, something he couldn't ever seem to get quite right on his own. She'd shaken her head the entire time while reading one of his early attempts.

"What's wrong with it?" he'd asked.

"Oh, nothing. Women *love* to read aggressive male-fantasy porn with zero sensuality."

John wondered what Lottie would think of his sex scenes. The thought of her reading one sent blood rushing downward. He cleared his throat, but that didn't flush the guilt.

"So, Idea Guy," Vicky said with a playful jab. "What's your big idea?"

"Okay . . . what if Marcus and Madison have to go off the grid, and they get separated at the end of act one? Then we write point-of-view chapters for each of them as they look for the other."

"Um . . . no."

"Why not?"

"Where's the romance, John? Seriously, we're outlining a romance and you just pitched splitting them apart."

"We're not writing romance. They're romantic *thrillers*."

"Right. *Romantic* thrillers."

"The romance comes from their separation," he argued.

"Or . . . we could start with a different story."

"But we haven't even *started* this one," John said. "We've talked more about our marketing plan for *after the book is written* than we have about the story itself. It took us all morning to decide on the enemies-to-lovers trope. You know how this works by now — that idea will lead to another and then to another after that. It's never where we start, it's where we go."

"Well, I'm not going to like where we're going if I hate where we're starting. And we need to have the marketing discussion because you know as well as I do that nobody — *including Sam* — is going to do that for us."

"We can —"

"No, John!"

She picked up his phone and hurled it across the room. It smacked the wall and hit the hardwood floor with a thud. John dug his fingers into the sides of his thighs to keep from running over and scooping it up. He'd deleted Lottie's voicemail and blocked her number, set his phone to silent and turned off all notifications. Changed his passcode, too. Even so, his heart nearly stopped when Vicky picked it up.

He took a deep breath, but said nothing.

Vicky was more difficult to get along with than a "regular" person, and her phasers were set to *detonate*. The smallest thing could trigger the cycle. She would erupt, John would retreat. Vicky would lash out, telling him to "be a man" while hurling things in his general direction. She seemed to want him to fight, but when he did, suddenly he was the villain and she was the victim.

He'd stopped trying to calm her — he'd learned that she only did that when left alone. His number one job had become shielding Dakota and Evie.

Vicky stopped pacing. She turned and snarled at John, as if on cue, "What, you're just going to stand there?"

Carefully, as though the words would burn his tongue if they left too fast: "Honey, have you —"

"Goddammit, John, of course I've taken them. I'm so sick of that bullshit. Every time I'm not wearing a flower crown and wanting to fuck you, it's because I'm not taking my meds! Go to hell, asshole."

Right. She's totally taking her meds.

"You think I don't know what you're thinking? You're such a pompous cock, John. You think you're better than what we're doing here, but what we're doing here is paying for the children's college, and getting rid of all the credit card debt we racked up while you were busy writing your *literature!*" She put that last word in air quotes, and actually curled her fingers for emphasis.

"I'm not thinking —"

"Yes, you are. I can see it. I can see you. I know what you think, and I'm tired of you thinking it. We've done this your way and we've done it our way. We can —"

"You mean *your* way."

"— do better. We can *write* more, if you'd let us. We could be making ten times what we are if you weren't so stubborn. Traditional publishing is *slow* —"

That wasn't fair, putting it all on him. But that was what she did when she was in a downward spiral. In an upward spiral, too.

When would it be Vicky's turn to take care of things?

That was a fantasy. Because she'd have to take her meds consistently, every day. She'd have to want to be the stable one instead of dumping that responsibility on John. Sometimes, he suspected she *liked* having the option of falling apart. That she enjoyed the adrenaline of a tailspin, and the safety of holing up in their furnished basement while John kept their careers — and lives— together.

John's job was to shut up and listen.

"— once we sign a contract, our shit essentially belongs to the publisher for the life of copyright. That's the life of the author, *plus seventy years after you die*."

"I haven't forgotten any of this since the last time we talked about going indie."

She glared at him. John swallowed, holding her gaze, wondering how long this particular standoff would last. *Until I convince her to start taking her meds again, probably.*

John finally broke the silence. "I agree with everything you're saying. And I really want to have this conversation —"

"Just stop it, John. Don't patronize me. I'm not in the mood for that shit — and no, it isn't because I'm *off my meds*. It's because I hate it when you're being pompous."

"I'm not being pompous."

"Whatever you say, Professor."

A deep breath. "Can we just —"

"No. We can't. I'm going for a walk."

Ten seconds later, the front door slammed hard enough to rattle the *Starry Night* print hanging beside it.

Evie started crying.

"Sorry, sweetie." John scooped her out of the crib. Just the feeling of her squirming as he held her to his chest eased some frustration. "That's a terrible way to wake up."

He patted Evie on the shoulder, bouncing his baby girl up and down, singing "Hey Ya" in a whisper. First, she stopped crying, then she started to giggle.

This was why he stayed. Dakota and Evie. They were the only thing in his life that was going right.

Eventually, once Vicky came down, she'd come to her senses, admit that she "maybe missed a dose or two," and would wind up apologizing and crying, asking, "Will I have to take them forever?"

She hated the answer, despite its truth. But John didn't see what was so terrible about taking them. It wasn't like she was hooked on Oxy. The medication stabilized her mood, drew her out of depression, and calmed her manic and anxious spells. They made life easier for her family. For him. She finally had what seemed like the perfect cocktail, and it worked. So why not take it?

Sometimes he wondered if she didn't take them specifically because they made life easier for him.

He shoved aside the unworthy thought as he turned to see Dakota standing in the doorway, her sad smile saying that she'd heard Vicky's meltdown.

"Sorry, Dad."

"It's okay," he said, giving her a sad smile back.

"It really isn't." Dakota came into the room, picked his phone up off the floor and handed it to him, then took

Evie from his arms. "Go work on your story. Mom will like it as long as you give her enough time to think it was her idea."

"Thank you." John kissed each of his daughters on the forehead and returned to his chair. While Vicky sulked, he'd have to figure out the story on his own. As usual.

He checked his phone, first to make sure it wasn't broken. No cracks, thank goodness. Then it occurred to him that maybe that was a bad thing. If he'd had an excuse to replace his phone, he also could've used that as a justification for making his number unlisted, so Lottie couldn't track him down.

He hadn't heard from her in a couple of days. Maybe she'd gotten the hint.

He checked his messages. Nothing from Lottie.

If he blocked her number, would that just piss her off?

His gut churned as he imagined how many ways Lottie could fuck up his life if she tracked him down. So, best not to piss her off. He wouldn't reply to her text or return her call, but there was no point in blocking — *yet.*

Chapter Six

"I'm sorry," Vicky said as she stepped into the breakfast nook.

Yep. There it was.

John lowered his iPad and looked up at his wife. She wore her happy face, eyes bright and smile wide. It felt like a promise, but that face had lied to him before. Things had been tense yesterday, concluding with a nighttime cold war that had them sleeping back to back, neither of them willing to concede the comfort of their bed for the distance of the couch.

He suppressed a sigh. A whiff of resentment would trigger her defensiveness. Possibly another cycle. And he needed her back on her meds.

"It's okay . . . really."

"No, it's not. You weren't doing anything wrong, and I went off on you for no reason. That sucks and I'm sorry."

"You called me Professor."

"I did."

"You know how much I hate that."

"Would it help if I want to hear your idea about Marcus and Madison going off the grid?"

"No," John said. "I already hate that idea. But you can pretend the next one is genius, even if it isn't. That will make me feel better."

"Done." She kissed him on the cheek. "Now, why are you sipping this? It's probably an iced coffee by now. Let me freshen it up for you."

Vicky picked up his half-empty mug and headed toward the kitchen. He watched her go, wondering how long that smile would stay on her face *this* time around the cycle.

She returned a few minutes later and set a fresh cup of coffee next to him.

Dakota entered the nook. "So, who's taking me to school?"

"I'm happy to volunteer," John said. "I just made it through email and would love to procrastinate for just a little longer. I appreciate your effort in making that possible."

Dakota laughed. He loved that sound. "I'll be in the car."

"Have a good day, sweetheart," Vicky said. Then to John: "Thank you."

He stood. "Sure thing."

Vicky took his hands. "Are we good?"

He looked into her eyes and kept things even. "We're good."

And then he kissed her.

Five minutes later, John was in the Odyssey, waiting at a red light. He glanced over at a squirming Dakota, her gaze fixed on the glove compartment. He knew that look. There was something she wanted to talk about.

So he broke the ice.

"I understand that anticipation for the Father-Daughter Dance is overwhelming you so much that you can't speak, but it's best not to overhype it." When she still said nothing, he added, "We can talk about it, you know."

"Not really."

"Come on, that's not fair. I always listen."

"So? Listening won't change anything."

"Especially with that attitude."

The light turned green. John stepped on the gas a bit harder than usual.

"Maybe you could just start telling me what's on your mind now, so you won't be cramming fifty words into the space of five while we're double-parked in front of the school." He pressed the gas a bit more. "Race ya."

"Why do we have to talk about it at all? Can't we just remember one of the other times we've talked about it and listen to Sirius instead?"

John suffered through another red light of silence before he tried again. "I'm feeling good about things . . . if that makes you feel any better."

"Don't you always 'feel good about things' until they're terrible again?"

"It's fine. Really. As long as she's taking her meds, there's nothing to worry about."

"Okay," she said, crossing her arms over her chest with a big sigh.

"I'm sorry —"

"Just stop it. Okay, Dad? Stop apologizing for her. Mom being a bitch isn't your fault."

"She's not a *bitch*, Dakota. Your mother is struggling with a clinical disorder."

"Okay."

"Stop okaying me, Dakota. She had a bad day. It happens. That doesn't mean it's always bad."

"Easy for you to say."

"What?"

"You never see it happening. You're always there *after* it happens."

"What does that mean?"

"Oh my God, Dad. It means exactly what it sounds like. Mom always gets craziest when you're not around. Like the time you were helping that lit major, Aubrey, and she was convinced you were cheating on her. You didn't have to listen to her screaming. Or watch her throwing things. She told me that I 'better get used to living in two houses,' and that when she was done with you, you'd never be able to stick it anywhere ever again."

Shit, when had Vicky started including Dakota in her tantrums? "That was highly inappropriate."

"Then she finds out that Aubrey was actually a guy and she's suddenly sorry all over the place. Then I'm supposed to keep her explosion a secret?"

"Well, thank you for telling me. Although, I did love all the awkward conversations."

"And that was all before Evie. She's even worse now!"

John hated the frustration in her voice. It wasn't fair that she had to put up with Vicky's meltdowns when he wasn't around. But how was he supposed to protect Dakota when Vicky insisted that John do all the traveling to promote their books?

He had to make her understand how not taking her meds was affecting Dakota. How it would affect Evie, too. If she wouldn't stay on them for him, surely she'd take them for their sake?

"Look, honey, I hear you. And I promise I won't let it happen again. I'm on this, okay?"

Dakota forced a smile, obviously wanting to believe him. "Okay."

Something inside him exhaled. It hadn't occurred to him that some of their distance might be fallout from his relationship with Vicky. He'd always been able to make Dakota laugh, and as she'd gotten older, they'd been able to talk about art and life with a depth that John never expected from a "moody teen." Then again, Dakota wasn't a moody teen. She was occasionally quiet and often loud, but said what she meant and meant what she said, even if she sometimes said it in the wrong time or place, or to the wrong person. She'd inherited his blunt honesty and Vicky's difficulty in reading the room.

He worried that she'd also inherited his tendency to bottle up his feelings until he felt a tick from detonation.

But at least she hadn't inherited Vicky's condition.

John swung a right onto Washington, six blocks from school. "Let's play a game. Tell me something I don't know."

"So you can know it all?"

John laughed. "Anything."

"We're almost at school."

"So stop wasting time."

"It's fine. I can tell you after school."

"I appreciate a good cliffhanger, but they're empty carbs. Right now, I think I'd prefer the protein of some closure."

Dakota laughed, and that got her going. "Do you remember Amanda?"

"Amanda . . . black hair, kinda dim, will definitely have to marry for money, the only one the big B-word Brittany wants to hang out with. That Amanda?"

"Exactly."

"I remember."

"Well, we're not friends anymore. We haven't really been friends since the start of the year."

"Is that because she's a bitch?"

Dakota laughed. "I should be allowed to swear if you're going to keep doing it."

"Swearing is part of my job." He didn't bother pointing out that she'd just called her mother a bitch.

"Not in front of me, it's not."

"Okay," John said. "I'll never curse in front of you again. But that means you can never curse in front of me, and if I hear you swearing in front of your friends, then I'm going to have to correct you."

"I don't swear in front of my friends."

Two blocks to go, John laughed. "Are you kidding? Is Josh not a friend? Because I heard a few of my favorite words when I was driving you two to the mall."

"Ugh, Josh."

He tried to bury his glee. "We don't like Josh anymore?"

"Permission to swear?"

"Permission granted."

"Josh is an asshole."

"Ah, well, that's too bad," John said, pulling up to the curb. "Okay, out of the car."

"But I didn't get to tell you about Amanda."

"You should have started sooner." John smiled, then waited. Dakota wouldn't be able to leave until her story was told.

"Yes, it's because Amanda is a bitch. She thinks she's too good for all her old friends. She started hanging out with this new girl, Tiffany. And yes, she's a bitch, too. An even bigger bitch —"

"That's three 'bitches' plus the 'asshole' for Josh. I think you've hit some kind of quota."

"Tiffany says mean things to me all the time."

"So she's bullying you?"

A pause. "Yes."

"What are you doing about it?"

Dakota shrugged. "Nothing, I guess."

"Have you told your mother?"

"About Tiffany?"

"No, about David Fincher's take on Gilligan's Island."

"That's not a real thing. And I've told her about Amanda, but not about Tiffany, and *definitely* not about the bullying. I didn't want to bother her, or set her off. Plus, well . . . never mind."

"What?" he asked.

Tears welled in her eyes. "I don't want . . . I don't want to complain."

"What is it?"

"I can't tell Mom these things because she gets all . . . I dunno, overprotective. Once I tell her something bad about someone, she *never* forgets, or lets *me* forget. If I told her everything, she'd never let me have *any* friends."

"You could tell me."

"You're always busy with some story or another. Even when you're with us, you're not *with us*, except when you're playing with Evie. I don't want to . . . never mind."

"I'm sorry. You're so important to me, Dakota, more than any story. I've always been one to get lost in my thoughts, and I sometimes assume that other people are like that, too. If I'm giving you too much space, let me know. I'm here for you, okay?"

She wiped her eyes and he hugged her.

"So, how long has this been going on with Amanda and Tiffany?"

"Most of the school year. Amanda told her some private stuff about me, and now she uses that stuff to antagonize me. It's like she's trying to make me mental."

"Does it work?"

"Sometimes."

"Do you have a picture?"

Dakota thought, then said, "I could find one. Why?"

"Because I was thinking that I could come by at lunchtime and punch her in the face. So I need to know what she looks like."

Dakota laughed. "They would arrest you."

"Ah, good point. It'll have to be you, then. The worst they could do is try you as a minor."

"It would definitely shut her up."

"I'll have your back when they call you into the principal's office."

"Punch your enemies. Solid advice. Thanks, Dad."

Dakota took off her seatbelt, leaned across the console and gave him a tight hug, then got out of the Odyssey and started walking toward the school's front steps.

It killed John to think that his Dakota had been putting up with bullies for months, while thinking that she had to deal with it alone.

Yet another reason to talk to Vicky about taking her meds. For Dakota's sake.

John was halfway home and a block from Hot Cross Buns when he decided to stop for donuts and coffee. To linger a moment in the reconnection with his daughter before returning to the eggshells surrounding his wife.

Buns wasn't just Vicky's favorite bakery — they made the only baked goods in the city that were, as she put it, "literally worth dying for." And this from a woman who hated the improper use of the word *literally* as much as he did. Their donuts were her favorite. You could order from behind the glass, same as any donut shop, but you could also order off a custom menu. And each of those donuts would barely fit on a salad plate. John planned to order three of Vicky's favorites so she could pick at them throughout the day instead of picking at him.

The bell jingled as he entered the bakery already salivating at the thought of a PB&J donut. He was third in line, his stomach growling.

He glanced outside . . . and saw the impossible.

No. It can't be.

John got out of line, ran outside, and squinted down the street.

The woman turning the corner could have been Lottie's twin.

Or maybe that was the guilt screaming inside his empty stomach? Could he be hallucinating?

Torn between the desire to chase her down and run back into the bakery to hide, John watched the woman disappear around a corner. She had the same color hair, the same haircut. The same sway in her hips. The same luscious ass.

Hands shaking, he pulled his phone out of his pocket and checked for messages. Nothing. If she were here, she would've called or texted, right?

It was a coincidence. It had to be. Someone similar enough that his guilty conscience projected the image of Lottie onto a woman he'd never met.

He took a deep breath and stepped back into Buns, gagging as the formerly mouth-watering scents of pastries done right turned cloying, suddenly too sweet in his nostrils. He would get the donuts for Vicky, go home, and finish the damned outline for their next book. He'd man up and talk to Vicky about her meds, get her on track once and for all.

And he wasn't going to think about Lottie ever again.

Chapter Seven

Two days later, John was preparing for a last-minute trip to Los Angeles — and having the inevitable pre-travel toe-to-toe with Vicky.

"What did Sam say, exactly?"

John sighed. "He said, 'We need to do everything we can to get you both in the room.' He knows that we're better together, at least when it comes to *Death*. It's not like I'm pitching one of my things here, Vicky."

"Oh. You mean something good."

"That's not what I'm saying." *Although that's true.* "I'm saying that these suspense thrillers are your babies, and you can talk about them with a lot more enthusiasm than I can."

"So I give a shit, whereas you don't?"

Another sigh. She seemed determined to turn this into a fight. "Come on, Vicky. Help me out here."

"I'm trying to help you out. Why don't you help *me* out? You know, by doing what you've been doing for years."

"I haven't been doing this for years. Talking to Netflix isn't like having a pitch meeting with Sam."

"You're not talking to *Netflix*."

"But I'm talking to Fable, and that's an open door to Netflix. How is that not the same?"

"Sam will be there with you. I don't see why you need me."

"Because these stories were *your* ideas."

She exhaled dramatically, then walked to the closet, pulled out John's suitcase, and plopped it on the bed. She calmly opened the lid and went back into the closet, speaking as if nothing had happened, her voice now muffled. "I think you should wear that checkered shirt from Lands' End. It's writerly, but not too frumpy."

Vicky had promised that London was it, that from here on, they were going to be a team. That she wasn't going to dump all the responsibility for marketing their work on him. But there they were, back where she swore they wouldn't be. "You promised that —"

"No, I didn't." Vicky emerged from the closet holding his Lands' End button-down with the tiny checks that made him feel squinty-eyed, and another Lands' End shirt that he hated even more. "Like always, you're picking and choosing the parts of our conversation that fit the narrative you want to tell. I've said it from the beginning — you're the frontman in this operation. I'm happy to come up with the initial ideas, and write all the sex scenes. It's your job to get out there in front of the camera, as it were, selling our shit."

"But I don't —"

"Of course you don't *want* to. Which is why I suggested that we self-publish. So you don't *have* to do it anymore."

"That doesn't even make sense! If we self-published, we'd have to be out there even more than we already are, because *we* would be the publishing company. You may not think the publishers are doing enough, but at least they do *something*. Isn't it hard enough getting the books written?"

"It doesn't have to be, John. There are better ways to do what we do."

This again. "Besides, even if we did self-publish, how would that be any different when we're pitching to Netflix?"

"You're not pitching to Netflix."

She stopped, seemed to notice John's wounded expression, then came over and took his hands in hers. Softly, she said, "I need you to be strong and do this for me, John. For us. I'm just . . . not feeling my best, and I'm worried that I could ruin things. If I had more notice . . . A day just isn't enough time."

She stared up into his eyes, her own starting to water, that same expression that always so fully disarmed him. He wondered if her welling tears were authentic or if she was manipulating him. Maybe she'd always manipulated him.

Did it matter? Dragging her along when she was emotionally fragile was a disaster waiting to happen. As difficult as it would be to do this on his own, it would be harder to spend the entire trip managing her sullen anger and the retreat into wounded helplessness that followed.

It was better this way. Besides, if he could land a deal for a TV show based on their latest series, that would give him the freedom to write a real book.

He wrapped his arms around Vicky's waist and pulled her close. "I understand."

He held her tight, rocking back and forth, thinking — even though it might not be fair — that London was Vicky's idea. And if she had gone with him like she promised before buying the nonrefundable tickets, then he never would have been in The White Lion, drinking French martinis with a local blonde.

There was a soft knock on the door.

"Yes?" Vicky said.

"Can I come in?" asked Dakota.

John cleared his throat. "Of course."

The door opened and Dakota stepped into their bedroom. "So, Dad's going by himself?"

Vicky nodded.

Dakota glanced at the checked shirt. "And you're making him take *that*?"

"I'm not *making* him do anything."

"She's totally making me." He winked at his daughter. She smiled back before turning to Vicky.

"He's a writer, and it's LA, Mom. Give him a jacket and the coolest T-shirt in his closet. Don't send him into a pitch meeting looking like a fancy lumberjack."

John laughed. "Thanks for your support."

"Where's Evie?" Vicky asked on her way to the closet.

"She's watching *Nightmare on Elm Street*. The first one, because it's hard to believe that's really Johnny Depp." Then, when no one laughed, she said, "She's playing with Mr. Fox."

Vicky emerged from the closet holding a T-shirt in each hand. "Which one do you like?"

John studied both tees, watching Dakota out of the corner of his eye to see her reaction. Not because he cared which one was better, but because he wanted her to feel like she had some input into a situation where she had no control: his leaving her alone with Vicky again.

He couldn't tell which one she liked from her expression, so he pointed to his favorite — black, with bright white lettering that read *The past, the present, and the future walked into a bar. It was tense.* — just as she raised her hand to do the same.

Like father, like daughter.

"Good choice," Vicky said, rolling her eyes.

But Dakota seemed happy that he'd chosen the same one, her eyes sparkling as she laughed, grabbing the shirt from her mom and stuffing it into his suitcase. "Knock 'em dead, Dad."

That's exactly what he would do.

Chapter Eight

John couldn't believe it. He'd scrambled to travel, getting to Los Angeles with less than twenty-four hours' notice, and now he was cooling his heels in a shitty hotel room? He felt shanghaied.

"Sorry, John," Sam said over the phone. "Harold can't meet until Monday."

"Did something come up? Is this about *First Degree* being too similar to our story? I don't understand how they can just cancel after someone flew out here to meet them."

"They didn't cancel, they *delayed*."

"But why?"

"I don't know why, I didn't ask. Harold is a busy guy. Trust me, he wants this to happen as much as we do. I'm sure whatever came up is important."

"So it's not about *First Degree*?"

"Honestly, I think *Worse Than Murder*'s similarities to *First Degree* work in our favor — do you have any idea how much that show is making?"

"What am I supposed to do until Monday?"

"Can't you just work on the new book?"

"Not without Vicky."

"Visit your parents, then."

"I don't want to visit my parents."

"Then take some time for yourself, do something you wouldn't normally do. You sounded stressed when you got back from London, and you sound even worse now. You're telling me there isn't a part of you that can see a weekend by yourself as a gift? No family, and nothing but freedom in one of the best places on the planet? Come on, most married men would kill for that."

There was a time when he would've too. But right now, he didn't *want* to be away from his family. He'd love to be watching something stupid with the girls, hearing Evie coo, eyes wide as she watched the pretty colors on the TV and Dakota laughing as she crunched through a bowl of popcorn.

"See you on Monday." John hung up on his friend and agent for the first time in his life. Then he collapsed into the room's only chair and called Vicky. She answered on the third ring, sounding agitated.

"So how did it go? You're calling early. Is that good or bad?"

"Neither, yet. Something came up. Harold can't meet until Monday."

"What does that mean? You're stuck there?"

"Apparently."

Silence on the other end of the line. *Now what?*

"Vicky?"

"Has your daughter texted you?"

"Dakota?"

"No, Evie. Her stuffed fox has been teaching her to use your old iPhone."

"Why would Dakota have texted?"

"Well, I could see her not wanting you to know that she

got suspended for fighting today, but I could also see her thinking you might be proud of her . . . *since you told her to punch another girl in the face.*"

John's stomach fell several floors. Not because he was upset that Dakota fought back, but because he could tell Vicky was teetering on the edge of another meltdown. And it was his fault. "That's not how it happened."

"Then how did it happen, John? Help me out here. Which is the scenario where you tell our daughter to punch a girl in the face and I say, 'Wow, John, that was a great idea'? Seriously."

"We were joking around. I actually said that *I* was going to punch the girl in the face —"

"Oh, *now* I'm relieved!"

"— but then I told her that if *she* did it, the worst that could happen was that she would be tried as a minor."

An exasperated pause. "Yes. I heard the story."

"But it was funny. We were joking."

"Well, looks like she got the punchline."

John could hear Vicky breathing heavily into the phone, as if just talking to him was a tax her body could barely cover. She wasn't about to melt down, she was already in the middle of one. Poor Dakota had probably already absorbed stage one.

He'd fucked up again.

Maybe he could break her out of the downward spiral by getting her to think about something good. "I don't want to do this when we can't even look at each other . . . why can't we just have a nice conversation? It sucks to be here alone, clear across the country, without you. We used to have a good time with each other . . . even long distance. Remember when we lived in Las Orillas and I would have to go to New York?"

"Oh, you want to have phone sex? Like in the 'good

old days'? We have video these days. That would be hot, right?"

He sensed the trap and tiptoed around it. "It *could* be."

"Then you could see me. And the giant mess in the living room, because Evie wouldn't listen to a thing I said this morning. Or the mountains of index cards that seem to be multiplying like I fed them after midnight. Or my hair, which is piled on my head like all the mountains of laundry that still need washing."

Would a joke break her tirade? "Mogwai multiply when you get them wet. They turn into gremlins when you feed them after midnight."

"Oh, *now* I'm horny."

"I'm not asking for phone sex. I'm just asking you to be nice."

"I'm not *trying* to be a bitch, John. I'm trying not to go crazy. Evie is *exhausting*. It's hard to have you gone. And it's a lot harder when I have to trek down to school and bring Dakota back home. Then I find out that you told her to hit someone? Joking or not, that wasn't smart."

"I'm not sure this is a matter of intelligence."

"I'd love to go to LA and just leave it all behind, but —"

"That's exactly what I asked you to do. I don't even want to be here! I'm here because you wanted me to be the 'face of our author platform.' If you'd been willing to come, all four of us could be waiting in line at Disneyland right now."

Could he actually hear Vicky's teeth grinding together or was that his imagination?

"Have you called your parents?" she asked. "Go visit them."

"No. And that isn't the point."

"Right. The point is that you want to say this is all

about me and my mood swings, but do you know what it's like to fly with an infant?"

"We could've left Evie with your mother. Isn't that one of the reasons she moved to New York, to spend more time with her grandkids?"

"My mother is flaky, and you can't stand her."

"That's not what this is about."

"Evie is driving me crazy, John."

"I told you before — I think we should hire a nanny."

"We . . . we can't," Vicky said, with less resolve than he'd ever heard from her on this matter.

"We can, and we should."

"I really hate that word."

"Queef? Same here."

She laughed. Finally. "*Nanny.*"

John wrinkled his nose, even though she couldn't see. "Eww. It *is* rather offensive, now that I hear you say it."

"I'm serious. It reminds me of all the spoiled rich girls I grew up with. I hate it."

"We'll make up our own word. We do it all the time. It'll be fun. But I really think you should start looking into it. Stop trying to do it all, because that's never going to happen, and you're just going to keep feeling worse about yourself. And as much as that sucks for you, it sucks for me, too. And the kids."

"I know." She hesitated. "I'm sorry."

"It's okay."

Evie babbled in the background.

"In a minute," Vicky said to her. "I gotta go."

"Sure."

"I love you and I'm sorry. Have fun." It sounded like something crashed to the ground. "Argh. Seriously?"

The line went dead, and John was alone.

Chapter Nine

"May I repeat that back to you, sir?"

"Of course," John said.

"Tonight, you'll be enjoying our antipasto dish. That comes with three types of artisan cheese, prosciutto, diced almonds, olives, and grilled flatbread. You'd also like a bottle of Freedom Cross Chenin Blanc."

The antipasto cost twice what it would've in a nice Italian restaurant, and the wine was over-the-top expensive, but he deserved some sort of consolation prize for being stuck in his least favorite city for an entire unwanted weekend.

"Correct."

"That will be forty-five minutes, sir."

He said thanks, hung up the phone, and headed straight for the minibar. He could wait for the cheese and bread, but hell if he was going to wait on the only thing that might soothe his ire at Vicky.

John opened the small door and pulled out two tiny bottles of SKYY vodka and a bag of pretzels. *There goes $50.*

He emptied both bottles into the room's coffee mug, opened the bag of pretzels, and surfed the hotel's crappy selection of television stations, shocked — and admittedly disappointed — to find that there wasn't any porn. It was petty, but he enjoyed imagining the look on Vicky's face when she saw the charge on his hotel bill.

He took a giant gulp of vodka, then turned off the TV and unloaded his laptop onto the bed. It was the internet age — who needed cable porn?

His phone buzzed halfway there. He looked at the number. *Unlisted.*

Flashes of Lottie's doppelgänger turning the corner entered his mind. He took another gulp and ignored the call, but then his phone buzzed with a text.

You around?

He texted back. *Who is this?*

His phone rang again.

This time he answered, the knot in his stomach tightening around the vodka as he did. Because he knew who it would be.

"Hello?"

"Grayson!"

No.

"Lottie . . ."

"You never called like you promised. Is everything okay?"

His heart pounding, his head spinning, his mind trying to connect dots that refused to stay in orbit. "How did you get this number?"

"You gave it to me."

"I thought I gave you my office number."

"You would know best." She laughed and the sound seemed to vibrate through him, settling in his groin. "I just dialed the number you gave me."

What the hell? Did I really give her my number?

Sigh. Time to rip off the Band-Aid.

"Lottie, I'm sorry. I enjoyed our time together, really I did. But it's like I told you — I'm married, and I shouldn't have done what I did. I wasn't being fair to you."

Lottie laughed. "*Fair?* I'm the one who got you back into my room. We both knew what we were doing. You don't have to apologize, sweetie. So . . . what are you doing?"

John looked around his empty hotel room. "Well . . . waiting."

"Waiting for what?"

If he was smart, he'd hang up. "I really should go."

"But you're not going to." Another laugh. "Wanna guess how I know?"

"No, Lottie." His phone buzzed with a text. "Hold on." John took the phone from his ear and looked down at the screen. *Holy crap.*

From far away, Lottie said, "Those are my tits. You just can't see my face because I'm pretending that I'm shy."

And there he was, already getting hard.

John brought the phone back to his ear. "If I was home right now, this could get me into a lot of trouble."

"Where are you?"

"I don't want to do this."

"So why haven't you hung up?" Lottie giggled. Not a laugh, but a little girl's giggle, designed to tease as much as challenge him. His cock loved that giggle. It wanted to hear her do it again while she rode it.

John thought. He swallowed. He almost killed the call.

But instead, he took another giant swig from his mug and waited to see what Lottie would do next.

"Wanna play a game?" she asked.

Definitely. It wasn't like she was here, about to fuck him.

She was just playing with him over a long distance phone call. Like his own wife refused to. It would serve Vicky right if he had phone sex with Lottie.

Was it the resentment or the guilt that made this even hotter than it would've been?

Guilt won a temporary victory. "Not especially."

"Of course you do."

Another buzz. This time, the text came with two photos side by side.

"The game is called, 'Which One is My Pussy?' It's really easy to play. You look at both pictures, then you decide which one is my pussy. The one with the heart, or the one that's like a little hairless clam. It could be either, since I had a basic bikini-line trim the last time you were licking me."

Now he was *really* hard.

Another swallow of vodka. One or two more and the thing would be empty.

"It's okay, Grayson. I'm sure you're already hard, and you're only going to get harder the longer I talk. And I know how this works. It's not like you're going to put that thing away, even if we hang up right now. So if you're going to spill all over yourself anyway, then you may as well pretend you're shooting it all over my tits, or my arse, or whichever one of those pussies you think is mine." And then, as if she had just nabbed an awe-inspiring idea right from the universe, "Or my *face*! You can pretend to come on my face!"

Another giggle.

John downed the vodka, lay back on the bed, and started stroking his cock.

"I can hear you breathing, Grayson."

John breathed harder, faster.

"I can hear you jacking off. Do you want me to join you?"

He grunted into the phone.

"Say it, Grayson."

"I want you to join me . . ."

"Join you doing what?"

"Jacking . . . off."

"Are you jacking off right now?"

"Yes . . ."

"Is your hard cock throbbing in your palm as you stroke it?"

Oh God.

"Yes . . ."

"Are you wishing it was my tight little pussy?"

Grunt.

"You probably just grabbed your dick as soon as you saw that picture of my pink little pussy, didn't you? But you might want to slow down, maybe moisten the head, so it's like I just stuck the tip of your dick in my hot . . . wet . . . mouth."

John wanted to jack faster, but he slowed down instead.

"I bet your wife never talks to you like this."

And now, faster.

"Say it, Grayson."

John said nothing. He didn't want to think about Vicky. He wanted to enjoy this guilty pleasure while it lasted.

"Say 'My wife doesn't do this for me' or I'll stop talking," Lottie purred.

A reluctant grunt, a growl, then, "My wife doesn't do this for me."

"I wish I was there right now, Grayson." Lottie's voice was mostly breath. "I wish you could see me right now, in this black little thing. I wish you could peel it off me. Or you could just lift the top to see my tits . . . slide my panties to the side . . . fill me with your cock .. . do whatever you want to me. My fingers just aren't enough."

Her breath chugged like a freight train gathering speed, and so did his.

"Are you going to come, Grayson? I don't want to come without you. Tell me when you're going to come."

"I'm . . . going to come."

And then he did.

Lottie screamed — John had no idea whether or not she was faking, but he didn't particularly care — then deeply exhaled.

John looked down at the gooey puddle on his belly, already drowning in guilt.

Lottie giggled. "Did you make a mess?"

He wanted to hang up. He got under the covers instead.

"You don't have to feel bad. That was great. I mean, not as good as the last time, but as good as a girl is gonna get over the phone. Next time you can come in my mouth again if you want to."

"We shouldn't have —"

"No, John, that's *exactly* what we should have done."

Oh shit. After several long and terrible seconds, he finally collected himself. "What did you say?"

"That's *exactly* what we should have done."

"No, what did you call me?" Pause. "What's my name, Lottie?"

She laughed, and this time it was terrifying rather than sexy. "You're John Treadwell, silly. You just told me that your name was Grayson James because you didn't want your one-night stand to track you down."

Fuck!

No.

This can't be happening.

I'm such an idiot.

"There's nothing to worry about, John. I'm not going to get you into trouble. You're my favorite author, by far. I've read all your books. *The Delicate Proverb* is definitely my favorite, but I love all the stuff you wrote . . . before you started writing with Victoria, anyway. I'm sure I don't have to tell you how much better your books are." Lottie laughed, waited for John to agree, then continued when he didn't. "Your writing speaks to me in a way that no other author ever has. You know how to reach right into my *soul*, John. It was like we'd been talking for years before we ever saw each other in the pub. You must have authors that do that for you . . . right, John?"

"I guess . . ." *I am such an asshole.*

"Don't get me wrong, the *Worse Than Murder* series is *good*, maybe even great. And I like the smut — well done, though I can tell that's not you writing those scenes. I had my suspicions before. But now I know they're all clearly Victoria."

John felt like he was dying, or maybe he'd forgotten what it felt like to be truly alive. Either way, his heart was beating far too fast and he had no idea what to do. Except maybe raid the minibar again.

He couldn't pretend that this didn't feel good. Not just her saying and doing all the things that Vicky wouldn't — Lottie's affection for his art seemed . . . genuine.

The Delicate Proverb was the best thing he'd ever written, by far. He knew it and so did Sam, even if Vicky and the public seemed not to agree. Vicky once said the book "rambled a bit too much, especially for the middle seventy-five pages or so." While she thought it was "beautifully written," she was sure to add, "I guess you just need patience to read it." A small part of him never forgave that.

John also couldn't deny that compliments always sounded nicer — and hotter — when delivered in a British accent.

This was all so dreadfully wrong and he knew it. He'd never meant it to go there, and wished he could erase it. But he couldn't change the past; he could only decide what to do going forward. Even buzzed, John knew that the right thing to do was to end this immediately. He still didn't know how he let things get so out of hand — all he'd wanted was affirmation by way of some meaningless flirting at a bar.

Vicky was his best friend, his wife, his partner in art and in life. He wouldn't throw that away for Lottie, no matter how much she stroked his ego. Or stroked anything else.

"So which authors?" The same giggle that had made him hard a few minutes ago now grated on his nerves. "Who gets you all wet, John? Besides me."

"I've gotta go."

A big sigh. "This again?"

"I'm a happily married man."

"No, you're not. You're a *married* man. A *happily* married man wouldn't have come all over his tummy right now — or at least he wouldn't have let me help put it there. I think the real issue is that you're afraid of getting caught."

"This isn't right."

"Was it right when you were eating my pussy?"

John was already getting hard again. And angry. "You lied to me. You knew who I was when we met."

"*I* lied to *you*? You gave me a fake name, *John*. I just didn't tell you that I knew who you were because I wanted to have a real conversation. I didn't want to gush all over you like some silly fangirl." Laughter sending tingles up his cock. "The gushing could always come later."

"I'm going to go. Please, can we just be grownups? I don't want any trouble. I have two daughters —"

"I know. You told me that they were the reason you were still with your 'crazy wife.' Before you fucked me."

God, he wanted this erection to fuck off. What was wrong with him that even Lottie's anger made him harder? "I didn't say that."

"You said a lot of things, John."

He couldn't imagine ever revealing his wife's medical condition or trashing her to someone else, let alone a stranger. That betrayal might even be worse than fucking said stranger.

"Regardless, I have two daughters, and —"

"Are either of them there right now?"

"Of course not."

"Then they won't know what we're about to do."

"Lottie . . ."

"'I have seen the face of God, but it is not any deity that lives in the sky. It is the eternity that lives in the molecules between us. It is only in those spaces where we can see the true isolation that festers inside even the fullest heart. When you meet someone who can see that pain, finally recognize it for what it is, share in it, revel in it, dance beneath the waning moon to its song, then you will delight in the most delicate proverb, and forge a deeper connection than mere mortals could ever comprehend.'"

John's heart wanted to stop beating so he could hear her better. His words sounded so beautiful coming from her mouth.

"You wrote that, and it touched me, John. Ever since I first read it, I've wanted to touch you . . . do you want me to touch you?"

"Yes," John admitted.

"Then pretend that I am."

Did it matter if he came once or twice during the same call?

He'd already started, he might as well finish.

Again.

Chapter Ten

"That wasn't an office," John said. "Offices have corners. That was a . . . playroom."

"Says who?" Sam dumped another creamer into his coffee, sitting across from him in the booth at the back of the retro 1950s-themed diner.

"Every architect in history." John looked at Sam's coffee. His stomach hurt enough, with guilt sitting like a gallon of acid in his stomach. That mug full of bitter brew would make it worse, but he wanted it anyway. "I still don't know how you can drink that so late and still sleep."

"I sleep like a baby, because I meditate. If you listened to me for once instead of insisting on doing things your way, you'd probably sleep like a baby, too. And I've seen plenty of round offices."

"Plenty? I doubt that."

"So what if Harold likes a round office. Why do you care?"

"Because it made me nervous. No corners or furniture . . . and he just kept pacing the room, swinging that bat."

Sam blew on his coffee and took a sip. "He wasn't

hunting zombies. He was thinking. I thought you wanted to work with people who were doing things differently. Harold does things differently."

"*Vicky* wants to do things differently. I just want the old way to work better." His balls hurt. Guilt always made his stomach hurt, but since when did it settle down there? Maybe that's why he was fidgeting, bending the straw and slowly shredding the wrapper.

"What's wrong with you? *I'm* supposed to be the curmudgeon. Harold loved the project, so Fable will pitch it to Netflix. Isn't that the homerun you came out here to hit?"

John shrugged. "I guess."

"You guess? Why do you have to be such an asshole? This is great news."

"It would be great news if I could count on Vicky to get on a plane."

"We'll figure it out."

"He made it clear, Sam. They're investing in a partnership, not a frontman. And I agree with Harold — I don't *want* to do this shit by myself."

"Like I said, we'll figure it out. This is the next step for us, for all of us. We've already agreed on that. Have I ever steered you wrong?"

"Have I ever stopped making you money?"

"No, but if we hadn't shifted course when we did, we'd barely be making anything now. And don't forget how long it took to get here. I always knew you'd succeed as a writer — that's why I took the chances on you that I did. But you never know. Crap books by shit authors can sell like half-priced hand jobs, while brilliance piles high in the remainder bin . . . that's publishing for you. Why wrestle with all the self-publishing nonsense when you could just play a bigger game and turn your books into TV?" Sam leaned closer to John. "Do you agree that this is the right move?"

"Yes."

"Then what's the problem? Is it only Vicky?"

"It's not a small thing. She sent me to London alone, and then here. She says it's my job, then acts like I'm going on vacation." John wished the edge wasn't there in his voice, but if he could hear it then surely Sam could as well. Regret over last night's call only pickled it further.

"Things bad between you again?"

Yes, he wanted to say. But if he told Sam that Vicky seemed to be getting less stable, would he consider dropping them as clients? "No. But . . ."

Sam sipped his coffee, looking at John. "But?"

"She *says* she's taking her meds, and I don't want to fight about it one way or the other, but it feels like she isn't."

Sam set down his coffee and squinted at John. "You've been through this before. Made sure she takes them every day. What's different this time?"

John looked over at the waitress, hoping for any interruption. But her back was turned, so he met his agent's eyes. He had to tell him.

"I think I fucked up."

"You *think*?"

"In London."

Sam raised his eyebrows. "Tell me you didn't cheat on your wife."

John said nothing. He wasn't sure if he was angry or relieved that Sam had guessed on his first try.

Sam exhaled with a heavy whistle. Then he sat back and folded his arms, shaking his head.

"I didn't mean to."

"Does anyone ever *mean to*?" Sam asked, loudly enough

for a couple of neighboring diners to give their table a glance.

"Yes. Plenty of people mean to do it."

"Not with Vicky. You've gotta be kidding me." Sam turned around and signaled the waitress. "Excuse me?"

She turned around, saw Sam, and walked toward their table. "Yes, sir?"

"What's your best pie?"

"Right now, it would be the chocolate coconut cookie. It's even better than the regular chocolate, and we don't always have it."

"Then two slices of that, please. And thank you." He turned back to John. "What happened? Tell me everything."

John told him everything down to the phone sex, omitting only the most embarrassing details. Sam stared at him, shaking his head repeatedly. He'd only spoken three times during John's story to ask clarifying questions, and when they'd paused to receive their pie.

"What are you thinking?" John asked.

Sam paused, then said, "Who am I right now? Your friend? Your manager? Your and *Vicky's* manager?"

John shrugged. "All of them?"

Sam chased his final bite of pie with a long swallow of coffee. Then he began. "You know marriage isn't my thing. Not because I don't believe in it, but because I keep marrying women who don't get me. Sure, I've had an affair or two or whatever, but what did they expect?" Sam shrugged. "They knew the deal when they said *I do*. None of the side dishes meant a damn thing. It was always just about sex, which I would have been perfectly happy to have at home. Anyway, point is, my wives knew the score. I've told you about Angela?"

"A little. Is she the one with the mob ties?"

"Yeah, and I've had reason to use those ties for special services on more than one occasion. She was a crazy bitch, just like wives one and three, but Angela knew people who could take care of things when shit got messy. Anyway, she practically begged me to get it outside the house, if it meant she didn't have to give it to me. That left her plenty of time to give it to Eduardo."

"The pool man?"

"Our chef."

"What's your point? That *everyone's* an asshole?"

"My point is that marriage *is* your thing and Vicky *does* understand you. She always has. She's always been good to you, John. Except for the stuff that isn't her fault, and that drives her just as nuts as it does you. I'm not one for keeping secrets — my affairs usually live in the closet for a month at most because I prefer to get shit out in the open and over with — but Vicky can't *ever* find out about this."

"Clearly."

"And I've gotta be honest, there are a few things about your story that bother me."

"*All* of it bothers me."

"I don't mean about the cheating. I mean about the actual encounter. With this Lottie. You really don't remember anything?"

John shook his head, shrugging. "Not really. I mean, I remember flirting at the bar."

"And how much did you drink? You said it wasn't that much."

"It wasn't enough for this to happen."

"That doesn't bother you?"

"That I didn't drink that much?"

"That you didn't drink that much, apparently had the wildest sex of your life, and don't remember a damned thing."

"Well, I guess when you put it like *that* . . . sure, that bothers me."

"Could you have been drugged?"

John considered that, shocked to realize that the possibility hadn't occurred to him before. "I'd know if I'd been drugged . . . wouldn't I?"

Sam rolled his eyes. "You said that she pretended not to know who you were, right? And admitted later that she actually did?"

John nodded.

"And she called you on a phone number that you didn't give her?"

John nodded again.

"What is it with you authors? Living in your own fantasies. You are seriously the smartest idiots I know."

"You don't have to get personal."

"You have a stalker, John. I've seen these situations go south plenty of times. You're lucky that this Lottie is in London."

"So what do I do if she keeps calling?"

"That's a good question," Sam said. "You need to be damn careful. Because this isn't just about hiding the truth from Vicky. You need to bury any and all evidence, so that no one ever knows that there's a truth to be hidden. This problem can't even fart if there's a chance that Vicky will smell it."

"*It can't even fart?* Really? Is that the best you have?"

"You're the writer. And apparently the cheater."

"I wasn't trying to cheat, it just —"

"But you did, and now we have to make sure that this doesn't send the rest of your life into a tailspin. As your friend, I'm worried for you — for you and your family and your marriage and your *career*. In that order. As your manager, I'm worried about your career. As manager for both of you, well, you already have me thinking about which of you would make me more money in less time, and I hate you for even making me wonder."

"Her?"

"Definitely her."

"Thanks."

"Brutal honesty, right?" Sam pointed to John's still-mostly-uneaten pie. "You gonna finish that?"

"I'll trade you for some actual advice. What if Lottie decides to keep calling? Or worse, what if she calls *Vicky*?"

"Fair enough." Sam slid John's pie closer and shoved the first bite into his mouth. "Proceed with extreme caution. I suggest that you wean her off and see how that goes. If she responds by clinging even harder . . . well, my friend, then you definitely have a problem and we'll need to revisit this conversation. With a lot more of this pie. But if she's like most women, she'll know the score and go away on her own."

That sounded reasonable enough. Except that *Lottie* didn't seem anything like "most women."

"Did you use protection?" Sam asked.

"I haven't worn a rubber in almost twenty years. So no, probably not. Even drugged, I think I'd remember *that*." John laughed, a sad, empty laugh.

Sam shook his head. "You're a dumb fucking bastard, you know that?"

"I do."

Chapter Eleven

"Ooh," John cooed, "that one is *very* pretty. May I?"

Evie gurgled through her smile, chirped several sounds that would someday soon be words, and handed him the necklace. He couldn't believe how fast she was growing.

John took great pains to inspect it, raising it to his nose and inhaling deeply. Then he handed the necklace back to his daughter, smiling wide. She grabbed the necklace by one of the rigatoni tubes and giggled when it rattled.

"That is very nice, young lady. It looks like Pottery Barn, but smells like uncooked lunch. Want to make a bracelet?" He held up the bag of macaroni and shook it. "We can use this."

Evie clapped and John poured a small pile of macaroni onto the table. He picked up one of their pre-cut pieces of string and carefully threaded it through the noodle. "See," he showed her, "it's harder than the big one, but great for your pincer skills."

John handed his daughter the string and pinched his fingers together.

"Oh, she loves making bracelets!" Vicky said as she came into the room.

John looked up. Smiling, he said, "You didn't love it so much the last time."

"I didn't mind the bracelet. It was all the paint that her 'pincer skills' couldn't quite handle."

John laughed sheepishly. "My bad."

Vicky smiled and sat on the other side of Evie and kissed her forehead, then Vicky's hand found his shoulder. "Thanks for taking her. I needed that nap. Now, I want to hear everything."

"First, any news on the nanny?"

"I don't want to talk about that right now — and I still hate that word. I want to hear all about Fable. How did all that go? Does Netflix want to make us rich?"

"Harold is . . . weird. How about 'governess'?"

"Well, we knew that. Sam told us he was weird."

"He's weirder in person."

"So?"

"And his office is round." Vicky looked at John like she was waiting for more, so he added, "There aren't any corners, and he walks in circles while he's talking, swinging a bat like he's waiting for his turn in the cage. It's weird."

"Got it. He's weird. What did he say about *Death*?"

Vicky looked hopeful. That look twisted the knife in John's gut.

"He likes it a lot."

"Then why don't you look happy?"

"I *am* happy."

"Someone should tell your face."

He sighed. John would've given anything not to have to bring it up yet. He'd barely been home for a few hours. He couldn't handle another fight.

"It's just . . . he wants to see the two of us together. He

says his production company is hiring a partnership, not mindlessly buying an IP. He also said he wants to see that dynamic in action."

"He has every right to. Thank you," she said to Evie when Evie handed her two rigatoni noodles and a piece of string.

How long were they going to pretend that everything was normal? "I was there alone. I get the feeling that will happen again."

"It won't," Vicky said, stringing her necklace. "I'm sorry. It totally sucks that you had to go to London, and it totally sucks that I stiffed you again for LA, and to prove how sorry I am, you can stiff me right now if you want to."

John laughed nervously. He glanced at Evie as if she were the root of his discomfort, rather than the instant guilt and a clear thought of Lottie's "arse."

You can slide my panties to the side . . . fill me with your cock . . . do whatever you want to me.

She followed his eyes to Evie, then shook her head. "I thought *I* was the prude. How about we do it later, then. I can make you some of those little pineapple upside-down cakes?"

"The tiny ones? I love those. Really?"

"Really. Except . . ."

"Except what?"

"Except I don't have any pineapple."

John smiled. "Are you saying that if I go to the store and get you a pineapple you'll make the little cakes . . . like, right now?"

"Yes, that's what I'm saying." Vicky kissed him on the cheek. "And I'm sorry for being so difficult. We'll figure it out. What's our next step?"

"We have to write a treatment."

"What's involved with that? How is it different from pitching to Sam?"

"It's not, really. We need to explain how we see the pilot working, and then we'll need to figure out how to best break down the books into seasons, assuming the show lasts more than one."

Vicky draped her finished necklace around Evie's neck. "That sounds fun."

"Don't get too excited. Sam said they'll change everything, guaranteed."

"Except the numbers on the check, I presume."

He was having a hard time believing her. But John smiled and took her hand anyway. "You seem great."

"I *am* great. And, again, I'm sorry. I am honest-to-God excited. You are a sexy, sexy man." She pulled him into a hug. "Now go and get me some pineapple."

John stood, saluted, and said goodbye to Evie. He drove a mile and a half to Provisions, the hipster grocery store that was just too close to their house to ignore — the one that John found himself loath to admit he was liking more by the visit.

He swung into the lot and parked between a Prius and a Tesla.

He grabbed a handbasket and walked toward the produce section, eyeing shoppers as he went. His eyes settled on a good-looking man in his early thirties.

Adrian Bates is a former homecoming king and high school quarterback. Now he's an internet marketer who has made an ungodly sum of money, and was living the life sleeping with supermodels before settling down with his girlfriend five years ago. Now he's under investigation from the FTC and his world is about to come crashing down around his ankles.

Then he found an attractive woman, but with tired eyes and hair that had stopped caring.

Alison Randolph just turned thirty-five. She's a wedding photographer, and one for whom photos aren't "just a job." She believes in trying to capture a moment's soul, and is excellent at what she does. Alison is fun, and funny. She takes few things seriously. When she was younger, she was a bit of a party girl. That's softened, but she yearns for the carefree nature of those days, before she had her son. Now that he's been diagnosed as being on the spectrum, and decent help is almost impossible to find, her world is slowly unraveling.

A nerdy kid with what appeared to be an entire world exploding behind his eyes grabbed a pineapple for his mother. John grabbed the one right next to his and gave the kid a smile.

Angus Rowe is an unsocial, extremely introverted fifteen-year-old whiz kid — the kind of introvert who has trouble ordering at a fast food restaurant because it gives him stage fright. But the boy is a genius, fascinated by figuring out how things work. He hasn't told anyone because he doesn't want to be laughed at, but Angus believes that —

No.

John saw a flash of blonde and something impossible.

Without a thought, he followed the blonde.

There she was, by the exit. It *had* to be Lottie, unless it was Lottie's twin, just like at the donut shop. Fat fucking chance.

She left the store. John hurried after her, his mind racing.

When Lottie discovered that her favorite author John Treadwell wrote romantic thrillers under a pen name, she couldn't believe it. She'd read all those books! Sure, they were literary candy and didn't have the depth that only people like her and John could understand, but they were great reads. Dark, and full of dirty sex. When she found out that he co-wrote the books with his wife, Lottie wasn't that surprised. That's *why they were so dumbed down — his wife clearly didn't have John's intellect. Or Lottie's. The violent nature of the books and the tension between the couples told her, somehow, that John's marriage wasn't so solid. Even better for her. Lottie hatched an elaborate plan to meet her favorite author. Sure, she has to drug him, but a writer would appreciate the intricate plotting. Even if he were more timid — hey, some guys are — he would eventually come around if she persisted enough. Would Lottie cross an ocean to catch him? To free him?*

John was outside the store, but the woman who couldn't possibly have been his stalker was already gone. His paranoia went nowhere.

I must be going nuts.

"Hey mister!" A shout from behind him. John turned around. "You gonna pay for that?"

He looked down at his basket, filled with a single lonely pineapple.

"Sorry," John said, face flushing hot. "I don't know what I was thinking."

Chapter Twelve

Finally, the weekend.

The last few days hadn't been easy. John couldn't get Lottie out of his head, but *these* unwelcome thoughts weren't anything like the ones from before. Zero chance of a boner with these.

That girl outside of Hot Cross Buns looked like she could have been Lottie's sister, if not her twin.

Or Lottie herself.

And then at Provisions, he thought he'd spotted her again.

John's mind kept circling that particular wagon, and every trip around stirred the mess in his gut further.

Lottie *couldn't* be here.

That's what he kept telling himself, like a vaccine to ward off a plague. Because if she was here from London, then there was only one possible reason. And that reason wasn't just nuts, it was downright dangerous. She could destroy everything in his life with one short sentence.

I fucked your husband.

The parts of John that were panicking most kept

insisting that he tell Vicky and at least get in front of the situation, attempt to control it. But his less impulsive parts told him to wait, observe, and only pull the trigger on the madness of confession if he had no other choice. Because telling Vicky would surely mean the end of everything. Besides, her mood was presently buoyant, and John wasn't stupid enough to throw a rock through a stained glass window.

Most of the time, John felt happy that Lottie hadn't called or texted since that night at the hotel. But the rest of him was constantly looking over his shoulder. He didn't know how she got his number — he'd scribbled something random. Did she somehow get it off his phone while he slept? Was that possible without knowing his passcode?

Shit. If she'd drugged him, she could have just used his thumb print while he was passed out.

By the time he made it back home and took the pineapple into the kitchen, Dakota was home from school and deep into a furious textathon with her friends on the couch. Vicky had parked Evie on a beanbag in front of something Disney, a plastic bowl of Cheerios balanced on her lap. Valentine sat beside her, waiting for an errant Cheerio or five to drop.

Everything as it should be.

John could almost exhale.

Vicky came downstairs carrying an open laptop, beaming as she showed him her work on the treatment.

"I really love it," she said as she handed the laptop to him.

Vicky was binary when it came to self-assessment. Her work was either *terrible* or *brilliant*.

"But I think I've taken it as far as I can," she continued. "You're better at all the plotty things, and explaining why stuff in the pilot will matter in season four. I can tell them why Madison Blue will tear up the screen. I'm excited about pitching this."

"Me too," John said, meaning it. All his paranoia melted away and he felt a sudden rush of pride for Vicky, encouraged by everything in his life not having to do with Lottie. "I've got the rest of this. I promise. You've already done all the stuff I didn't want to do. The stuff I *can't* do."

"Thanks for saying that."

John closed the laptop. "So, the nanny?"

Vicky shrugged.

"Not going well?"

"I've talked to a few people, but I haven't really clicked with anyone. At all. I do think I have a new word, though."

"Oh yeah, what?"

"A poppin. You know, like Mary?"

John made a face.

"You don't like it."

He shook his head. "Not my favorite."

"Then *you* give it a name."

"I don't really have a problem with 'nanny.' It's definitely better than *au pair*. How about governess? Or Maria? I would rather have the *Sound of Music* nanny than Mary Poppins. I don't trust anyone with a bottomless purse."

"Maybe Julie Andrews is the common denominator."

"Where are you looking for your . . . poppins?"

"April gave me a few names. She's a gossip and knows everything about everyone, but as I talked to every person on that list I got the distinct feeling I'll eventually find myself on some sort of underground nanny newsletter. *'That bitch is sooooo crazy.'*"

John laughed. She might not be wrong. "You tried LiveLyfe?"

"Already posted. I got a couple of responses, but really,

it's not a big deal. I'm thinking maybe we should just forget the whole thing."

"But it *is* a big deal. It's not about how you feel right now, it's about how you feel the next time. And the time after that. Getting you the help you need to keep you at some sort of baseline, and working, will be good for you. And for us. And for the writing."

"I know, I just . . . I don't really want to share my space, you know?"

"Is that what this is about?"

"A little." She looked away, embarrassed.

John took her hand. "Call an agency. This can't be hard, people do it every day. Give it a try. If you don't like it, we won't do it. We'll figure something else out. But I want you to stop thinking that *you* have to do it all. There's no shame in getting some help for us."

"Okay."

"Promise?"

"I promise." Her lips formed a little smile and gave him butterflies. "Thank you."

Vicky looked up at him, her eyes adoring. She was in a good place. So *they* were in a good place.

He wished they could stay there forever.

"How about if I take Evie to the park and then come back with some lunch? I can take Dakota and Valentine, too. Then you can have the house all to yourself."

"*And* you're going to finish the treatment?" She shoved him playfully in the chest. "What do you want?"

"A happy wife," he said. *And forgiveness.* Then he kissed her.

Five minutes later, John was pushing the stroller on their way to the park. Dakota walked beside him, holding Valentine's leash as she stopped and sniffed every bush they passed. Dakota had been mute since leaving the house.

"Are you giving me the silent treatment?" John asked.

"No. I just don't have anything to say."

"You *always* have something to say. Should we text instead?"

"Maybe I didn't want to go for a walk."

"That's fair," John said. "Maybe I didn't want to go for a walk either. But your sister did, and so did Valentine. Your mother deserves at least a few minutes in the day with the house to herself."

"I could've gone to my room. She wouldn't even know I was there."

"It's not the same, and yes, she would."

"Okay."

"Whether you wanted to come or not, here you are. So now you get to decide whether you're going to be miserable for the next hour, or be nice and maybe talk to me. Come on, dude, I'm dying here. Your sister isn't quite the conversationalist that I expect she may be one day."

"Fine. What do you want to talk about?"

"Why don't you tell me about the fight?"

"You already know what happened."

"Yes, because your mother told me. *We* still haven't discussed it, though." John put his hand on her shoulder. Dakota let it stay there.

After another six cracks in the sidewalk, she said, "I know you didn't *explicitly* tell me to punch Tiffany, but I really wanted to. I was in the locker room getting dressed and she came up to me and asked if I minded if she took a picture and tagged it hashtag-whatnottowear."

"You punched her for that?"

"No. I punched her because she said that my mom wrote my dad's books for him."

John stopped. "What?"

"Yeah," Dakota said. "I told Brittany one time that I

wished you still just wrote by yourself. Don't tell Mom . . . it'd just make her mad or sad or both. But I like your other books better."

"You shouldn't be reading *any* of them."

But it made him proud that she'd wanted to. Not that he was one of those dads who expected his kids to follow in his footsteps, but John hoped that he could at least inspire her to figure out what *she* wanted to do with her life, and do it.

If she ever finds out what I did with Lottie, Dakota will never look up to me again.

Oblivious to his inner turmoil, Dakota rolled her eyes and resumed their walk. "I'm old enough and that's not the point. Brittany never should have told Amanda, and Amanda never should have told Tiffany. I was just so mad. There were like six things between her first comment and that one, but I don't remember any of them. I just started yelling, and then I was punching her, and then Coach Carlin was pulling us apart. And here we are."

"What did you tell your mother?"

"That she kept calling me names and getting in my face. That's totally true. She doesn't need to know the other part."

"No. She doesn't."

They were silent for the last block before the park. As John opened the gate and held it for Dakota, he said, "I'm glad you like my books."

"Of course I like your books. They sound like you."

"Don't the books your mother and I write sound like us?"

"No. They sound like the person she wants you to be and the person she wants everyone to think she is."

"Ouch."

"Sorry, Dad. You asked me to always tell you the truth.

You fold to her too much. You're always so afraid of setting her off that sometimes you just do whatever she says."

"I don't do *whatever she says.*"

"Okay." Said like she wasn't buying it.

"I *don't,*" John said, getting louder. "But I *do* want peace, and we both know how bad it can get."

"I'm not blaming you. I just think that it sucks."

"It does suck," John agreed. He was realizing more and more that it didn't just suck for him. He'd thought they were hiding the worst from Dakota, but apparently they'd been failing.

He looked down at Evie, clapping and pointing at the swings. "Will you take her to the swings?"

"So you can sit and do nothing?"

"My 'sitting and doing nothing' has been putting a roof over your head for years."

Dakota rolled her eyes again and took Evie to the swings, leaving John with Valentine.

John brought the dog over to the benches and took a seat, scratching Valentine behind her ears as he watched his daughters on the swings. Eventually his eyes began to scan the park, drifting from one well-coiffed mom to another, crafting backstories for each of them.

But then his eyes were pulled toward a woman jogging just past the playground, coming around the bend in the path. Black yoga pants. Pink hoody. Blonde hair pulled back in a ponytail, whipping back and forth as she ran.

She jogged closer and John swallowed hard.

He'd seen that jogger before.

One regrettable evening across the sea.

You can pretend to come on my face!

It was Lottie, no doubt about it.

And she was jogging right toward him.

Chapter Thirteen

Lottie yanked the earbuds out of her ears. "Hi, John!"

Valentine's tail wagged as Lottie bent down and petted her on the head. Lottie was bright and chirpy, acting like a long-lost friend, smiling big, as if this wasn't completely fucking insane.

"Lottie?"

A laugh. "Who did you *think* it was?"

"Have you been following me?"

"Of *course* I have," she said. "Ever since *Behind the Curtain* — one of your best books, by the way."

"You know that's not what I mean. Have I . . . you know, seen you around?"

"I don't know." Lottie smiled. "*Have* you?"

Panic boiled in his guts. It took everything John had not to lose his shit in front of his kids. Dakota was out of earshot, still playing with Evie on the swings, but she was definitely in their line of sight, and looking toward them now, surely curious.

Please don't sit, please don't sit, please don't fucking sit —

Lottie sat. "What's wrong? You seem on edge, John."

John didn't know what to do. This woman was either totally fucking with him, or completely insane. Lottie was a good-looking girl, and vivacious in the sack, but now he wondered how much of his initial attraction was simply her stroking his ego, so he couldn't see the cracks in her very nutty shell.

"I'm not *on edge*, I just don't know what to think."

"What do you mean?"

"What do you *think* I mean, Lottie?" He stole a glance at his daughters. Tried to seem casual.

Lottie followed his eyes. "Them? You don't have to worry about that. I'm not going to say anything. So you really don't have to be shy."

John shifted on the bench and moved a subtle few inches from Lottie. "What do you want from me? I told you, we can't keep talking."

"We're talking right now."

"The last time I saw you was in London, and now you're here in Tivoli, thousands of miles from your home. Am I not supposed to think that's *weird*?"

Another laugh, this one with a slap to his knee. Dakota looked over again.

"What makes you think I live in London?" Lottie asked.

And then he noticed it, something that he'd failed to notice before. An icy chill ran through his body.

Lottie was no longer speaking with a British accent.

In fact, she didn't have any accent at all. Maybe something faintly Midwestern.

The question caught in his throat, but he forced it out anyway. "So . . . where do you live, Lottie?"

She looked at John as though *he* were crazy. "I live in New York. Same as you."

John felt like a block of ice, sitting there in the sun.

"Why all the lies, Lottie?"

"Lies?" Lottie laughed, and the sound that was once sweet as cream became nails on a chalkboard. "When did *I* lie?"

"You said you lived in London!" John realized that he was talking too loud, so he lowered his voice. "You said you lived in *London*, Lottie."

"I never said I *lived* there."

Again, too loud: "But you were speaking with a British accent!"

"You've never done that? Traveled to a foreign country and tried out their language?"

"The Brits speak fucking English, Lottie."

"I went to Paris for three months after college, you know, and I didn't speak English even once. I used my really terrible French the entire time. It's a great way to immerse yourself in the culture. But if you want to talk about lies, John, you told me you were a producer, and gave me a fake phone number and a fake name."

"What do you want, Lottie?"

She looked confused. "I don't *want* anything. Well, that's not *exactly* true. I did want to say hi. It's not like I could see you sitting on a park bench and not come over and say *something*." Lottie lowered her voice to a conspiratorial whisper. "Not after what we shared in London."

"We never should have done that."

"Yes, you keep saying that. But I know that's just what you have to tell yourself because now you're home with Victoria. But you don't have to worry about me, because . . ."

Lottie glanced over at the girls while she was talking. She watched Dakota lift Evie out of the swing, then take her hand and start walking toward them. Then she turned back to John. "Like I said, I'm not trying to get you into trouble. But I did want to say hello, and I don't want you to freak out every time you see me. Especially if you're ever with Victoria. That would just be *weird*!"

"*Every* time I see you?" John repeated her words numbly.

Lottie stood fast, then made a big show of shaking John's hand. She patted Valentine on the head before popping her earbuds back in, jogging back to the trail, and disappearing into the wooded nature trail that extended beyond the park.

"Who was that?" Dakota asked, looking after her.

John swallowed, prayed that his daughter couldn't see right through him like she always did, and fumbled for the safety of a half-lie. "She's just some fan. I guess she recognized my face from the book jacket and wanted to say hi."

"Must be one of *your* books." Dakota nodded in approval. "Good taste."

Dakota laughed and John forced himself to laugh along with her, even though he was feeling anything but amused.

Chapter Fourteen

They stayed at the park for what felt like the longest hour of John's life.

Evie still wanted to play on the slide, and then on the bars, and finally in the sand. And even though Dakota hadn't wanted to come, she didn't seem to be in any hurry to leave. Valentine could have stayed forever. All the while, John kept waiting for Lottie to come jogging by again. *Oh, hi there! These must be your daughters. So lovely. Say, girls, did your dad happen to tell you how he fucked my ass — or "arse," as the Brits say?*

Dakota kept looking at John, her eyes curious. He expected her to start questioning him at any moment about the strange blonde who had been sitting next to him on the bench — had she really bought his half-lie?

Why was she really sitting here, Dad?

Was she flirting with you? It seemed like she was flirting with you.

Did you fuck her in London? Because she flattered you and let you come in her mouth?

"Is everything okay?" Dakota finally asked, after his

series of noncommittal grunts to her attempts at conversation. It felt like a fitting role reversal, considering his recent attempts to get her to open up.

"Yeah, everything is great. I'm just . . . thinking hard about our treatment. That's part of the reason I wanted to come out here." John looked down at the dog. "Valentine usually helps, but today she's been worthless."

Dakota let it go, but John couldn't tell if she actually bought it.

He was lost in his head, thinking in circles, looping back to the "incident" with that lit major, Aubrey. He hadn't done anything wrong but Vicky had threatened to chop his balls off anyway.

What if Dakota mentioned Lottie to Vicky?

What if Vicky didn't believe him when he said Lottie was just a random fan out for a jog?

What if Vicky read the truth in his eyes and knew that he'd cheated on her?

He'd do anything to keep that from happening.

By the time they got home, the house was spotless, and filled with the scent of meat on the grill and pineapple upside-down cake baking in the oven. It was hard to believe they'd only been gone for an hour and a half. Vicky bounced into the living room before "We're home!" was all the way out of his mouth.

"The place looks great," John said.

"It's a miracle what I can get done with one hour and an empty house. *This* one" — she pointed at Evie — "is like a reverse vacuum cleaner. Seriously, thanks for getting them out of my hair."

"Out of your hair?" Dakota said. "I was going to go to my room and not bother anyone."

"You're right." Vicky smiled, then came over and kissed her eldest child on the cheek. "I knew you wouldn't be in my way. But it was still nice to have an empty house and to cross a lot of items off my to-do list."

"Perfect," John said. "I did some good thinking at the park. I'd like to get at least a little of it on the page before dinner."

"Good idea." She tilted her head at him. "You have that stationed-on-Pluto look."

"Sorry. I'm just . . . ." The lying was coming easier every day. "Just thinking about what order things should go in."

Forty-five gut-twisting minutes later, John sat next to Dakota at the dinner table, across from Evie and Vicky. Evie was mashing bananas all over her highchair, face, and hands. She tried reaching across the table to smear some on John.

"No thanks," he said. "I think I'll stick with the chicken."

Evie laughed.

"So how was the park?" Vicky asked.

Cold sweat leaked from every pore on his body. He took a gulp of water.

Vicky prodded, "Was that mom with the unitard there?"

Dakota's fork stopped halfway to her mouth. "Unitard?"

"There's a woman with a toddler a few months older than Evie," John said. "Apparently she wears a bright yellow unitard every day. Your mother's obsessed."

"You guys should really let me stay home every once in a while. It's amazing the things I'm not learning in school."

"How *is* school?" John asked, eager to divert the conversation away from the park.

Dakota looked at her father. "Fine . . . I guess? Same as always. Mr. Graubner's a jerk, and the school day is a few hours too long."

"You get out at three o'clock," Vicky said.

"Read up, Mom. Americans spend more time than most in class, but we're still not learning as much. Russia has like half the hours that we do. And did you know that kids in Finland get no more than four hours of homework a week? And there are no grades or tests. We are literally the worst in every way." Her eyes flashed across the table at Vicky. "And please don't tell me that you're disappointed in my use of the word *literally*."

"I wasn't going to." But Vicky's expression turned a little sour, her lips tighter than before.

And so went dinner. The park did eventually come back up, but only because Dakota wanted to talk about Evie's courage on both the swings and the slide, and about how she stood up to a baby half her size who dared to play with some adjacent sand. They also talked about how unfortunate it was that the mom with the yellow unitard was MIA. But there was no mention of the "pretty jogger in the park," despite John's ever-present worry that the subject would bubble up like boiling lava.

His fingers twitched with the compulsion to get out his phone and check the ringer, to make sure it was silenced. In case Lottie called again.

She didn't. But the idea that she might ruined the evening anyway.

"I'll do the dishes," he said after dinner, even though it was Dakota's turn.

John wanted to think, and stare out the window. He wanted his back to his family and, for fifteen minutes, to the rest of the world.

When the dishes were done, he went to his office, where he tried and failed to add a single cogent paragraph to their treatment for Fable. He finally surrendered and went to tuck Evie into bed.

Bedtime had always been easy with Dakota. Evie was a different story. Even when she showed all the signs of exhaustion — rubbing her eyes, yawning on repeat, falling apart at the smallest provocation — she couldn't stand to miss out, or be away from the family. Even though she didn't have the language to express it, John knew that she somehow saw bedtime as a punishment.

He told Vicky that he'd take the lead, then handled it like a project, starting with knowing that he had to teach Evie to fall asleep alone. If she could only go to bed with her parents around, she'd form other bad habits that would be hard to break later.

Now they followed their nighttime ritual religiously, unless John wasn't home. Ten minutes before lights out, he asked, "Do you want a story, or do you want to listen to the music box?"

Evie would point to either the box or the bookshelf. Tonight, she pointed to the box.

"Music it is." John smiled, then walked over and picked up the music box. He opened the lid, and filled Evie's bedroom with "Für Elise."

Then he kissed her on the forehead and sat in the rocking chair next to her crib. He started to rock, knowing that she would be asleep in minutes.

John woke up an hour or so later, jolting out of the rocking chair and looking wildly around the room. He shook his head to clear it, then checked on Evie once more, tucking her in before going to his bedroom.

Vicky was already sleeping, loudly snoring. He closed the door, went into the bathroom, sat on the toilet, and checked his phone.

His stomach dropped. Two messages from an unlisted number.

John hit the button for voicemail and raised the phone to his ear.

"It's me. Lottie." Still sounding slightly Midwestern. "I was thinking about our little chance encounter at the park and, well, I really don't want you freaking out. I started imagining all this from your perspective and I can understand if it looks a little crazy."

She laughed, but this time it sounded surprisingly reasonable and understanding, almost self-effacing. More like the laugh he'd fallen for in London.

"Even though I never *said* I lived in London, I can totally see how you thought that I did, since I was using the accent and didn't tell you I was staying in an Airbnb." Her voice fell to a whisper. "*That's where you fucked me.*"

Normal voice resumed, as if she hadn't said anything of the sort. "Anyway, I'm a big fan, but I didn't want to come off like a big stupid fangirl, you know? You weren't a speaker, so I thought that maybe you were trying to stay on the down-low at the fair, especially after you told me that you were a Hollywood producer and then gave me the fake name."

Another laugh, this one less reasonable. "I guess we both like to tell stories. Anyway, I'm sure we'll see each other again at some point, and I don't want you to think I'm crazy when we do."

She ended the message abruptly. No goodbye.

John looked at the phone.

He played the second message. Silence for thirty seconds or so, followed by a click.

John left the bathroom, looked at his sleeping wife, and wondered if the walls of his world were about to start crumbling down around them all.

Chapter Fifteen

It was Sunday, and just like most Sundays, John was whittling his chore list to nothing.

Before they were a writing team, it was John's job to write all week and do some of his "husbandly chores" on the weekend, while Vicky tended to the household's day-to-day duties. She did the cooking, cleaning, laundry, ironing, sewing, decorating, gardening, and all of the shopping — including all the gifts for family and friends.

It was never a conversation. They just sort of divided the chores in the way that seemed to make the most sense. John filled his weekends with mowing the lawn, pulling the weeds — which Vicky didn't consider part of gardening — and general maintenance, plus all of the grungier scrubbing that Vicky hated and John genuinely didn't mind all that much.

It was almost an escape. John could clean for hours and not remember even five of those minutes. Though the soap coated his hands, John's mind was usually marinating on story, working on solutions, untangling narrative knots. But today he was orbiting a more personal tale — still working on a solution, but now untangling the narrative knots of *his* life.

Because this thing with Lottie was one nightmare of a knot.

One that could ruin everything if he didn't untangle it, and fast.

As if fate were taunting him right there in his kitchen, John's phone buzzed. He knew what it would say before he shook the suds off his hand to check it.

He was right. *Unlisted.*

Vicky sat at the dining room table, poring over a pile of notes. Evie played with her Little People activity center at Vicky's feet, and Dakota seemed to be everywhere, flitting from the TV to the kitchen for regular snacks.

John wanted to deal with this right now. Answer the phone and yell at Lottie. Call Verizon and change his number. Get Sam on the phone and see if he had any suggestions. He was starting to feel like his life was a waking nightmare, hallucinating the phone buzzing in his pocket even when it wasn't, and imagining all of the things he'd say to Lottie once given the chance. But dealing with it now was impossible.

He let the call go unanswered and finished the dishes.

There were a few times during that day that he found himself alone. He wished that Lottie would call so he could end things once and for all. He considered calling her. He even thought of a few things he could say that might drive the point home for her.

But of course, she didn't call again. And he didn't dare call her.

Later that night, the whole family gathered around the dining room table to play a game.

Soggy Doggy had been one of Dakota's favorite games when she was little, and even though it was still a bit sophisticated for Evie — ages four and up, the box said — it was still entertaining. Dakota was moving her piece back to the start when the phone rang.

Not his cell phone, but the house phone, the one plugged into the wall that the cable company made them pay for even though no one ever used it.

John, Vicky, and Dakota all looked at each other in confusion.

Vicky raised her eyebrows. "When was the last time we heard *that?*"

"It's been a while," John said. Then he stood up to answer.

Dakota bounded up from the table. "I got it, Dad! It's your turn."

John stared at the board, forgetting the rules of *Soggy Doggy*, his heart pounding and his ears straining, waiting for Dakota's return.

He heard her in the other room, a faint, "Hello?" then, "*Hello?*"

She returned and sat back down at the table. "Weird."

"No one there?" Vicky asked.

"Someone was there, they just didn't say anything. I could hear them breathing. And then they hung up. The Caller ID said Private Number."

John's eyes were all over Vicky, studying her for the slightest hint of suspicion. But he saw only mirth.

"Remember how fun crank calling was in the eighties?" Vicky asked him, snickering. "Did you ever do that?"

If this kept on, his heart was going to explode. "Not much."

"Oh, I did," Vicky laughed. "Me and Jenny Morrison used to do it *all the time.*"

"Like?" Dakota said.

"Like we would call some random person and ask for

Samantha. Then we'd hang up when the person told us that we had the wrong number. Then we'd call back later and ask that person if Samantha had any messages." Vicky laughed harder.

"I don't get it," Dakota said. "What's the joke?"

Which only made Vicky laugh harder.

John tried to fake it. He couldn't. Still barely clinging to his facade of calm, he said, "I have to go to the bathroom."

He had been sitting on the toilet for five minutes, clutching the phone and waiting, certain it would buzz in his palm at any second. But it had remained horribly silent. How much longer could he spend in the bathroom without arousing suspicion?

Because suspicion was a trail that led to the horrible truth.

Another minute without a buzz. John checked his email, just because.

Then one more minute, and still nothing.

He needed to get back to the table. Apparently he'd have to deal with Lottie later.

But just as he stood, the phone buzzed in his hand.

Unlisted.

"Hello?" he growled into the phone.

"Hello!" Lottie said, a thrill in her voice.

"You need to stop fucking calling." After nearly thirty seconds of silence, John could no longer stand it. "Are you there?"

"I'm here," she said, her voice brittle. A long, uncomfortable pause. "I'm really sorry. I just . . . I miss you, John. I needed to hear your voice."

Another long pause. John thought of a dozen responses, none quite right, and discarded them all. Finally, she ended the silence. "I was hoping that maybe you would want to hear from me, too."

"You *get* that I'm married, don't you?"

"Yes, I'm sorry, John, I —"

"I love my wife. Can you understand that?"

"Yes . . . but what am I supposed to do? Your words are inside me — just like you were. I can't stop thinking about you, about us, about all the things you did to my body and that I'm dying for you to do again. Do you remember those things, John?"

"Yes — *no*."

"I do . . . and I don't want to remember them alone anymore."

"You have to. I can't do this. Listen, do you really care about me?"

"More than anything."

"Then I need you to stop calling me. Because this *will* ruin my life. And that won't mean that the two of us are together, it will mean that everything I have will be taken away. I'll lose my wife *and* my daughters. Would you really want to do that to me?"

Soft, almost a whisper. "No . . . I don't want to do that to you."

"Then please don't. Please stop calling."

After a long silence, Lottie finally replied. "Okay, John. I'll stop calling you. I hope that everything works out with you and Victoria."

Impossibly, she sounded sincere.

"Thank you," he said with a heavy exhale.

"But John . . ."

"Yes?"

"You still need to know that I will always love you."

And then the line went dead.

John stared at the phone in his hand, not quite knowing what to do. Lottie was crazy, and as much as he wanted to believe she was out of his life, it was hard to imagine her detonating an "I love you" bomb before disappearing forever.

He practically crashed into Vicky outside the bathroom.

"Who were you talking to?"

"Sam," he said, the lie flying from his mouth before his brain worked out the finer details.

"In the bathroom?"

John shrugged. "I was sitting there when he called."

"And you couldn't call him back?"

He forced a grin. "I wanted to get back to *Soggy Doggy*."

"Is everything okay?" She was biting her bottom lip. That wasn't good.

"Of course. Why?"

"Because you've never taken a call in the bathroom before, not once. And you look pissed."

He had to be careful. Tiptoe. Measure every move. The wrong one would tip Vicky into a terrible place. Protecting himself *was* protecting her. So his second lie came even faster than the first.

"I didn't want to tell you, but . . ." — dramatic sigh — "Sam wants to pull out with Fable. He doesn't like the deal."

"*What?* Are you kidding? What's wrong with the deal?"

"He thinks we can do better."

"Based on what?"

Shrug. "He says he's been sniffing around, and has his fingers on the pulse."

Vicky held out her hand. "Give me your phone."

"We already have our ten o'clock with him tomorrow."

"I want to talk to him now."

"It's Sunday night."

"He called *us* on Sunday night, John."

"This is why I didn't want to tell you. Can you please just trust me on this? Honestly, I think he's been drinking and was just feeling a little mouthy. It's Sunday night, he's alone, he probably got to thinking —"

"Thinking what? About fucking us out of the deal we've been working toward for a year?"

"I've handled it."

"You better have. For Sam's sake. Because if he isn't licking our assholes with 'sorry' on his tongue by tomorrow morning, then I'll — I'll — *ugh*. Now come on." She gestured toward the living room. "Let's put this Doggy to bed."

John followed Vicky back to the game, wondering how fast he could get ahold of Sam and make sure they were on the same page with their lie — *his* lie — before morning.

Chapter Sixteen

John was walking a razor wire of alertness, despite his exhaustion. *Stay awake, John.*

Vicky liked to hit the sheets around nine or midnight, depending on her mood. Unfortunately, she was still laughing at reruns of *It's Always Sunny in Philadelphia* at 11:37.

"One more?" she asked.

"Okay," John said. "One more."

Eyes open.

He wouldn't normally have minded. Because he wouldn't have typically been awake, anyway. But tonight he was waiting for Vicky to start snoring so he could get out of the house and on the phone with Sam.

Forty-five minutes after the "Dennis and Dee Go on Welfare" episode ended, John was donning his jacket and sneaking out the back door into the cold night air.

He dialed Sam's number.

"John?"

"Yeah, it's me. Sorry, were you sleeping?"

"Barely." Sam's voice sounded even older than he was.

"What's up? Everything okay? And what's that sound? Are you dodging bullets?"

"It's the wind. I'm walking."

"The two of you get in a fight?"

"No. At least not yet. She's sleeping. But I kinda fucked you and you need to know before our ten o'clock tomorrow. Because she's going to rip your dick off."

"It's always good to know when you're being fucked. And double fuck-you for this after waking me up. So what did I do?"

"You had too much to drink, then you tried to convince me that we shouldn't take the Fable deal."

"That sounds highly irresponsible of me. Why would I do that?"

John sighed. "She called."

"Lottie?"

"Yeah."

"What happened?"

"I knew she was going to call, so I went into the bathroom and waited."

"Why not just put your phone on Do Not Disturb?"

"Because when you see a bomb in your house, you get it out of there as fast as you can. Do you want to hear the story or not?"

"I *did* wake up for it." Sam coughed. "Jesus, can you walk in the other direction or something?"

John crossed the street and started walking with the wind.

"Well? Get on with it."

John took a deep breath. "So she called and I told her that she had to stop, but then when I left the bathroom I ran into Vicky. She asked me who I was talking to and I said you, because that makes sense, even though it was in the bathroom and she definitely thought *that* was weird. But then she asked me why I looked so mad and —"

"The first thing you thought of was that I wanted to fuck the Fable deal?"

"I'm sorry."

Sam sighed. "It's fine. I'll fix things with Vicky. But we need to talk about your international stalker."

"She doesn't live in London."

"Where does she live?"

"Here."

"In America?"

"In New York."

"She moved to New York?"

"No. I think she already lived here. Maybe the whole time."

"Oh, wow, my friend. You *definitely* have a stalker. You said she had an English accent. Even went on like an idiot about how sexy it was."

"It *was* sexy, but it was also totally fake. She came up to me at the park."

"She came up to you at the park?" Sam repeated, now sounding twenty years younger. Sounding like he'd finally woken up to the situation.

"While I was there with Evie and Dakota."

"What happened?"

"She jogged right up to me, sat next to me on the bench, and just started talking like we were old friends or something."

"Did Dakota say anything?"

"*See* anything or *say* anything?"

"Take your pick."

"She didn't say anything, at least not to Vicky. But she noticed. I told her the woman was a fan."

"So . . . *fuck*. This is serious."

"Right. And tonight, Sam? I think she called the house. Our landline. When Dakota answered, no one was there. That's why I went into the bathroom. I figured she was trying to get my attention. I'm worried as shit that she's going to keep calling the house phone, or showing up at the park, or, worse, on my doorstep. What if she approaches Vicky directly? Or wants money, threatening to tell her if I don't?"

"Do you think that's what she's doing?"

"I don't know. You've seen Vicky when she's having one of her highs?"

"Of course."

"Lottie's a little like that, except her high has no end in sight. She's always laughing, and even when she's not, her whole face seems to glow. It makes you want to smile right back. And when she said she was sorry, she really sounded sorry. But fuck if I know."

"I could see how a stalker sounding sorry would really convince you."

"Are you going to help me or not?"

"Of course I'm going to help you, you dumb fucking bastard. That's why you're calling me at fuckyou in the morning."

John stopped walking. "So what do I do?"

"Nothing. I'm going to look into this. I have people I can call. In the meantime, just make sure that you're on Do Not Disturb and stay on top of the house phone. Hell, unplug the thing if you think it'd go unnoticed. Make sure that *you're* the one taking Evie to the park. And leave Dakota at home next time."

"I'm pretty sure she was also at Provisions, and outside Hot Cross Buns."

"Jesus . . . I'll move fast."

"Sam. What if she tries to extort me?"

"Don't pay. Call me. We'll get a fixer, someone who can maybe take care of this without anything ever getting to Vicky."

"What, is that like an actual job?"

"I represent a lot of authors, John. You'd be surprised at how many *problems* I've had to take care of. Way worse than this, trust me. We'll be okay."

John said nothing, hoping that Sam would continue. He did.

"Remember Angela?"

"Mob ex-wife. Crazy bitch."

"One and only. Thanks to her, I know a guy named Danny, and I'll tell you, Danny alone is worth the alimony. One of my authors — I won't say who because I wouldn't do that to *you*, but he's a household name and a royal fucker — he got himself into a little pickle with an underage prostitute. His wife didn't give a shit — she was fine with him giving it to hookers, even young ones, so long as he stayed on the bestseller lists. But the public *would* mind. Award-winning writers can drink themselves sick, drug themselves into oblivion, get bored and nail whoever they want. They can suffer from any possible combination of mental disorders. But what they can't do, because they're not some Hollywood fucking producer, is have sex with underage hookers."

"What happened?"

"Danny. Danny's the one who made the problem go away. I swear the guy could get a murder rap to disappear."

Something ugly and black belched in John's stomach.

"How *noble* of him."

Part of him wanted to ask how Sam could feel okay with getting that author's problem "fixed" — but the moral high ground would have to wait for another time, prefer- ably when John wasn't dick-deep in his own mess.

"Everyone should know someone who knows someone who knows a fixer, John. You need Danny, and you'll be glad you know me. Besides, this isn't about protecting *you*."

"It's not?"

"Shit, no! John, this is about protecting your family."

Chapter Seventeen

"So we don't get to pick *any* of the songs?" John asked.

"No, Dad. I already told you a bunch of times, we have no say."

"What's the point of a Father-Daughter Dance if we can't dance to 'Barbie Girl'?"

Dakota laughed. They were leaving Macy's and heading through the mall toward Nordstrom, their third and hopefully final spot to find a dress for the Father-Daughter Dance. Dakota wasn't usually as picky as she'd been today. John was trying to figure out if her opinions were getting stronger with age or if she was merely milking the time alone with him.

"The point is the dance itself. You're thinking about a Father-Daughter Dance at a *wedding*." Dakota blanched. "That's totally different."

"Ohhh . . ." John said, playing along. "And you're probably too young for that."

"Gross, Dad."

"I'm just saying! We'll figure out the song now, then have a good fifteen years to anticipate it."

"Fifteen years?"

"And not a year earlier."

They rounded the corner, with Nordstrom now directly in front of them.

"So what kind of personality are we going for? Do we want your bridesmaids laughing or crying?"

"Definitely laughing. Except for my maid of honor. She should be crying."

"Why?"

"She's a total brat."

"Oh? Who is she?"

Dakota shrugged. "Not sure. Probably haven't met her yet. Maybe Evie? How about you? Are you more of an 'Ain't No Mountain High Enough' kinda dad, or are you thinking 'Macarena'?"

"'Macarena.'" John's tone grew mock-serious. "Are you okay with that?"

"I think we'll have to talk about it."

And they did, laughing harder each time Dakota emerged from the dressing room in a different gown. By the time she chose her final dress — a two-piece with a crop top and high-waisted skirt, simple and in the perfect shade of blush — they also had their lineup of songs, though they might have been the worst wedding selections in history. Kanye's "Gold Digger," REM's "It's the End of the World as We Know It," and "D-I-V-O-R-C-E" by Tammy Wynette, all suggested by John but immediately agreed upon by Dakota based on the titles alone.

"Can we get a Cinnabon?" Dakota asked, leaving Nordstrom and eyeing the food court across the way. She added a long and drawn-out "*Pleeease!*" before John could even answer.

"It's like two hours until dinnertime."

"Mom doesn't have to know. And we can split it."

"I don't want any of your Cinnabon. I'm too damned old to be putting that into my body. I'd probably gain twenty pounds with the first mouthful."

"Does that mean I can have one?"

"Fine," John said, "but please don't tell your mother. I mean, I don't want you to lie. So if she asks you, 'Did you have a Cinnabon?' then you need to say yes. But don't bring it up. And you have to wait in line, because I'll want it if I smell it."

Dakota laughed and thanked him. A few minutes later she was standing in line while John waited at a table, scrolling through his phone. Mercifully, he saw nothing from Lottie. No calls, no texts, no emails to his johntread-wellauthor email address. He looked up and around him. He didn't exactly feel safe, but —

No.

A flash of blonde, then a look back his way before the woman that couldn't possibly be Lottie darted into Forever 21.

He bounded up from his seat, glanced over at Dakota still waiting in line with her back to him, and took off after the woman.

But inside the fast-fashion mecca, John saw only shoppers — a third or so blonde, and none of them looked like Lottie.

But no, there she was at the edge of the store, riffling through a long row of graphic tees. John had a fat half-minute while crossing the floor toward her to consider all the stuff he would say. What kind of game was she playing?

He came up behind Lottie, grabbed her roughly by the shoulder, and spun her around.

"What the fuck are you doing here? And —"

The woman — who, he clearly now saw, definitely

wasn't Lottie — looked up at John with wide, horrified eyes. She didn't seem scared so much as affronted. She shook herself out of his grip and said, "Excuse me?"

John fell a step back. "I am so, so sorry. I thought you were someone else."

"And you were going to grab that person and yell at them?"

"She . . . it's someone who is putting my daughter in danger."

"Oh . . ." The woman's face seemed to relax a bit. "I'm . . . sorry?"

"Thank you," John said. "And again, I'm so sorry."

He gave her an awkward smile, then, feeling like a nutjob, made his way back to the food court.

"Where did you go?" Dakota asked through a mouthful of sweet-smelling garbage, her lips ringed with frosting. "And why do you look like you just goosed a pony?"

"I — I had to run to the bathroom." He looked down at her Cinnabon. "Maybe it's the fumes."

"Whatever. You know you want this. But it's too late now." She shoved the last bit of bun into her mouth, barely chewed, then swallowed.

"Freedom!" John said, though he really did want one now that the scent had found his nostrils.

Ten minutes later they were in the parking lot . . . and ten minutes after *that* they were still looking for their car.

"Usually I agree when you say that you're crazy, but yes, we definitely parked here." Dakota pointed to Sears. "Because I said, 'Who even goes there?' and you said, 'They used to have a catalog.'"

Dakota was right. John was trying not to flip out. He was on edge after seeing a Lottie who wasn't *that* Lottie.

And now his car was missing. Had it been stolen, or was this something else?

"Excuse me!" John raised his hand at a security guard in a passing golf cart.

The man rolled to a stop. "Yes, sir?"

John gave him a self-deprecating smile. "I'm sorry to bother you, but I think our car might have been stolen."

"Are you sure this is where you parked it?"

"Positive," Dakota said.

"Because a lot of people think they parked one place when really they parked somewhere else."

"We parked here." Again, Dakota pointed to Sears. "Right over there."

The guy looked unconvinced still. He shrugged. "Well, you can hop in the cart and I can drive you around the lot if you'd like. If you keep clicking your key fob, your car will eventually beep."

"*If* it's here," Dakota said.

"Sure," the guard said.

He was smug when John and Dakota got into the back of his cart — but much more so when they found the Odyssey on the other side of the lot. It chirped, then the guard smiled and drove right up to it.

"A lot of people think they parked one place," the guard repeated, "when really, they parked somewhere else."

John thanked the guard, who waved goodbye as he sped off in his cart. John helped Dakota lay her dress flat on one of the Odyssey's bench seats.

She got into the front seat and closed the door. "That was weird."

"It was," John agreed. His heart was beating too fast, too loud.

He backed out of the space and the Odyssey made a loud *THUMP*, followed by a dragging sound.

"What's that?" Dakota asked.

"A flat." John fell down the cliff face from nervous to scared. "We have a flat tire."

Chapter Eighteen

John wasn't sure that he would ever be able to sleep again. And when you don't sleep, your mind takes the opportunity to drag all your skeletons into the bright light of a burdened mind.

Once upon a time, he almost lost everything *and he hadn't even been cheating.*

That entire episode with Aubrey had been crazy. He never wanted to go through that sort of hell again, and Vicky promised that he'd never have to. He believed her. But this . . . this he had brought on himself.

His life was about to tear apart at the seams, thanks to his stupidity. And Vicky was oblivious to his turmoil — at the moment, at least — snoring with the corners of her mouth twitching in a little smile. He wondered what she was dreaming about. At least for now she was far away from the nightmares that would surely come.

He didn't deserve this. He had been tricked. He'd told Lottie to stop. She had probably drugged him. Raped him?

But the only thing he'd had in his system the night of

the hotel room phone sex was vodka, and not all that much.

Wanna play a game? The game is called, "Which One is My Pussy?"

I can hear you breathing. I can hear you jacking off. Do you want me to join you?

Say it.

"I want you to join me . . ."

Vicky snored and John rolled over.

Half in a panic, he reached down to the floor and flipped his phone face up, making sure that all of those texts and pics were deleted before checking to see if Lottie had sent something through his Do Not Disturb in the half hour since he last checked.

Four missed calls. Fuck.

His heart leaping into his throat, John swallowed and swiped over to the recent calls, expecting to see an unlisted number.

But it was his mom.

His heart was still pounding, but now for a different reason.

He slipped out of bed, hitting Send on his mother's number before his foot hit the top stair. He didn't even hear it ring before she picked up.

"I'm sorry, John, I know it's . . . late," his mom managed to say before her voice split down the middle.

A cloud of emotion hovered above him, pregnant and angry, ready to spill.

"What's wrong, Mom?"

A terrible sound, like a coughing cat, followed by an awful silence that yawned an eon too long. John waited, knowing and hating that there was nothing he could do.

Then, finally: "Your father . . ." Another long pause. "He's gone, John."

John bit his bottom lip, unsure of what to say. What did *gone* mean? Had he finally gotten fed up with John's brother, Barry? Had he left like he'd been threatening to for the last thirty years? Or was he . . . *gone*?

"Did you hear me?"

"Yes," John said. "Just processing. How did it happen?"

"I found him on the bathroom floor."

"Oh."

"He said he wasn't feeling well, but you know your father . . . when's the last time you heard that man say anything else? The toilet flushed, and then there was a thud. I checked on him, because it was so loud and he didn't answer when I called. But I never expected to see . . . that. Sixty-eight isn't that old. We were going to Alaska in two months. He was excited because we've never been that many miles away from Barry —" Her voice had been steadily rising into panic.

"I know, Mom. I'm so sorry."

"I tried to get him to wake up. Thought maybe he slipped and fell and that was all it was. But he wasn't moving. He was just . . . not there anymore. Gone."

"Oh my God."

"The doctor said it was a pulmonary embolism. A blood clot from his leg lodged itself in his lung. There's nothing that anyone could have done."

"I'll be there tomorrow."

"Thank you, John."

He wandered the kitchen while finishing his call, then said goodbye and poured himself a drink from the first bottle his fingers closed around when reaching into the cabinet. Tequila.

His father was gone. The world was a bog, and John was lost inside it.

Andrew Treadwell had been old school. Blue collar

and proud of it, with no desire for that color to ever change. He'd worked as a field service technician. John never even knew what that meant growing up, and didn't bother to find out until his character, Arnold Coffee, needed a nine-to-five in *Diner Fires and Kindling*.

The tequila bit back as he sipped.

The old man kept his emotions a planet away from everyone else, believing that too much affection spoiled his children, and that a good wife knew her husband loved her without all that "lovey-dovey crap." In many ways, John was grateful for the terrible example. It made him a much better father. John always liked taking Dakota to the mall or dance class or wherever she needed to go. He never saw it as a chore on those days when he was in charge, when Vicky just couldn't deal. Even when Evie fussed and Dakota withdrew into her phone.

But even though John wasn't much like his father, that didn't mean he wouldn't miss him. Or that he didn't love him. Or that for the rest of his days John wouldn't be thinking up things he wished he had said to him.

Three drinks and two hours later, he finally wandered aimlessly back to his side of the bed and fell asleep. Still, his eyes were back open before Vicky's the next morning.

He went downstairs, turned on the coffee, and booked his flight. He was leaving in five hours — and paying three times the usual price for the pleasure of doing so. The timing couldn't be worse. He felt vulnerable, his life's many windows all open for Lottie to crawl through.

John considered just taking everyone with him, insisting that it was the right thing to do. Vicky wouldn't like it and Dakota wouldn't understand. The flight would be miserable with Evie. But he could do it. He could play the *My Father Just Died* card and get them all to go with him.

But then his house would be empty, and Lottie could

have unfettered access to his home and riffle through his shit even more than she already had. She wouldn't just be getting into his life, she'd be getting into his family's as well.

"Did you sleep last night?" Vicky asked, yawning as she entered the kitchen. "You were gone for a while."

"Vick . . . my father died."

Vicky was immediately awake. "Shit. Shit, John, I'm sorry."

She came over and gave him a hug. Then she kissed him on the cheek and pulled back just enough to look him in the eyes. "Are you okay?"

"Yes. But I need to go help my mom."

"Of course. Any idea how long you'll be gone?"

"No idea. I don't even know when the funeral is."

"Do you know when you're leaving?"

"Five hours from now. 12:35. But I need to lie down. I barely slept and I feel like I'm going to fall over."

"What do you want me to tell the children?"

"That I love them, and you, more than anything else in the world."

Chapter Nineteen

John hated airports even more than small talk.

Flying was a miracle, yada yada, but he loathed the whole experience. Driving to the airport, leaving his car behind for $27 a day, rushing to wait in the security line . . . It didn't matter what time he left, John always felt harried once he stepped into the airport terminal. Maybe that was because half the people around him were sprinting toward connecting flights. Plus, waiting in line for a filthy urinal while he tried not to get piss on his luggage was a special kind of hell. Food choices that would delight Dakota — he'd yet to find an airport missing its Cinnabon — but priced several times higher for a captive audience. Boarding was always miserable, with everyone worming their way to the front, hoping to cram their carry-on into the overhead bin without getting it checked. And the cherry on the shit sundae? Paying for motherfucking WiFi.

But the thing John hated most about the airport was that it seemed to bring out the worst in humanity.

Airports should be slightly more complicated than a bus stop. Instead, they buzzed with anxiety — excitement, stress, or nerves for the greenest fliers. People were rude, or distant in a way that they didn't seem to be in any other context. Not just the travelers, either. The people who actually worked in the airport were the worst, their sense of empathy strangled by the doldrums of a daily life they hated.

There was also something about the airport that made John excessively paranoid. Like the thought of spotting Lottie, or finding out his seat was right next to hers, *hardee-fucking-har*.

But how could he not be at least a little suspicious? After all, he could be standing right next to a terrorist and not even know it. John was a writer, after all — he could make up a story for everyone.

The most dangerous people always sat alone, often with their back against a wall or a bank of windows. They had carry-ons, usually black like their clothes. These people almost always wore glasses, either prescription lenses (though they could also have been clear glass) or sunglasses, even when indoors. All the better to hide the lies that might be otherwise visible behind their naked eyes.

Today, John's paranoia felt instinctive and primal, something he had no control over. He kept glancing around, at everyone and everything. For the first time, he felt justified, and not like he was being unnecessarily neurotic. He was being careful, searching for someone specific.

His quiet phone was driving him crazy. He felt like an idiot — or perhaps a Millennial, checking his phone every five seconds, unsure whether he wanted to see a message from Lottie or whether her silence signified something more ominous.

The flight felt three times longer than it actually was, and when John landed at LAX, the six and a half hours in the air had done nothing to quiet his nerves. If anything, he felt more uneasy than he had before boarding in New York.

He checked his phone for the billionth time. No texts from Lottie or anyone else. Not even a text from Vicky saying *Have a safe flight!* or *Text me when you land!*

He texted her anyway — *I'm here! Love you, love you!* — then stood inside the ground transportation exit, staring down at his palm, waiting for her to text back. Was everything okay at home? A few minutes was torture. Finally, he saw the three dots. He watched them for a while — a *long* while — then:

So glad you're safe! Do you think it would be cruel to get a muzzle for Evie? Do you think Children's Place carries anything like that? She's sleeping now, but OMG this morning! I still managed to get a couple of ideas down, but I'm not going to text them because I want to see your expression.

John texted back, *I can't wait to hear it. About to grab an Fastr. Will check in later.*

A few swipes later and John was waiting for an Fastr, still wondering if Lottie would attempt contact, or try to mess with his car or family in any way. He wondered if she somehow knew he was gone. If she had been watching him.

Would she show up at the park or his house? Or do something even worse that the writer inside him was afraid to imagine?

Chapter Twenty

The Fastr had been gone for more than a minute already, but John hadn't taken a single step toward his childhood home.

He just stood there, staring at it, sorting through too many emotions at once.

Was it because his father had passed, giving this homecoming additional weight? Or was it all this stuff with Lottie, making him afraid that he'd abandoned his family when they needed him most?

The outside of the house was unchanged, with the same manicured landscaping that had always been his mother's pride and which his father said was a "useless waste of time and money." The windows gleamed and the blue paint still appeared relatively fresh, even though it hadn't seen a brush in more than twenty years. His mother's yellow Mini Cooper was parked in the driveway, right in front of his brother's beast of an old Bronco. Despite the fact that it would be immaculate inside, he braced himself for his mother's fussy apologies for "the mess."

John swallowed and stepped onto the porch, his heart beating faster than it should.

He knocked twice, waited a beat, then turned the knob and walked inside.

"Mom?"

No one answered, but she couldn't be far.

"Mom!"

Still no answer. John went to his old room to drop off his stuff. It was still a museum of his childhood, but Barry had left his big brother a present on the bed.

It was a pink box, exactly the kind that would hold a dozen donuts. But John knew what would be inside the second he saw it. Barry was so unoriginal. His brother had always been an asshole, and there was nothing John could do to fix or change it. He had four decades of trying as proof.

Barry was an unsocial, inconsiderate sloth of a human, but being the youngest in the family gave him a halo that John had never understood. Their father finally grew disenchanted, but Mom never had. Barry was spoiled and entitled, not to mention verbally abusive to everyone who would take his bullshit.

Growing up, Barry got away with everything while John got away with nothing. Barry barely had to take out the garbage, while John had more chores than both of his other siblings combined. John started doing his own laundry when he was seven years old. Mom made him do Barry's and Sherrie's when he was nine, and that continued until John went off to college. Barry was loud and obnoxious out of the womb, but his bratty tantrums, belches, and farts eventually turned to misogynistic bro-speak and a stream of crap that never stopped falling out of his mouth. It had been at least twenty years since John had heard his brother go a full minute without swearing.

John peeked into the box — yep, it was a giant black dildo, just like he'd expected — then put it in Barry's room. In the kitchen, he found his mom, stirring something in her largest pot.

"Hi, Mom."

She looked over at him and smiled. "John! I'm so glad you're here. I'm making ribollita."

"What's in it?"

"It's good for you and you're going to love it."

"What's in it?"

"It's half cabbage and half beans."

"Why didn't you tell me the house is infested with termites? I would've sent you money to fumigate."

"Very funny. How long have you been here?"

"Just a few minutes. I called out when I came in, but no one answered."

"I was in the back with your brother. He was showing me his new car."

"You mean his new *radio-controlled* car."

"He loves those things. They mean a lot to him."

She turned back to her ribollita. John waited until she couldn't see him to roll his eyes. "It's a really stupid hobby for a fully-grown man, Mom."

"Don't tell your brother that. It will hurt his feelings."

"I tell him all the time. It's a stupid hobby. He spends way too much money on it."

"What else is he going to spend it on?"

"Growing up? And how much of that is *his* money? That new car he just showed you, did he even buy that himself?"

She turned back around. "Be fair, John."

"I'm always fair. But Barry is —"

The back door opened. Barry walked through, then let

it slam behind him. "Hey, John. What are you two mother-fuckers talking about?"

"Hey, Barry," John said. "We were just talking about how stupid RC cars are, and how your newest one sucks the hardest."

"The Axial Racing Yeti SCORE Trophy Truck RTR? Fuck you, suckfucker. That shit runs on awesome. Authentic solid rear axle with a four-link setup, aluminum King shocks and springs, replica BFGoodrich Baja T/A KR2 tires, 105 Method Race wheels, a massive 3150KV brushless motor, an Axial Hi-Lo two-speed transmission, an actual WB8 HD Wildboar driveshaft, and a full inde-pendent front suspension. Fuck your mother."

"She's right there." John pointed to their mother.

"I don't mind," she said.

"You don't know shit from sherbet, shitwhistle. And that's a fact."

"When is Sherrie coming in?" John asked, ignoring his brother.

"She'll be here tomorrow," Mom said.

John made his face thoughtful. "I hope she doesn't bring her home waxing kit."

"You know that wasn't my fault!" Barry protested.

Mom turned to John. "Is this really necessary?"

John said, "I'm just saying, Sherrie should probably leave that at home. She has enough to deal with coming back here to bury her father, and she shouldn't have to go through *that* again." He turned to his brother. "And how was it not your fault? You took *her* wax from *her* waxing kit, from under *her* sink. Then you applied it to your tiny little junk. I'm sure she still has nightmares, listening to you scream while she shouted about olive oil from the other side of the door."

Barry scoffed. "You probably wouldn't know, since

you've been married for a hundred years, but girls like a guy to have his garden weeded. A bitch shouldn't have to hunt through the forest to find a deer."

Their mother interjected, "Women aren't bitches —"

"I'm sure you give them a nice path of daisies to run down," John said. "Do you leave rose petals in a trail from the door to your bedroom in the back of Mommy's house?"

"I'm meeting with a possible agent next week," Barry said.

"For your screenplay?"

"It's really good." Mom stopped stirring and turned toward John. "He added a dog."

John smiled. "Sounds like the script practically reads itself."

"Shut up, John! I bet we're watching my shit on the big screen before yours."

John didn't say anything.

Barry had spent a lifetime being jealous of John, and relentlessly competitive. But John hadn't ever felt that way about Barry. Mostly, he'd felt sad that he was never going to have the brother he'd always wanted. If it hadn't been for their mother keeping the family together, mostly through guilt and grit, John would have cut ties with Barry a while ago. And Sherrie would've done it even sooner.

Barry relaxed a little through dinner, though not nearly enough for John. He still took out his phone and texted repeatedly, chewed with his mouth open and talked with it full, blew his nose and showed everyone the damage, picked his teeth, burped, farted, and licked his fingers after every other bite.

"You live with this?" John asked his mother.

"He's usually not this bad."

Barry belched.

His mom was serving a simple sheet cake when John realized that he was . . . not as bothered by Barry as he usually would be.

Because navigating his brother's bullshit had moved his mind a few inches from Lottie. And yet, not thinking about Lottie was like not thinking about the pink elephant in the corner after someone challenged you not to. *Of course* you were going to think of the goddamned elephant, and of course it would be pinker than Pepto-Bismol. So now, he was thinking of Lottie. She'd sunk her claws deep into his brain.

He wanted to check his phone, see if she'd called. But he couldn't take it out at the table. Not after the dirty looks he'd thrown his brother's way. No stooping to Barry's level, no matter what.

"How was London?" his mother asked.

"You went to London?"

His mother cut in, "Barry knows you went to London."

"London was fine."

"Fine?" She was better at reading him than anyone else in the world, including Vicky. Had he said something with his face? "That doesn't sound very exciting."

"I was alone."

"No, you were without Vicky and the girls," his mother corrected. "You couldn't have been alone."

"What do you mean?"

"Yeah, what do you mean?" Barry said. "No one wants to be with *him*."

"You were at a conference in one of the world's biggest cities. Being alone is a choice."

John looked at his brother and said, "You should consider it."

Since he didn't want to risk his mother suspecting what he'd done in London, he changed the subject to the talks with Fable, and a possible Netflix show. Mostly to infuriate Barry. Not surprisingly, Barry left the table almost immediately, slamming the back door on his way out of the house to play with his remote-controlled car.

John offered to do the dishes after dinner, partly because he knew it would relax him and partly because he knew that Obama had probably been in office the last time Barry had lifted a finger in the kitchen to do anything other than eat.

He checked his phone before he turned on the sink.

Nothing from Lottie.

But he couldn't stop thinking. Wondering. *What if?* The wrong *what if?* would ruin him forever. John wouldn't have a family, or a career. At the very least, he'd be starting over on both fronts.

He finished the dishes, then went to his room and closed the door behind him.

He dialed Sam. It rang three times, then, "Hey John, what's up?"

"I need your help."

His voice sober, Sam said, "Lottie?"

"Yes."

"What do you need? What has she done?"

"Nothing yet, or that I know of. But I feel . . . I don't know . . . vulnerable, I guess. I'm out here and she's back there, batshit crazy. If she finds out I'm gone, then —"

"You're not exactly a social media type. How would she know?"

"How does she know where I shop, or which park I take my children to? Are you being serious here, Sam?"

"Okay, I'm sorry. Calm down."

"Did you find anything out?"

"Still waiting. Did you want me to call my —"

"No. Not yet, and hopefully not at all. But can you just

. . . I don't know, maybe drive out there and check on Vicky and the kids?"

"Yes. Of course. I have plenty of reasons to drive out and talk to Vicky that won't make her suspicious. How is it, being home?"

"I beat Sherrie here by a day, my brother is still an asshole, and my mom still puts up with every ounce of his infantile crap, for some reason that I'll never understand."

"Isn't it enough to know that your brother's an idiot? And that you've done something big with your life?"

"Yeah," John said. "If I haven't fucked it to pieces."

Chapter Twenty-One

"You sure you're not going to regret getting rid of this?"

John was looking at the old acoustic guitar in his hand, but he'd meant all of it — every one of his father's possessions now sitting in a giant pile in his mother's living room. It left a numb, hollow feeling in his stomach, seeing these objects as the remnants of a person's life.

Dad is gone.

"I'd rather have the space than the reminders," she said.

"So blunt." John looked up at his mother. He expected her to look bitter, but she was actually smiling. "Are you . . . *happy* that Dad is dead?"

She looked horrified. "No! Of course not. Why would I be happy that your father is dead?"

"You've never had a problem admitting that he's an asshole."

"That doesn't mean I didn't love him. Like I said, if you see something you want, take it. If it's something Sherrie would want, maybe wait to ask her."

"She won't want anything. And honestly, neither do I. Except maybe for this." John held up the guitar.

"You don't want any of his old clothes?"

John waited a second to see if she was kidding, realized she wasn't, then said, "No."

He was turning back around when something caught his eye — a brown leather volume. It was probably filled with pictures, though the album itself didn't look familiar. He set the guitar gently on its side and picked up the book.

On the second page, John realized that something wasn't right. He recognized his father, but not the others in this particular family photo. The woman who wasn't his mother was apparently playing her for Halloween, standing right beside his father, hand around his waist — wedding ring on the appropriate finger — and head lolling onto his shoulder. The kid between them, smiling wide and showing off her missing tooth, was nine or maybe ten years old.

She had the same thatch of matted brown hair as John's father. It just hung in longer clumps. She shared John's smile, the one Vicky had said was "so real it hurts." John had seen it in a few pictures and videos, but Vicky said it was something felt more than seen. Dakota agreed.

Looking at this girl, John thought he might finally understand.

His father was wearing a vest, the one that John's mother used to say made him look like Geppetto, and that he wore far more than any reasonable man would have, until he abruptly stopped one day. That meant the picture was at least twenty years old, and surely not much older than that.

"What's this?" John shook the album to nab his mother's attention.

She looked over and lost most of her color. "Oh, John."

"What? What is it?"

"I was going to tell you."

"Tell me what, Mom?" John shoved the album into her hands. He wanted to see more photos only slightly less than he didn't. "What is this?"

"I promised your father that I wouldn't tell you while he was still alive. And yes, I actually used those words. Because he's a coward, and didn't want to have to face you. But I told him that I refused to keep on lying for him after he died. You just found that before we could talk."

"I was here all night. And this morning."

"Your brother is home and . . . you know how tired he makes me."

"You should really kick him out."

"I can't kick him out."

"You can and you should. He's an asshole and he doesn't respect you. Now . . ." John cast an accusatory glance at the book. "Can you please tell me what that is about?"

She sighed. "Did you ever see *The Familiar Stranger*?"

"No. What's that?"

"Of course you didn't. It was a TV movie from a long time ago. Lousy picture. Some guy commits suicide, then fifteen years later his wife is struggling to raise their two sons and she finds out that he faked his death."

John looked at his mother, confused. "And?"

"Well, your father didn't fake his own death, but the husband in that story faked his so he could be with another family. And your dad . . . had another family."

"*What?* How is that possible?"

"He just . . . fell for another woman. I was clueless for a while. He was surprisingly good at keeping secrets."

"Dad?"

"Yes, your father."

"But Dad could never keep a secret."

"That's because he was always so busy keeping *this* one."

"How did you find out? *When* did you find out? How could you not tell me? And . . . who else knows?"

"Kathleen."

"Your therapist?"

"And my sister, because I've told her everything forever. That's why your aunt stopped coming around. But that's it."

"Shit, Mom." John sat. "You didn't even tell Bonnie?"

"No, not even my best friend. And *shit* is right, okay? I wish I could say that I caught him, but I didn't. He just came right out and told me. Right in the middle of the *ER* season finale."

"What did you do?"

She sat too. "I died. Right here on the sofa. I couldn't move my legs. The ache came from a place so deep it was liquid. I couldn't swallow and I wanted to vomit for so long . . ." She stopped and ran a hand through her hair. "It was awful, Johnny. We had our issues, but I thought we were happy. Like, the *real thing* happy. And right then I realized that it had all been a lie. I had to grieve — what I lost and what I had and what could never be again. And I had to do it alone."

"You didn't have to —"

"I did and you know it. I sat in the pain because I had to, and I wouldn't have had it any other way. I took my time and did my thinking. Eventually I had to let it go."

"Let it go? How could you just *let it go*?"

She shrugged. "I didn't want to be alone, and I loved your father. We even broke up for a few months after it happened, but eventually everything settled. He chose our family and I chose to let it go."

John sat, speechless.

Then finally, "What do you mean you 'broke up'?"

She laughed softly. "Your father still lived here, but I made him sleep on the floor by the bed."

"Why didn't you just kick him out?"

"I didn't want Barry to know, in case everything worked out. And good thing, because it did."

John shook his head, still mired in disbelief, and getting more upset by the second. He stood and started to pace the room while his mother watched in silence.

He picked up the photo album and turned through every page, studying each picture for several seconds before flipping to the next. He stayed longest at a picture of the girl on his father's back, with each of them making a strongman pose. It stopped his heart, both because they looked so happy, and because the photo was so similar to one of John's favorite pictures, where *he* was the one on his father's back, also flexing his scrawny arms.

John dropped the album on the sofa where he'd been sitting next to his mother. She was still there, hands folded in her lap, waiting for her son to explode.

Instead, he deflated, and with barely any air left inside him he said, "I can't believe you didn't tell me any of this."

"I promised him I wouldn't."

John shook his head. "I get not telling Barry, and even Sherrie, but shit, Mom, you should have told me. You know I never would have told him that I knew." He looked into her eyes. "You wouldn't have felt so alone."

"I didn't want to bother you."

"Why would that *bother* me?" John held her gaze, still shaking his head. "You're my mother. I always want to help you."

"When was the last time you weren't busy when I called?"

"That's not fair."

"I'm not trying to be unfair, and I'm not trying to guilt you. But you're always busy, and you don't ever call. If I want to talk to you for more than a few minutes, then I need to wait for a holiday or make an appointment." There was a quiet moment and John thought she was finished, but then she added, "And if I want you to visit, I apparently needed to wait for my husband to die."

That one was an arrow, right through his neck. He looked at her, feeling a bit off-kilter, fighting the urge to cry. "I thought you said that you weren't trying to guilt me."

She smiled back at him sadly. "I'm sorry. I'm not trying to, but that one was a little too obvious. I'm not sad or bitter or anything else. Life moves on and I understand. I'm just trying to move forward, John."

"What are you going to do next?"

John was surprised to see a mysterious and slightly mischievous look on her face. "Do you really want to know?"

"Of course."

"Bonnie and I are going to start a catering company."

"A catering company?" John thought for a second, then carefully chose his next words. "That seems like an ambitious undertaking."

"Maybe 'company' is too big a word. Bonnie and I are going to start a small catering business."

"Okay," John said, waiting for more.

"You know how much I love cooking for others, and I'm always the one making everything for everyone else. So why not turn my passion into profit?"

"Wasn't Dad insured? Aren't you doing fine?"

She dismissed him with a wave. "I'm not doing this for

the money, John. I'm doing it to keep busy. It's the perfect business for me, and for Bonnie. She's two streets down and her husband may as well be gone too, for all his time on the couch. We can start small, get a couple of helpers — her daughter is already interested — and focus on catering only for people we already know."

He smiled. "Just, please don't hire Barry."

"Oh God, no."

John laughed. "Does Sherrie know?"

"Of course. She's helping me figure out all the business stuff. She's going to stay for a few days after the funeral, to help me and Bonnie plan." She saw the look on John's face and added, "But you got to be the first to hear about your father's secret family."

She smiled as if everything was suddenly better.

Your father's secret family.

And again, he thought of Lottie. But this time, there was a glimmer of hope, gleaming from the end of a very dark tunnel.

Because his mom was easy to talk to, and she had already been through this. Cheating could test even the strongest, most resilient relationships. Hers had survived. Maybe she could help John to salvage his.

If it hadn't been for the episode with Aubrey, John would probably have confessed already. He didn't want to keep secrets — he hated secrets, and as a storyteller he knew the damage they dealt to every character who had ever been unlucky enough to have a big one.

Maybe this affair could save their relationship . . . or at the very least improve it. After all, it wasn't really an affair. It was a mistake, one he didn't even remember making.

You remember jerking it in the hotel room, though.

He shoved that thought aside, hard, and refocused himself on hope.

Perhaps the answer to navigating all this was right there in front of him. John looked at his mother.

"I have a secret of my own," he said.

Chapter Twenty-Two

He moved the photo album containing his father's secrets and sat in its place.

His mother looked at him expectantly. "What is it, John?"

He could only imagine the look on his face, and could barely face hers. But he couldn't chicken out now. Not if his mother could show him a path to bringing his mistake out into the open and finally making it right.

Not if it would take away all the power that Lottie held over him.

"I . . . cheated on Vicky."

Something died inside his mother's eyes. He saw it, and it killed him.

"Oh, John . . ."

Her hand found his.

"I'm sorry," he said, his voice catching.

"Don't apologize to *me*." She sighed. "So, do you want to talk about it?"

"No." John wheezed what was probably his life's most

uncomfortable laugh. "Not at all. But I think I should. I think I need to."

His mother said nothing. Her eyes said, *I'm listening.*

John drew a deep breath. "It was in London. And it was an accident. It's nothing like Dad, and I know it's cliché, but it didn't mean anything. Honestly, I don't even remember."

"You don't remember? Were you drunk?"

"We'll get there," John said. He drew another breath. "I was flirting with this girl in a bar on the last day of the conference. It was innocent, I swear, just a . . . I don't know, confidence boost. I don't remember anything until I woke up the next morning."

"Do you think she . . . *drugged* you?"

"Why would you ask that?" John understood why Sam's mind had immediately gone there, but his mother's too?

She leveled her eyes at him, the mother's equivalent to rolling her eyes. "You said that you didn't remember. You also said 'we'll get there.' And I've been listening to your stories since you could talk."

"Yes. I think she drugged me. At least that's what I think now."

"Why now?"

"Because I've had more time to think about it, I guess."

She narrowed her eyes, surely knowing that something was up. Her mother's intuition was firing on all cylinders. But John didn't want to tell her about the phone calls or the surprise visits to Provisions.

Or jacking off to Lottie's dirty talk in a hotel room.

This was about him figuring out how to handle the situation as it pertained to his marriage. This was about him getting a woman's perspective — a married woman's perspective, his mother's perspective. This wasn't about making an already-grieving widow fear for her grand-daughters' safety.

"There's a reason you're telling me."

He tried to shrug it off. "We tell each other stuff. Except for that time you didn't tell me about Dad's secret family. Remember that?"

She slapped him on the knee.

John continued. "I was wondering if I should just tell Vic —"

"Absolutely not."

"You didn't let me finish my sentence."

"I didn't need to. Telling Victoria is about you, not her. You and Dakota were both miserable during and after that whole ridiculous thing with that lit major. How can you possibly think that telling her about *this* is a good idea?"

"Because it's honest. And the right thing to do. Look at Dad, Mom. The secrets we keep are what kill us."

"Bullshit. It's the secrets that keep us safe."

"So if you had to do it over again, you're saying that you wouldn't have wanted to know about Dad?"

"Of course I wouldn't have wanted to know! I *hated* knowing. I loved our life before that. I was fine living in ignorance. It was when I had to live the *lie* that it all became unbearable."

"So you'd take the blue pill?"

"What?"

"Never mind." He'd have to remember that one for Dakota later. She'd love it.

"I forgave your father, but it was the hardest thing I've ever had to do. And even after everything was technically okay between us, I would still think of the two of them together and either feel like murdering someone or stuffing my head in the oven. I'm not sure if I ever went more than a day without at least a part of me wondering if maybe he loved her more, and was only with me because he had simply invested more in our life."

John looked at his mother, helpless. This wasn't going how he'd wanted — or expected — it to go, at all. Sitting here listening to her story was like watching helplessly as a train derailed.

"I never went looking, and probably never would have found out if your father hadn't told me. And that confession was all about him. About him living a lie for a really long time and finally wanting it off his chest."

"Doesn't that prove that he loved you more? That *you* were the one he was confessing to?"

"Not in the slightest." She gave John a hard stare. "After he told me, *he* felt better. I had to live with it rotting inside me until a couple of days ago."

John put his hand on his mom's shoulder. Neither of them spoke.

After a few moments, John said, "But it's good that I'm telling you, right? Because you're my mother and I need to tell someone. Isn't it better to be honest?"

"No. It's selfish, like your father was selfish."

John flushed, not sure if he was more angry or embarrassed. The last thing he wanted was to be like his old man.

"Of course you should tell someone, John, but why are you telling me? Why not tell your agent? Sam, right? Tell *Sam*. Or someone else. Someone who won't be hurt by it."

"This is a private matter and you're my mother."

"Exactly. I'm your mother. Do you think I want to see my son as a man who cheats on his wife?"

John blinked. He felt slapped. "No. I guess not."

"Of course I don't. Sometimes telling makes sense, and other times it's selfish. If you did the crime, then you should be a big enough man to live with the burden. Guilt is a natural consequence. This is *your* cross to bear, and it isn't fair for you to put this on me, or Victoria."

"The stress of hiding this is killing me."

"Exactly! It's killing *you*. And you want to ease that strain on yourself by making things more difficult for the person you did this to in the first place? What about Dakota — how do you think *she'll* feel? Or Evie, when she's older? Really think about this. Your next step here is important."

He'd thought confessing to his mother would be freeing, but instead, the bars of his prison were thicker than ever. What if he figured out how to get rid of Lottie — and he still felt like this? Could he live with this festering secret for the rest of his life?

Or would it drive him insane?

More silence.

A moment later, Sherrie entered the living room. "Oh great," she said, looking around. "We're sorting shit!"

His mother laughed as she and John stood up to hug Sherrie.

"It's good to see you," he said, embracing his sister.

"You too." Sherrie smiled and punched him on the shoulder. Then she looked around the room with her eyes narrowed and her nose scrunched, as if hunting for something rotten. "Where's Barry?"

Mom said, "He's at a race."

"You mean playing with his toys," Sherrie said, flashing John a knowing look.

"Or himself," John suggested with a smirk.

"Don't start, you two," their mother said.

Sherrie rolled her eyes.

John turned to his sister. "Wanna go for a walk?"

"Sure. Can we walk down to Nev's and buy some of those cinnamon toothpicks?"

He laughed. "Just like old times. Sounds perfect."

They hadn't even reached the stop sign on the corner before Sherrie was loudly bitching about Barry — a nice change from his mother's infuriating passivity.

"She needs to kick him out. Remember when we thought this was funny? It's not funny anymore. She's just enabling him, and it's going to be way worse now that Dad is gone. And you can't say anything to Mom, because she's always like, 'Barry is Barry,' as if that's an excuse."

"Dad had a second family."

Sherrie stopped walking and turned to look at John. "Fuck did you say?"

"It's not a joke, Sherrie. Mom just told me and I'm sure I'm not supposed to tell you, so just act surprised when —"

"You think the surprise on my face is an act? The fuck do you mean, 'Dad had a second family'?"

"Exactly that. We were going through his crap this morning and I found this old photo album. It was fucking weird, Sher. Dad in his stupid Geppetto vest, and he was with some Mom clone and another fucking kid. A girl. She didn't look like you, even though you both look like him."

She stared at him for a beat. "I gotta walk, do you mind?"

"Of course not," John said.

They turned the corner and started toward Nev's, the liquor store exactly one mile from their childhood home. They used to sneak out of the house, run the forbidden trip to Nev's, quickly buy whatever contraband they could afford — usually cinnamon toothpicks, the cheapest thing by the counter — then race back home without getting caught.

"What are you thinking?" he asked after she had fallen mute for maybe a minute.

"So. Many. Things."

"Care to share?"

"I'm just . . . so *pissed* at him. I can't articulate. But now at least I understand *Barry*."

"What do you mean?" John asked. "A team of Swiss scientists couldn't understand Barry."

"I always wondered why he tolerated it, you know? I get why Mom lets that piece of shit still live at home, but I never got why Dad put up with that crap. Now I get it." She smirked. "It's the price he paid for the affair."

"It was more than an affair."

"Fuck you for telling me this. Do you have any idea how hard it's going to be to pretend I don't know?"

"Would you have been happier if I didn't?"

"Of course not."

They were two blocks from Nev's. John wanted — needed — a second opinion. He was going to confess, tell his sister all about Lottie, his mother's "silent burden" advice be damned. There was no one outside his home that he trusted more than Sherrie. *She* would see a way out, because that was one of the things she was best at. But she started talking before he opened his mouth.

"*Fuck you, Dad!*" Sherrie was yelling at the night sky, furious. "He always said that 'cheating is lying and lying's destructive.'"

"I know."

"Did you know I almost caught Alex cheating?"

"Oh, shit. Seriously?"

"Sorta," she said. "He was sexting."

"With who?"

"Some barista bitch at Hill of Beans."

"Did they actually sleep together?"

"What do you mean, *actually*? Is telling her that he'd like to see how many fingers he could fit inside her not enough?"

"Ouch," John said. "I'm not saying that's not cheating. I'm just asking how far the affair went."

"Thank you for using that word. Alex doesn't agree with its usage. He says they didn't sleep together, and for what it's worth I believe him."

"Why?"

She laughed. A strange sound in the moment. "Because he's the one who showed me the sexts."

"*What?*"

Another laugh, drier this time. "Yeah. He was feeling guilty as shit, you know Alex, and so he just came into the kitchen while I was making ravioli. Like, from scratch. It's his favorite. He handed me his phone and said, 'Look.' So I did. And then I stared at him. There were a *lot* of texts, and they went back and forth for about two weeks. They were fucking nasty, John. Really filthy. I gave you one of the cleaner ones. He said that it started as fun. Her name is fucking Honeydew, if you can believe that."

"Fucking Honeydew, or just Honeydew?"

Sherrie ignored the joke. "Alex doesn't know how adorable he is, which is one of the things I've always loved most about him. But it can make him a time bomb. Apparently, fucking Honeydew got his number from his Hill of Beans loyalty card and texted him, *Who has two pink nipples and thinks you're cute?* I don't even have a dick and that makes *me* hard."

John laughed.

"So that went on for a week. Alex swears that he was never going to sleep with her. It was just fun and exciting for him. I get that."

"So he just felt . . . guilty? And had to tell you?"

"That, and he thought if he didn't come clean, he might actually sleep with her. Like, it was getting more serious. Telling me was insurance against what he saw as inevitable."

John opened the door for his sister. She entered and headed straight for the counter. They each bought a pack of cinnamon toothpicks, and Sherrie grabbed a Snickers. Her go-to snack when upset. Then they started back home.

One more block. Once they turned left onto Lemon, he'd tell Sherrie everything. Then she would tell him what to do.

But first he had to ask, "So you're glad that he told you, right?"

"Of course I'm glad. It saved our marriage. In a weird way, we're closer than ever. But if he *had* cheated, I don't think I could have forgiven him. Or, I could have forgiven him but I couldn't have lived with him anymore. It would just be . . . over. Because how could I ever trust him again?"

"So you don't *really* consider the sexting cheating."

"No, I mean, it's still cheating. But it's different. I don't know . . . maybe I'm just grateful he was self-aware enough to know when things were getting dangerous."

It was now or never.

John opened his mouth.

But again, Sherrie spoke first.

"I guess I don't consider the sexting *truly* cheating because I think of cheating as being the lowest form of selfish. And when it came down to it, Alex did put me first. I could give a shit if he's on Pornhub, that's never going to be a relationship. He hasn't been back to that Hill of Beans since her first text, because he didn't want to see her in person. He didn't want the temptation."

"Have you gone in to see what she looks like?"

"Of course."

"And?"

"She looks like a girl named fucking Honeydew. If I was a dude, I have a pretty good idea what I'd want to do to her."

"And the reason you're so cool about all of this is because he told you?"

"Well, yes, that, and because he didn't actually fuck her. If he had, then there would have been at least a small part of me that would never, ever have forgiven him." She laughed, loud enough to highlight the absurdity of what she was about to say. "Can you imagine if you had actually cheated on Vicky with that Aubrey dude?" Sherrie shook her head. "She would have handed you your dick. And dude, you would have deserved it."

Chapter Twenty-Three

The urge to tell Sherrie was scratching a hole in his guts, but John couldn't muster the courage back at the house, or after dinner when they were crammed into their old treehouse, chewing on toothpicks, sharing a six pack, and hiding from Barry.

Nor could he tell her the next day, even though Sherrie asked him more than a few times why he was constantly checking his phone.

"You're like a fucking teenage girl with that thing," she said. "Dakota rubbing off on you? I bet you sleep with it next to your bed."

"No, I don't," John said, even though he really had been — ever since he got back from London.

John definitely couldn't tell her anything the morning of the funeral, or during the funeral itself. They shared the front pew. Sherrie sat on his left, leaning over to whisper inappropriate jokes in his ear every couple of minutes.

Barry was seemingly omnipresent after the funeral, rendering any sort of private conversation with Sherrie impossible.

"I don't want a memorial service when I die," she said, plucking a shrimp from the buffet. "Just toss me in the box and turn it to ashes."

"I wouldn't mind a funeral," John said, "so long as it doesn't cost a lot, or put anyone out."

"I want a PAR*TEE*!" Barry said, then belched.

There were a few awkward moments, including when Sherrie straight-up asked John if he had anything on his mind.

"I'm just wondering what they're really hiding at Area 51," he said.

The reception wasn't any better, because then John had to talk to relatives he'd never been close to and hadn't seen in more than a decade. He hadn't cared for Aunt Lily's condescending tone when he was twelve and certainly didn't care for it now that age had sharpened her holier-than-thou tongue.

"It's great that you were able to turn that hobby into something," she said from behind four pounds of foundation. "If you hadn't become a writer, I'm not sure what we would have done with you."

"Yes," John said, "I'm sure my family is grateful that I can feed them."

The reception was held in the back of the church. After the first hour, it was too much. After two, John's throat was itching from thirst and he needed to leave a week ago.

He waited for the swarm of well-wishers around his mother to disperse, then he approached her. "I should go. I still need to grab my stuff from the house before I get to the airport."

"You're leaving? Right now? Isn't your flight at six?"

"Yes, but I'd rather be safe and get there an hour earlier than I need to. And besides, you're fine. There are a lot of people here. You're not going to miss me."

She looked like he'd slapped her. "I always miss you. Are you calling an Fastr?"

"No," he said. "Sherrie is going to take me."

"Oh, that's great. I'm glad that you two have had a chance to reconnect, though I wish it was under better circumstances."

They embraced for a long minute. Then they parted and she looked right into his eyes. "Remember what I told you, John. Keep Victoria safe."

"Okay, Mom. I will."

John walked outside to meet Sherrie, then hesitated, thinking about the remnants of his father on the living room floor, then about Barry, who still didn't know who their father really was.

If he died, Barry would never know.

Maybe he should make the effort, one more time. Reach out and try to connect with his little brother.

He followed the sound of revving thunder and found Barry in the back of the church parking lot, racing one of his RC cars.

John yelled, "Barry!"

The sounds stopped and his brother turned around. "What up, dick dork?"

"I just wanted to say goodbye."

"Later," Barry said, turning back around. The thunder sputtered and resumed.

"Barry!"

He turned back around. "What?"

"It's been a couple of years, and it might be a while before we see each other again. Don't you want a better goodbye than this?"

Barry looked at him, and a rare flash of seriousness found his expression. Something washed over his face. John wasn't sure exactly what it was, but he hoped for understanding. Barry walked over to John and gave him an oversized hug, still holding his remote control.

Deep in the hug, Barry farted. Loud and long and reeking. It sounded wet.

"You're right. That felt great."

In the car, Sherrie said, "What did you expect?"

"I don't know. Maybe for him to not act like he's twelve *all* the time."

"What're you, new?"

John tried a thousand confessions on their way to the airport, but none made it more than a breath. Two exits away, Sherrie finally sent a shot across the bow. "Is there something you want to talk about?"

"No," John said, like a coward. "Why do you ask?"

"Because you're acting weird."

"How am I acting weird?"

"I don't know, you're just being weird. Like you have something on your mind."

"Can you be specific?"

"I don't know, John. I can tell when you're . . . off."

He swallowed. "Give me one example."

"Okay. The last couple of days, you can't even take a compliment. I told you that I'd finally read *The Delicate Proverb*. You love it when people read your shit, and you seem to especially love it when *I* read your shit, even though it's not always necessarily my thing. I would have expected something like, 'Oh, you read it? That's great, sis! Thank you! What did you think?' Instead, all I got was, 'I don't even know how they let me publish that.' And then, like five minutes later, you shit all over the stuff you're writing with Vicky."

"So I'm feeling a little self-doubt. Isn't that a writer's prerogative?"

"You asked for an example. I gave you one. Now we have two minutes until I'm idling in front of JetBlue and some dude in an orange vest is yelling at me to move it. If you have something you want to say, now is the time."

Instead of confession, a laugh erupted from somewhere inside him. "I'm fine, Sher. I just hate everything I'm writing right now. I'm trying to finish this last book for Sam, and we're waiting to see what happens with Netflix. Also, I just lost my father. I'm a ball of nerves."

Sherrie gave him a pointed look. She wasn't buying it.

"Really," he said.

She stayed quiet until she pulled the car up to the JetBlue entrance. "Promise you'll call if I can help with something?"

"I promise," John lied.

Sherrie got out for a quick hug, then took off before the guy in the orange vest — who turned out to be a lady in an orange vest — started to yell.

John entered the airport and looked at his phone.

Still no Lottie.

Her voice echoed through his head as if summoned.

You wrote those words and they touched me, John. Ever since I first read them . . . I've wanted to touch you . . . do you want me to touch you?

It was easy to imagine the worst. That she had shown up at his home or the park or somewhere and told Vicky everything. But even if Lottie *did* tell his wife, and she was waiting for him to come home so she could scoop his eyes out with a melon baller, Dakota would have called him and demanded that he tell her mother it wasn't true.

Or would she have? She'd recognize Lottie from the

park. She'd still probably call him, ask if it was true, or if that crazy woman was lying.

The thought of having to admit to Dakota what he'd done made him want to vomit.

He checked in, shuffled through security, and made it to his gate with nearly two and a half hours to spare. Sitting in his uncomfortable fake-leather seat, he sifted through calls, texts, and emails, but saw nothing from Lottie. He called Sam, got voicemail, left a message. The fear that Lottie had gone after his family was making him want to crawl out of his skin.

His chickening out with Sherrie was pressing on him. Everything he'd said — and not said — flashed through his mind. He hadn't been completely untruthful. He *did* hate everything he was writing. Fuck it. At least that could change.

He took out his laptop, deciding that he would write something new, something different from everything else he'd ever written. Maybe science fiction. Because right now he felt like making shit up.

John had no idea what he was going to write, but he was thrilled to be writing it. He wouldn't tell anyone, not even Vicky. Maybe he would try this self-publishing stuff. Use a pen name and keep it a secret. Though really, another secret was the last thing he needed.

John wrote for an hour, but there wasn't a single word of sci-fi on the page. Instead, Lottie bled through every word of the rambling mess. Shit. What if he couldn't write anything until he told Vicky? What if the guilt shattered his creativity forever?

He deleted every word, just as the announcement came over the speakers. His flight was delayed by two hours and forty minutes.

Fuck.

So he wrote some more garbage. And deleted it.

After the flight, while disembarking from the plane, John looked at his phone and, for the first time, wondered if maybe everything *was* okay. If maybe Lottie had just given up. Because if she wasn't showing up at home while he was gone, or calling or texting or emailing, then maybe she had seriously gotten the hint and the worst of this was behind him.

Maybe he could make everything right. Be a better husband and father. He and Vicky could start having a date day, time during the week that wasn't about the children or work. Just them. And a father-daughter day, too. He shouldn't be waiting for Dakota's school to schedule a dance to spend time with her.

John called Vicky. No answer. Shit. Instead of leaving a voicemail, he dialed Dakota.

She answered on the first ring. "Hey, Dad! How's Uncle Barry?"

"Really? That's the first thing you ask?" But he relaxed a little. If Vicky was in crisis-mode, Dakota wouldn't sound so cheerful.

"Uncle Barry's always good for a story."

"I'm glad you think so."

"Remember the time he farted so hard that he pooped, but he wouldn't admit that he had poop in his pants and we all had to pretend that we couldn't smell it?"

"Unfortunately. How's your mother?"

"In bed."

"A migraine?"

"It's bad. All yesterday, too. I'm keeping Evie busy with *Lazy Town*. It's not nearly as awesome as I remember. Robbie Rotten is creepy. He looks like Jim Carrey made of wax."

Now it was John's turn to laugh. "How is your mother's

mood?"

"Fine, actually. She's annoyed about her headaches, but she's not being a . . . she seems good. She actually seems excited about the nanny, or whatever stupid thing you guys are calling it. She's interviewing her favorites tomorrow."

"That's smart, handling them all at once."

"Oh, she wants you to help her decide. She said if you didn't, she'd probably hire a hot Swedish guy."

John laughed again. "Anything else going on?"

Dakota made a noise. He pictured her shrug.

"Did we get the tire fixed? Any other flats or anything like that?"

"You're really reaching for things to talk about, Dad. Come on, you must have *one* Uncle Barry story. Did he fart on you? Just tell me if he farted on you."

"Several times. And I'm not 'reaching for things to talk about.' I just want to make sure that you're all doing fine.

He imagined Dakota rolling her eyes. She made fun of him for being weird, then he made fun of her back and ended the call.

He needed to stand. And stretch.

Really, John needed to walk.

He grabbed his bag and pulled it toward The Habit, a decent-looking airport restaurant, considering his options. Halfway there his phone buzzed. There was a text, but it wasn't from Lottie. His flight had been delayed again — this time until tomorrow.

Fuck. Fuck.

An hour later, he checked into a dump whose staff acted like they worked in a castle, then dialed Dakota as he dropped his laptop bag onto the bed.

He kept the call short. Told her that he loved her and Evie and her mother, and to please make sure that they all knew. His flight was delayed and he'd see her tomorrow.

"Okay," she said, even though he could hear in her voice that it wasn't.

He expected to toss and turn, like he'd been doing for weeks. Instead, John slept like a lamb who trusted the sheepdog to keep watch all night.

He woke up surprisingly refreshed. He practically sprang out of bed, fresh with a story idea that had been teasing his dreams. Not quite formed, but it had something to do with a solution to global warming going horribly awry.

He got all four acts of his idea laid out on the page, three paragraphs each.

Then, feeling better than he had since . . . before London? . . . John showered, dressed, and went to the airport.

There were no delays and the flight was smooth. They touched down thirteen minutes earlier than promised and it was almost as if the wheels were kissing the asphalt. Fastr said his driver was four minutes away when John booked the ride, but the car was already pulling up as John stepped outside.

After the brief trip home, he got out of the car and studied the pink VW Beetle parked in his driveway. The back was plastered with stickers. *Star Wars*, *Dr. Who*, a hand-drawn *Game of Thrones*. John smiled. This had to be one of the applicants, and hopefully the one that Vicky was going to hire. He was definitely a fan of her cultural touchstones.

He opened the door and entered his living room.

Vicky was sitting on the sofa, next to a brunette that was surely the applicant.

The applicant turned around. She smiled. And then she spoke.

"You must be John," said Lottie.

Chapter Twenty-Four

This wasn't happening.

John wanted to run, to throw his luggage at her, to scream at the top of his lungs and let the insanity out. Because if this was real, his life was over.

"This is Becca." Vicky stood, beaming, and walked toward John. "She. Is. Amazing."

Lottie followed. She held out her hand to John, smiling, her eyes sparkling, her perfect skin practically glowing. She was the same, but different somehow. Her posture was less slouched — not that it was frumpy before. But now she walked erect enough to have a line of kindergartners marching behind her.

Not knowing what else to do except maybe die right there on the living room carpet, he held out his hand. "John."

"Victoria said that you're a writer! I can't believe that. Is writing books, like, the best job in the world?"

Fuck me. Is she really going to do this?

"It's a good job."

"What's wrong, honey?" Vicky asked John, looking concerned. "Was it the delay?"

He was drenched in sweat. Hell, maybe he'd shit his pants and had yet to smell it.

"I'm sorry. It's been a really long week." He held up his carry-on, then glanced down at his rolling bag. "Mind if I just get settled in for a few minutes?"

"Of course," Vicky said, still beaming. "I just wanted you to meet Becca."

"I'm so glad to be here. I'm your *Help*," Lottie said, laughing. "Victoria wanted a different name for nanny. I said, 'You can call me whatever you want once I work for you, but I'm here to help you with whatever you need, so you might want to start there.' So *Help* it is — like the book!"

John had no idea what to say to that. He managed a bone-dry "Thank you for helping us."

Then he went to his room, hoping to avoid Dakota and Evie. He couldn't see them right now — he couldn't see *anyone* right now. Were his girls even home? He had no idea. Maybe they were at the park.

He closed his bedroom door.

His heart was pounding, his head was splitting, his frayed nerves were peeling into crippling splinters.

Why was she doing this?

What was her game?

And if Lottie was the eventual winner . . . what would that mean for John as the loser?

Fortunately, this would be over soon. There was zero chance that Vicky would actually hire her. Surely she could see through those phony glasses and conservative clothes. His wife was paranoid to a fault.

And that meant that John could handle this. All he had

to do was go back into the living room and take care of this situation like a man.

After taking a moment to gather his calm, John marched into the living room. Lottie was no longer there, but Vicky bounded up to him, her eyes and smile equally wide. She threw her arms around him and kissed him on the cheek like he might have expected, and then on the mouth like he didn't.

"I'm *so glad* you're home. Dakota and Evie are playing out back. Becca is out there with them now. I'm sorry for hiring her without you, but you weren't here and I couldn't *not*. She's the best. You're going to love her. Funny, smart —"

And hot? What the fuck are you thinking, Vicky?

"— and Evie *loves* her. You should see them. You *will* see them. And Dakota? It's a wonder. I know, I know, it's only been a couple of hours, but when you know, you know, right?"

John itched everywhere. He wanted to claw at his own eyes, dig right into the sockets to get at the screaming voice inside his skull.

"Did you interview anyone else?"

"*God*, no. Becca was first in line and I already loved her on the phone. Then she got here, and . . ."

Vicky was lost for a second, swimming back to a moment John hadn't been a part of, even though it had surely been designed around him.

"Evie just loved her, and you could tell how much Becca loves children. You know how some people treat kids like furniture? She's not like that at all. You can just see it in her eyes, that girl was born to make children happy. She's a child-care specialist with a ton of experience. She's a 'lifelong advocate for children,' as she put it — don't you just love that? And her *energy*, John . . . remember Dakota's friend, Lacy? Imagine that with an extra decade of life experience. That's *exactly* what Evie needs. And what I can't give her, because I'm so damned tired most of the time. Now maybe writing won't feel like I'm digging all day just to end up with a pile of dirt."

Vicky stopped, drew a breath, and smiled. She took his hands.

He was still frozen.

"You're going to love Becca," she added.

Hate filled every cell inside him.

Lottie toddled into the room holding Evie's hand, Dakota in step behind them. His girls ran up to him, and he hugged them hard and held them tight as he eyed their new . . . *Help*.

"So, what did I miss?" Lottie asked.

"I was just telling my husband how wonderful you are," Vicky said. Her voice was so sweet it made him sick.

Lottie laughed. "Oh, he doesn't want to hear that!"

John looked right at her. "I hear you're a childcare specialist."

Evie walked away from him, and John's heart raced as his little girl, oblivious to the threat, went to Lottie's side and took her hand. That same hand that he'd imagined —

Lottie clapped. "I am! I've worked with children my whole life. I used to babysit my brother all the time. He was born when I was seven, and I seriously thought he was the most adorable thing in the world. I wish I had a baby picture right now so you could see him." She squealed at the memory. "I was a camp counselor as soon as I was old enough to be one, and a CIT before that." She turned to Dakota and Evie, as if this were a perfect teachable moment, and said, "CIT means 'counselor in training' if you've never been to camp."

She looked back at John. "Have you ever been to camp, Mr. Treadwell?"

"You can call him John," Vicky offered.

Lottie didn't wait for his answer. "My first job was at the Sunshine School, a small preschool near where I grew up. The place was like a sandbox fairytale — at least that's what I always thought when I was playing with the children. My parents were never really around, and it seemed like I always got along better with kids than grownups, you know? Even after I was finally one myself." She laughed. Again. That damn laugh. "I guess it's still true even now."

John could only stay speechless so long. Eventually he'd have to open his mouth. And words would need to come out. But right now, he had nothing. Because if he did open his mouth, it wouldn't be to speak. Surely he would lose himself to a scream, one horrible moment before he lost his total fucking mind.

He wanted to grab this woman and drag her out of his house by the hair. He had always wanted to protect himself and his family. But for the first time that order had flipped. His family came first, and this woman was dangerous. There was nothing innocent or flirty about this. He needed to do something. *Anything.* Call Sam. Get Lottie alone and force her to leave. Tell Vicky everything, if that's what he needed to do. But right now, he had to say something. Because everyone was staring at him, including Evie.

She giggled and saved him. Lottie scooped her up and looked over at John. "She misses her daddy *sooooooo* much."

She crossed the room and handed Evie to John, nestling her into his arms — and getting uncomfortably close as she did so.

"Hi, sweetheart," John said, kissing Evie.

He set her back down. Never in his life had every moment felt so heavy, as if any one might crush him.

"I think she's going to start talking any day now," Lottie said. "I've seen this a hundred times. There's this light in her eyes and it doesn't stop burning. You can see her reaching for the words."

"I think she's right," Dakota agreed, walking up beside Lottie and then crouching down next to her baby sister. She looked into Evie's eyes, then up at John. "Becca showed me at the park. She definitely wants to talk. Can you see it, Dad?"

"Do you see it, Mr. Treadwell?"

"John," Vicky reminded her.

Everyone was watching him. He looked down at Evie, then back up at everyone. He smiled carefully. "Yes. I see it."

"What do you think her first word is going to be?" Vicky asked Lottie — as if she would have any fucking idea. Vicky had swallowed Lottie's childcare bullshit to the last drop.

Lottie put a finger to her chin in thought. "I'm going to guess some version of *daddy*."

She touched Vicky gently on her arm, and John had to resist the urge to slap Lottie's hand away from his wife.

"But don't take that personally," she added. "It's just so much easier for a baby to say than *mom* . . . and she obviously loves her daddy."

Another playful laugh.

Then she just stood there, smiling at him, as if expecting John to smile back.

This woman was insane. She was staring at him as though she hadn't come on to him in a pub, thousands of miles and an ocean away. As though she hadn't drugged him and stalked him and infiltrated his family.

"My first word was *daddy*," Dakota said.

"Of course it was," Vicky said, rolling her eyes.

Lottie turned to Vicky and whispered, loud enough for everyone to hear, "They can both say *daddy* first, Victoria, but they'll never know what his heart sounds like from the inside."

Vicky and Dakota traded surprised, satisfied smiles, as though they had just heard something truly wise, rather than some more of Lottie's fortune cookie bullshit.

He had to get out of there.

Robotically, John asked when dinner would be, then said he'd like to lie down until then and maybe slay his monster headache.

"It was so nice to meet you, John," Lottie said, extending her hand to shake his.

He reached out and took it, squeezing it tight, wanting to rip her arm off and beat her with it. Their eyes locked and her artificial smile didn't even waver.

"Nice to meet you, too . . . Becca."

Upstairs, he lay in bed, slowly going out of his mind. He pretended to sleep when Vicky came in to check on him, though John wasn't sure if she bought his possum act or not.

"Dinnertime," she said. He hated how happy she sounded.

He got up and splashed water on his face, hoping to wake up from the nightmare.

Dinner was served at exactly 6:30 — the time it always used to be, before Evie.

"What is this again?" Dakota asked with her mouth full.

Lottie said, "Chicken tikka masala."

"Isn't it delicious?" Vicky was looking at John, though she didn't wait for his answer. "The best part is, I didn't have to make it. When we decided to hire help and then I decided to let her cook, I was sure we'd be eating fish sticks, chicken nuggets, and maybe veggies from a can if that help didn't also happen to be health-conscious. This is truly amazing." Again, looking at John. "Isn't it amazing?"

"Amazing." He swallowed a bite, hating that it was indeed delicious. "So, when do you clock out?"

"Clock out?" Lottie laughed and looked at Vicky. "Friday at five still sound good to you?"

John dropped his fork. "What?"

Vicky said, unapologetically, "I didn't get a chance to tell you, but Becca will be staying with us. She lives in New Haven, so a daily commute just isn't possible. But she can live above the garage and go home on the weekends. I know what you're going to say, but you haven't written in there *once* since we started working together. It's wasted space, so why not use it to make our lives better? Now that we have help."

She laughed, apparently in love with the new word.

"And that's exactly what I promised to do," Lottie chimed in. "I said, 'If I can live here, then it's my job to make your lives better — every day!'"

John leaned across the table toward Lottie. "Why not just find a job closer to home?"

"John!"

He shrugged, looking at Vicky before turning back to Lottie. "I don't mean to be blunt. I'm just wondering why anyone would want to drive so far when they could just work somewhere closer. Surely you could find a job anywhere with your experience."

"Her friend Jasmine lives here," Dakota said.

Lottie nodded. "It's true. She's my best friend and I've known her since middle school. We both had Mr. Graubner." She winked at Dakota, who laughed. "Now she lives in Tivoli with her husband, so I drive down here to visit all the time. She's the one who told me about the ad when she saw it on the local LiveLyfe feed."

For the rest of dinner, John kept his mouth shut. He wasn't sure whether he felt worried or hopeful that Dakota would recognize Lottie from the park. Sure, she looked different as a brunette, but it was reasonable to think that his daughter would find her at least *familiar*. Dakota had his eye for detail and rarely missed things. But . . . nothing. And Lottie had an answer for everything. When he finally fell silent, she fired a different sort of shot into their fray.

Her foot snaked beneath the table, up his leg, and then right between his legs, touching his cock through his pants. He spilled his drink and started to sputter. It felt like Lottie was writing the alphabet with her toes on his hardening shaft.

The legs of his chair scraped against the Spanish tile as he pushed back abruptly.

"Everything okay?" Vicky asked. "You look —"

"He just doesn't know what to do with all of this excitement!" Lottie laughed.

John picked up his half-full plate and fled to the kitchen.

Chapter Twenty-Five

He spent the rest of the evening trying to avoid Lottie, while also watching her closely. A balancing act that might have been easy for a character in one of his books, but which was pretty fucking difficult in real life.

John had never hated anyone more.

He hated how Dakota kept looking over at her with adoration, and the way Evie seemed to giggle at their every interaction. He hated the way Vicky kept affectionately touching Lottie on her arm, as if she were her long-lost sister instead of a vicious parasite. It wasn't that John didn't want Vicky to have help — or *Help* — but Lottie wasn't there to help anybody but herself.

Mostly, though, John hated his attraction to her. He wanted only to abhor her, but John couldn't deny his genuine biological response. Perhaps if she hadn't tried to give him a footjob at dinner he could have continued to steep in his loathing. But now, seeing the sway of her hips or her hair or her breasts . . . it did something to John that it shouldn't. He'd never been angrier at his dick.

And Lottie herself was infuriating.

She kept catching John watching her, but clearly misinterpreted his gaze. She would glance up, see him looking, then offer him a smile and a wink that suggested they were sharing a delicious secret. But John tasted only poison on his lips and a desperation to have her gone.

What did she want? And what was her endgame?

"Isn't she awesome?" Dakota asked, running into John just outside the bathroom.

He assumed his robotic act again. "She's great."

"Why are you saying it like that?"

John looked at Dakota as if he didn't understand. "What do you mean?"

"I don't know, but you seem . . . bothered."

Softly he said, "Yeah . . . honestly, Dakota? I guess I was just really looking forward to a quiet night at home. It's been a long week. I missed you. And I didn't expect company."

"She's not company, Dad. She's another member of our family."

"No," John said. "She's not."

"Mom said she is. That's why she's going to be living above the garage."

"I'm not sure how I feel about that."

"I don't get it, Dad. You told Mom to get a nanny, and she found someone we all love. Isn't that —"

"You've known her for less than a day!" That was way too loud, and now Dakota was staring at him, confused. Much softer he added, "I'm just saying . . . do you remember when we ate at that place called Spoons?"

"Unfortunately."

"Right. But do you remember when we first got there?"

Dakota shrugged. "Sure. The menu looked great."

"But what happened later?"

"We got sick. But that's already a dumb comparison. Becca isn't bad food."

"I'm not saying she is, I'm just saying that maybe we're ordering appetizers, an entree, and dessert before checking Yelp to see if anyone else spent the night on their knees in the bathroom. Or worse — the hospital."

Dakota looked at him with her *I feel so sorry for you and your lack of intelligence* look. She was a master at that expression, and John usually found it amusing. But then again, the look was rarely leveled at him.

"Okay," she sighed.

"I hate it when you *okay* me."

"What else do you want me to say? 'I hope you get a good night's sleep, so that you're not all weird tomorrow'? Something like that?"

John looked at his daughter and forced a laugh. "You're right, sweetheart. I'm exhausted. From the travel, from the funeral. And hell, from your uncle." Another little laugh to prove that everything was cool. "I'll be much better in the morning."

He gave Dakota a hug, and she hugged him hard back.

As soon as he let her go he started cycling through ideas, thinking of any possible way he could get the parasite out of his house.

His house.

This was his house. He would pull her aside the second he got a chance and tell her that she needed to leave immediately. He wouldn't allow her to hold the threat of exposure over his head. Not anymore. And not in his house.

John followed his daughter into the living room.

Lottie was just heading upstairs. Evie was in her arms, half asleep, her head resting on Lottie's shoulder and a blissful smile on her tiny face. Lottie looked right at John and said, "Time for night-night, Daddy. She had a big day," then left the room.

Vicky came up to him, beaming, and put a hand on his arm, but before she could speak he said, "I'm exhausted." He kissed her on the cheek and went into his bedroom.

He heard the door open and then loudly close a second after he started brushing his teeth.

Vicky appeared in the bathroom doorway. "You're being kind of an ass, John."

He took the toothbrush out of his mouth. "I'm sorry?"

"You heard me. What is your problem?"

"I don't have a problem." John let it sit for a second as he rinsed his mouth, then added, "I'm tired. My father died and I couldn't come home when I was supposed to. I spent the night in a shitty hotel and all I kept thinking about the entire time was how much I couldn't wait to get back home to the three of you. Not to a fourth person that I haven't met who's now suddenly 'part of the family.'"

"She's great, John. *This* is great. For me. For us."

"You've known her for less than a day!" John felt like he had one song in his mental playlist, set on repeat.

"And how long did I need to know you before I felt sure of a thing or two?" Vicky offered him one of his favorite smiles. "You told me to hire some help, so I did. I'm sorry I didn't wait for you, but I'm telling you that Becca is perfect. So please be okay with it."

He dropped his toothbrush in its holder and dried off his mouth. "I'm fine with you hiring her, I guess. But she's *living here*. You really don't think that deserved a discussion?"

Vicky blinked. Opened her mouth, then closed it. Took a breath. "Absolutely. You're right. I'm sorry."

"I'm sure everything will be fine in the morning," John

said, though not at all in the way that he meant it. "I just need to get some sleep."

Another smile. "I can help you with that."

But unlike just about every other time he'd come home from a long trip, John didn't want to have sex. Because he would surely fall right to sleep, like always. And John needed for Vicky to be down and out so that he could slip away and exterminate the rat living above their garage.

She took a step forward. Reached up and bit his ear. Grabbed his hand and pulled him toward the door. "Come on, let's go to bed."

"Don't you have to finish up downstairs?"

"Not tonight." Another smile, this one with a dab of her tongue. "Thanks to our new help. *Now* are you glad?"

No.

John followed Vicky to the bed. She pulled him atop her and they kissed.

The whole time, he couldn't stop thinking about Lottie. Imagining her peeking through the window of the apartment above their garage, trying to see what he was up to. Imagining her sneaking into the house, listening at the bottom of the stairs, to see if he was still awake.

Imagining her bursting into their bedroom and asking to join them.

Somehow he managed to make Vicky come, even though he was only half-hard most of the time. Finally, he gave up on his own orgasm.

"Sorry," he said when she frowned up at him. "I'm just too tired."

"We'll try again tomorrow." Vicky smiled coyly before turning her back to him and snuggling under the covers.

Mercifully, Vicky was snoring soon enough. John waited for what felt like a half hour, then slipped out of bed and into the hallway.

Dakota's room was dark.

Good.

He crept downstairs. The living room lights were out, but the kitchen was throwing a few beams into the darkness.

Lottie was on her knees, scrubbing the oven. She looked up when he entered. "Hi, John!"

In a low growl, he said, "What the fuck are you doing?"

"Do you know how excited Victoria is going to be when she wakes up in the morning and her oven is all clean? This thing hasn't been scrubbed in years." She resumed the scrubbing, but this time she arched her back and made her ass prominent.

His cock tingled. *Not again.*

She kept talking in her bubbly nanny-voice. "You should have seen it an hour ago. Totally black and really sticky. But don't worry, I'm not using any harsh chemicals or anything, not with Evie in the house. It's just baking soda and vinegar."

John stood there, dumfounded. All his rehearsed arguments had taken flight.

She reached up and grabbed a towel, cleaning her hands while still on her knees, remaining level with John's crotch. She grinned right at it, as if his cock needed a *hello*.

He glared at her, then entered the kitchen the rest of the way while keeping out of reach.

"I mean, what the fuck are you doing *here*?"

Lottie looked up at him, perplexed. She shook her head ever so slightly. "I'm helping Victoria with Evie. And Dakota, I suppose. I don't think that's part of the *official job*, but their relationship definitely needs my touch."

Lottie gave John a knowing look, then she stood and came closer to John.

"You have *such* a beautiful house. I imagined it a lot, but I dunno, I thought it would look . . . different. For some reason, I thought it would be more Victoria than you, with a lot of Restoration Hardware and Williams-Sonoma. You know, so she could point to a page and say, 'I want my room to look like that!' But your personality" — she placed a hand on his chest — "is *everywhere*. The big red chair in the living room looks at least fifty years old. Victoria probably hates it. And she probably hates that *Grindhouse* poster in your office, too."

Yes. Vicky very much hated both of those things. And he hated Lottie for being able to see it so easily.

"Anyway, it's great to see that. Your personality is what brought me here, after all." She whispered, "My friend Jasmine didn't really show me the ad."

"You need to leave."

She looked at him, her eyes wide. "Why?"

This woman was either schizophrenic or Meryl fucking Streep.

John grabbed her by the arm — not hard enough to leave a bruise if she didn't resist — and dragged her toward the garage. He opened the door, pushed her inside, then followed, closing the door behind him. "Are you crazy?"

Lottie laughed. "Of course I'm not crazy. But that *is* a crazy question."

"You need to get away from me and my family. Now."

Lottie looked up at the ceiling. "You know what's up there?"

"I don't care."

"My bed is up there, John. That's the place where you can do anything you want to me."

Her accent was back, and so was his boner.

"But we don't have to go up there. We could do it right

now. I'll just pull these down" — Lottie tugged on her pants — "and then you can tear my knickers off and bury it in me from behind. I can put my hands on the wall . . . over there."

She pointed to the far wall.

John said, "Get the hell out of my house right now. Before I call the cops."

Lottie looked slapped. "Why would you call the police?"

"Because you're in my house!" He was trying not to yell. "And you're crazy! I don't want you anywhere near my family, or me."

She took a step toward John and reached out for his traitorous cock.

"But you're hard . . . and I'm wet. Why not have what we both really want, John?"

She peeled off her shirt and dropped it on the floor. She wasn't wearing a bra.

"Lottie."

"*Becca*," she laughed.

"This will never happen."

She stopped. Blinked. Looked down at her shirt.

Had he finally gotten through to her?

He picked her shirt up and handed it to her. She put it on, and then, seeming embarrassed, she said, "I'm sorry."

Her hesitation emboldened him. His rehearsed speech came flying back. "Stay the night so my wife doesn't try and track you down. In the morning, say that you've given this a lot of thought, and that you just don't want to be that far away from your family during the week. It was a really difficult decision, but you're firm. Do you understand?"

Lottie looked up at John and nodded, all of her mirth now but a memory.

He turned around without another word and returned to his bedroom.

Vicky was still snoring.

In less than twelve hours, all of this would finally be over.

Chapter Twenty-Six

Dakota dropped her fork as if she had a big announcement. She turned to Lottie, looking at her as if the demon sitting beside her were an angel gracing the room with her halo. "These are so amazing. Where did you learn to cook like this?"

Lottie smiled. "I'm not sure where I picked up this particular recipe, but I've just loved cooking forever." Then, to John: "Do you like your waffle?"

John looked down at his carrot-cake waffle. The whole thing was buttered in a layer of gooey frosting. It was dessert for breakfast, but it wasn't like he was about to rock the boat or say anything untoward now, not with Lottie on her way out.

"Delicious," he said, actually smiling.

"I just love that you got the girls to eat something healthy for once!" Vicky shook her head, clearly ashamed of her own failure as a mother to get her children to eat cake for breakfast. "I mean, I know this isn't exactly quinoa, but we're still getting fiber and whole grains."

Vicky speared another piece of waffle and popped it into her mouth. "And *ohmygod* . . . they're delicious."

Lottie turned to Dakota. "So how are things with Brittany and Amanda?"

"Ugh," Dakota said. "I don't want to talk about it."

Something scraped at John's brain. Had something happened since Dakota punched Tiffany in the nose over something Brittany — or Amanda — had told her?

"You know," Lottie said, "I had my own Brittany and Amanda when I was your age. Their names were Miranda and Leslie. Miranda had been my best friend since kindergarten and then all through middle school. We lived three blocks away from each other."

"What happened?" Dakota asked.

"Once we got to high school, everything changed. All of a sudden she didn't want to be my friend anymore. But I guess I can't blame her. You should have seen me in high school. I was mostly braces and acne."

Vicky raised her hand. "Been there."

Evie squealed, probably because she was having so much trouble getting her waffle-cake into her mouth. Her entire face was frosted.

Valentine hovered beneath Evie's highchair, just in case she dropped anything.

Lottie continued. "In my experience, Dakota, it's important to be aware of what's happening, then stay ahead of it. I waited way too long with Miranda. It took me an unreasonably long time to realize how much effort I was putting into the relationship compared to her."

"What do you mean?" Dakota asked.

"I would buy her things, offer her my stuff, always be available for whatever she needed, whenever she needed it. The relationship was totally one-sided, and it *hurts* to like someone a lot more than they like you —"

A barely perceptible glance at John. He dropped his eyes and took another bite of his own waffle. The sooner breakfast was over, the sooner Lottie could tell Vicky that she'd changed her mind.

"When I finally approached Miranda and told her how I felt," Lottie continued, "she said that she understood. But then she turned into an excuse factory. Take it from me, Dakota — if someone tells you that they want to be your friend, but then they can't ever make time for you, they don't really want to be your friend. And once you know that's true, the best thing you can do is take control of the situation."

"How?" Dakota asked, awaiting more of Lottie's wisdom.

Vicky seemed equally interested.

John stared, wondering what crazy shit she had *really* done to drive Miranda away. If there was really a Miranda at all.

"You just have to be honest," she went on. "With her and with yourself. The first and most important thing you can do is take care of yourself. A part of you knows that this thing you really want is now over. You've been hurt, and you feel dumb or maybe awkward for trying so hard. You made all this effort, did everything you could to make this person like you, and now they want to just cut you out of their life? Like I said, forget her and take care of yourself. Get sleep and eat something delicious — like carrot-cake waffles!"

Lottie laughed that sickening laugh, and Dakota beamed back at her.

"Then spend time with someone who *wants* to be around you. Go to the mall or watch some Netflix. I'm happy to be a person who *wants* to spend time with you, Dakota."

Lottie put her hand on his daughter's, and John felt murder in his blood.

"Friendship is a two-way street, Dakota. And Amanda isn't acting like your friend."

Dakota hugged Lottie, and with slightly wet eyes she said, "*Thank you.*"

Vicky looked at Lottie, beaming.

John's rage continued to grow through the morning. After Dakota left for school, Lottie tended to Evie, to the dishes, and to the rest of the kitchen cleanup as if last night's conversation had been roleplay. He even overheard her asking Vicky if she would like her to take care of the downstairs guest bathroom today or tomorrow.

It was as if last night had never even happened.

Maybe that's because Lottie is totally fucking batshit insane, dumbass. She clearly doesn't care what you say to her. She knows no boundaries.

He and Vicky started work at 11:30, as usual. Vicky showed up, with a ton of ideas. But John was so mad, he could barely sit still.

"What's with you?" Vicky asked, her voice playful.

"I guess I'm just not thinking straight."

"Really, honey, is everything okay? Is it your dad? Or is there anything else you want to talk about?"

She reached over and touched him. He smiled, trying to forget the bloodsucker still in his house, at least long enough to finally finish some work. But then, speak of the devil, said bloodsucker entered their office.

"I brought you a plate!" Lottie announced.

Vicky turned to Lottie. "Oh wow, what's that?"

Lottie set a full plate between them with a bowl of guacamole in the middle, surrounded by four clusters of snacks. Walnuts, blueberries, some sort of chips, and a few pieces of crumbled dark chocolate.

"It's brain food. You two are making magic in here and you need plenty of fuel. Those are baked kale chips. And don't think of the chocolate as dessert, think of it as something your work deserves. This stuff is loaded with antioxidants and it's a great mood-booster. But you already knew that, right, Victoria?"

They traded a look that got John chewing on his bottom lip. "Becca."

"Yes, Mr. Treadwell?"

"Would you mind if we had a couple of uninterrupted hours? Brainstorming is hard when you have to keep switching gears."

"Oh, of course! You won't hear another peep from me." Lottie turned to Vicky. "Did you still want to nap at three? I can make sure that Evie is ready to go down then, too. Good idea?"

"You are wonderful. Thank you."

Vicky watched Lottie leave, her face softening with affection in way that broke John's heart.

He had to fix this. His wife deserved a nanny who was every bit the person Lottie pretended to be, and he would make sure she got it. But first he had to get this monster out of his house.

Vicky turned back to John. "How can you not be in love with her?"

He was pretty sure Lottie was wondering the same thing. Damn it.

He flicked his eyes to the monitor, and the day's work that they'd barely started. "Shall we?"

"You sure there's nothing you want to talk about? It's Becca, isn't it? You're mad at me because I didn't wait for you to hire her, and now you're pouting."

"I'm not pouting."

"You're pouting a little."

"Really, I'm not. I just want to work."

"Okay," she said, clearly not believing him. "But I *am* sorry. I just . . . you can see why I hired her on the spot, right?"

"Of course. She's perfect." Robotic voice. "I'm really happy that you have her." Then he smiled, hard enough to hurt his jaw. "That *we* have her."

If Lottie hadn't been consuming his brain, the next few hours would have flown by. Vicky was happy. Laughing, excited, engaged. Her ideas were bright and abundant. By nap time, they'd gotten a quarter of the novel nailed down. Vicky looked at the monitor, satisfied.

"Well, *that* was an afternoon," she said.

John laughed despite himself. "It was."

"How much are you looking forward to a nap?" On cue, Vicky yawned. "So. Much." She kissed him on the cheek. "Thank you. That was fun." She walked toward the doorway, then turned around. "Can you do me a favor?"

"Of course."

"Try to like Becca while I'm napping?"

How about I try not to kill her while you're napping?

"Let's get you and Evie down for a rest, and then" — from behind the hardest smile of his life — "I'll do my best."

Down in the living room, Lottie was stacking blocks with Evie. They both looked up when John and Vicky entered.

"She's *tuckered*," Lottie said. "And ready to nap with her mama."

Lottie scooped Evie into her arms and handed her over to Vicky.

"Thank you, Becca," Vicky said. "This is officially the life."

Lottie smiled and touched Vicky on her arm. "I'm happy to be here."

Vicky looked from John to Lottie. "Well, you two have fun. We're going night-night."

She was maybe a second out of earshot when Lottie giggled. "Did you hear that? She told us to 'have fun.' What do you say, Daddy? Shall we have some fun?"

He had to stay calm, measured, despite his rage. "You need to go."

Lottie looked at him, confused. She blinked, seemed to reset, and turned her head as if in thought. Then she turned back to John, her eyes wide and appearing filled with genuine wonder. "Why?"

John stared. He wanted to grab her, shake her. But he kept his hands firm at his sides.

"I'm sure that deep in your selfish heart you know how cruel this is. Evie won't remember, but Vicky and Dakota will. The longer you stay, the more heartbroken they're going to be when you leave."

She laughed. "If you want to yell at me, you're going to have to help with the laundry. I promised Victoria empty baskets by dinnertime."

She walked toward the laundry room. John followed a moment behind her, but Lottie was already sitting on the washing machine, legs open like she planned to wrap her legs around his waist and pull his cock into her.

"Wanna help?"

"No. I can take care of the laundry myself. How about I help you to your car?"

She eyed him. Then she shook her head. "You don't look like much of a laundry man to me. Tell you what . . ." Lottie looked up at the cupboard above the washer. "If you can tell me what kind of detergent is in there — the brand, the color of the bottle, *anything* — then you can do the laundry all by yourself, and I'll go write a *Dear John* to Victoria right now."

John thought, hating her, trying to remember the last time he'd even *been* in the laundry room.

Her legs opened wider. "Color or brand, John?"

Tide was probably the most popular brand, since it was the first to come to mind. So it definitely wasn't Tide. John couldn't think of a single time when Vicky had ever done the most popular thing. He thought harder. Went deep and imagined the laundry room the last time he'd seen it.

Color or brand, John?

He pictured yellow and knew he had it. "Arm & Hammer."

Lottie sighed, as if she were genuinely sorry. Then she twisted around to open the cupboard, revealing the detergent bottle. It was yellow. But . . .

"Nope. Victoria likes Tide. The Coldwater Clean scent. Your wife is a smart lady — this detergent uses less hot water *and* saves energy."

John didn't know what to say, or do. He still wasn't sure if this was an elaborate game, or if the woman was truly insane. Should he call the boys in blue or the men in white coats?

She slid off the washer, then stacked one empty basket into another and set a third on top of the washing machine. She pulled out two pairs of panties and held them up for John. One pink and the other black.

"Remember these? Oh, no," she laughed, shaking the black pair. "You wouldn't remember *this* pair." Then she shook the pink one. "But these were the ones I was wearing the night you fucked me. The night you came in my mouth. Remember, John? Remember my arse?"

All he could remember was waking up in her bed, head and bladder pounding in unison. His guilty retreat from what he thought was her apartment. The sweaty agony of flying home.

Her accent trailed into the laugh. She raised the pink panties to her nose and deeply inhaled. Then she smiled at John and chirped, "Still smells like us!"

She dropped the pink panties into the basket and brought the black pair to her lips. "This is the pair I wore after you left. Do you know why I chose black?"

He stared at her, speechless, not wanting to encourage her but suddenly desperate to see where this was going.

His cock was at full mast again, too.

Like a secret, she whispered, "I chose black because I still had your cum inside me. I knew it would dribble out, and I could see you better in black."

And then she showed him.

John pictured himself choking her. But still measured, he said, "Last chance, Lottie. I won't play this game with you. It isn't fair to my family."

Another laugh, but this one came from someplace deeper. "You can't be serious." She held up the black panties again. "Was this fair to your family, *Grayson*? Was it fair to your family when you were beating off in your hotel room while on the phone with me? How many times have you thought of me while fucking Victoria? Is that fair to her? Don't be ridiculous. This is about *both of us*. You're already in deep." She licked her lips. "You might as well be balls-deep."

Furiously hard and hating it, John said, "You can't prove a thing. The moment you tell your story you'll sound like a stalker. No one will believe a word you say."

Lottie laughed until tears glistened in her eyes. John stood there, hating her, refusing to nibble on her bait.

She finally said, "Please tell me you don't mean that, John. I can't stand the thought of you thinking so little of me. Do you really think I would do *nothing* to protect myself? A girl has to be careful. I met this guy once, Garry, he found me in a dark club one night. We did a lot of drugs and got to know each other real well, real fast, if you know what I mean." She smiled. "What am I saying? You know *exactly* what I mean."

John glared.

"Garry taught me a few tech-nerd tricks, assuming I was just a dumb blonde he could fuck and show off in front of. He didn't know that I was watching everything he did. Learning. And when I was finished with him, I started applying what I learned. Maybe I couldn't hack like Garry, but I could do well enough, get into anyone's phone with just a few minutes. So I started digging into people's identities, discovering their aliases, their bad habits, their addresses and phone numbers. I felt so alive, John. And do you know what else I learned to do?"

He was terrified to find out. Lottie was still smiling like always, but now her grin belonged to the Joker.

"I learned to record things for my collection. And I have a couple of recordings that you might really like to see and hear. That *Victoria* might really like to see and hear. Like our time together on the phone. I have it all. My favorite part is when you said, 'My wife doesn't do this for me.' You were grunting so hard you sounded like an animal. I've listened to it a lot. I also have video from London, in case your wife wants to see how she might actually satisfy you."

John was going to kill her. Snarling, breathing heavy through his nose, he stomped toward Lottie with murder in his eyes.

"John — please!"

She raised a hand, palm out, her voice suddenly serious.

"I'm not trying to hurt you. I just want the two of us to be closer. Believe me, the last thing I want to do is cause you harm, but I really need this job. For just a little while longer, until I get back on my feet. I'm good for your family. They like me and I like them. And you used to like me . . . once upon a time. Maybe you might like me again." Lottie smiled, almost seeming reasonable. "If you're a good boy and you keep your mouth shut, there's no reason I can't do the same." Her smile widened. "Of course . . . I can always *open* my mouth when you need me to."

John grabbed Lottie by the neck.

She seemed almost to lean into his violence, as if she expected it. As if she enjoyed it.

"Just like that," she said, panting.

He pulled back, and she ripped her blouse open.

Buttons popped off and skittered onto the floor. Again, no bra. Her breasts were full, her nipples hard and pink.

As loud as he possibly could without screaming, he growled, "Get the fuck out of my house!"

And then her hand was snaking into his pants, wrapping around his cock.

He couldn't breathe.

He couldn't move.

John couldn't stop her, even if he wanted to. He wasn't sure his body would let him.

Her hand moved, up and down. "This doesn't feel like someone who wants me to leave. This feels like someone who wants to come inside me."

Lottie took a step back until her body was pressed against the washing machine, her nipples erect and staring at John.

She pulled down her pants — no panties — and he

caught something he'd missed before. Faded scars on her inner thighs. Some looked fresh.

She grabbed him by the face, pulled his gaze up to her eyes, and said, "You can do anything you want with me. *To* me." She whispered, "I bet you want to choke me. Well then, I want you to choke me, John. I just want to please you, to feel you inside me."

She brought his hands to her neck.

"Choke me, John," she moaned.

She was insane. He squeezed, feeling her pulse in his fingers, thinking how easily he could end this all right now.

His heart raced.

He was harder than maybe he'd ever been in his life.

There was something so wrong, so terrible, and yet so intoxicating about the moment.

She shuddered, pulling his cock against her.

"Choke me while you fuck me, John," she said, pulling his pants down. She bit her lip as his dick pressed against her wetness.

He squeezed her neck harder, enough that he was afraid he might not be able to stop himself. She gave his cock a firm tug, making his entire body shudder. With excitement. With loathing. With rage.

She stared at John, daring him.

Something inside him snapped, and he did the unforgivable.

Chapter Twenty-Seven

As he lay in bed that night, John waited for Vicky to fall asleep.

It was quiet. Peaceful. The kind of silence that sounded black. A cloak for the chaos that promised him calm. He wanted to sink down inside it. But he couldn't.

Because John had to wait.

She wasn't snoring, and he needed to be sure she was out, so that he could get the hell out of their room and start righting some of his many wrongs.

Today, he'd gone too far. Well, that was an understatement.

Today, he'd destroyed his life.

He'd never felt guilt like this. And this time he couldn't claim that he had been drugged, couldn't pretend that he'd been drunk out of his gourd. Yes, he had been manipulated, and yes, Lottie had known exactly what she was doing, threading the strings of his life through her fingers just so, then making him dance to the tune in her head.

But he was the one who said yes. He was the one who put himself inside her. He was the one feigning sleep beside his loyal wife while the interloper plotted downstairs.

I am the world's biggest asshole.

The guilt was even worse than the terror. Because whatever happened, now he was sure he deserved it. Lying there staring at the backs of his closed eyelids, it was easy for John to imagine the worst. Whether he confessed or she snitched, there would be no coming back once Vicky knew. She would leave him and take the children and he would have nothing.

There was a moment when he'd been on the edge, and he wasn't sure if he was going to fuck Lottie or strangle her.

He had to talk to Sam.

Sam had dealt with problems worse than this. He'd said so himself. Sam could put him in touch with his fixer. It wasn't too late. He just needed to get his agent on the phone.

But first he needed to get out of bed.

An excruciating hour and a half later, Vicky finally choked, snorted, and turned her back to John.

Outside the house, he pulled out his phone, feeling a glimmer of hope as the evening air kissed his overheated skin.

Three rings, then, "John. Let me guess. Lottie?"

"Lottie." John drew a breath. "She's here, Sam. In my house. Right now."

"What do you mean she's in your house? You mean she's told Vicky?"

"No. Vicky doesn't know anything. I came home from California and she'd already hired Lottie to be our nanny."

"Shit."

"A giant pile of it."

John could practically hear Sam thinking. After a

moment, he said, "So I assume she's perfect, and getting along with Dakota?"

"You've sold this story before."

Another sigh. "Shit, John. We need to be careful. Obviously, you know to stay the hell away from her. The last thing you need is —"

"I'll stop you right there."

"John."

"I'm not going to say it wasn't my fault, because obviously it was. But she knew *exactly* what she was doing, Sam. The whole thing was a trap. She's playing me, and I'm not smart enough to keep up with her."

"I doubt this girl is a genius. She's probably just crazy, and used to getting what she wants. You're plenty smart. Problem is, you're *acting* stupid."

"Yeah, a dumb fucking bastard, you said that already."

Sam paused. "We need to call Danny."

"Your fixer, right? Is that his real name?"

"I doubt it. I've seen him a half-dozen times in person and he's never been the same guy twice. Good-looking enough to charm the ladies, but always with a face you can trust. He knows how to get his back scratched, after a lifetime of scratching himself. He could be anyone: a street thug, a man in Armani, or a schlub in khakis. You'll see."

"Do I have to? Can't we do this over the phone?"

"Not a chance. Danny insists on looking into every client's eyes. He needs to know whether they're lying. He told me once that it won't necessarily determine whether he'll take a job, but it will absolutely affect the way he'll handle it. He won't even want me there the first time, because he's going to want to see how you handle all of his questions on your own."

"She's in my house *now*. This can blow up at any moment."

"This is what he does. Give me the green light and I'll call him right now. I'm sure he can meet you in the morning."

John thought. Considered. Wanted to say no.

But he swallowed and said, "Do it."

Chapter Twenty-Eight

Given Sam's description, John hadn't known what to expect from Danny Hayes.

Still, he managed to be surprised by the man sliding into the booth across from him in The Kitchen Sink, the greasy spoon Sam ordered him out to. It was nowhere near the airport, or John's house. Equally inconvenient for them both.

Danny held out his hand. "I'm Mercer. Good to meet you."

The man looked part forty-something rock star, with his long dark hair, Sex Pistols tee, and seven-day beard, and part Special Forces, with his large frame and muscles stretching the seams of his tailored blazer. His accent was somehow both New York and everywhere else.

John shook the man's hand. "You're not Danny?"

He blinked. "That's right, you're one of Sam's. Let's do that again." He took back his hand, smiled, and held it out again. "Danny Hayes. Good to meet you."

John didn't shake the hand this time. "Sam said you

were the best. I'd think you'd remember which fake name you're supposed to use."

"You're a writer?"

Slightly uncertain. "Yes."

"You ever write something and your editor hands it back to you, says maybe you mixed up some of the names, called one character Bobby when it was supposed to be Greg or whatever?"

"Sure. Of course."

"Well, there you go. Verbal typo. Now how can I help you?" Danny leaned back in his chair and started reading the menu.

"There's a girl —"

"There's always a girl."

"— and it's getting out of hand."

Danny dropped the menu and looked at John. "I don't know why I even bother. It's always pancakes." He scooted his menu to the edge of their table, then turned his head and scanned the area. Seeing that their waitress was busy, with her back to their table, Danny turned back around and found John's eyes. "Getting-out-of-hand out of hand, or *Well, shit. Looks like my dick is in the doggie again* out of hand?"

"The last one. But not again. This is new for me."

"I got the gist from Sam. You and me, we can fill in the blanks. That her job app?" Danny pointed at the thin pink folder on the table. John nodded, then slid it toward him.

Danny opened the folder, took out the two papers inside, and studied them.

After a couple of silent minutes, John said, "So, what are my options?"

Danny kept staring at the pages. He already looked like a different person than he had just a few minutes ago. Now, he seemed almost professorial. Finally, he dropped the sheets atop the empty folder.

"This is dog shit."

"I'm sorry?" John said. "What does that mean?"

"I don't believe a word that's on this thing. She's probably using a fake name, and I imagine her real one isn't either of the ones you've heard. Now, that in itself is something. Because if she's using a fake name, we can pressure your girl to get lost or we'll report her use of a fake ID. That could get her into a fair bit of legal trouble, depending on how far she's gone."

"Please — she's not 'my girl.'"

"You fuck her?"

John said nothing.

Danny smiled. "Why don't you tell me the story? Your words. Pretend I don't know shit."

He told Danny everything — at least everything as he knew it. The whole thing felt like Confession, although he couldn't imagine this guy on the other side of the screen. John held nothing back. There was no reason to make himself look like a saint in front of this man. Danny Hayes and his many aliases had surely seen it all.

Danny Hayes is a fixer, with the perfect combination of qualities to do the job. He was raised in the Bronx — before the place gentrified itself into a crap-ton of Starbucks and Pottery Barns — so he has the sharp eye of a native New Yorker who's learned to take shit from no one. He's disappeared evidence for cheating politicians. He's had billionaires' problem daughters "straightened out." Sometimes he even did the straightening out himself. After all, some of those women just needed the attention Daddy never gave them. He's helped Wall Street assholes out of bankruptcy, deprived entitled wives of their alimony. He's even killed people, when they deserved it. He's done jobs for the mob, but made it clear that he's a free agent and won't respond well to being strong-armed. They've learned to respect him and keep their distance, once they saw that he wasn't interested in any of their pie.

"What's your take?" Danny asked.

"I just told you."

"No. You told me what *happened*. Now I want to know your take. I need the stuff between the lines." Danny turned around again. He'd been looking for the waitress all through John's story, but it was like their table was invisible. Now she had vanished. Danny turned back to John and made a *hurry up* motion with his hand.

"Well, she was in London using a fake accent, and I can't help but think that she targeted me in that bar."

"You, my friend, are a genius. I might actually get coffee before you figure this out. I'm asking about the drugs. You say you don't actually remember what happened after you got back to her place, right?"

"Right. I don't even remember what happened at the bar. It's not even cloudy . . . it's just not there."

"Yeah, you were roofied."

"How do you know? What does that look like?"

"It looks like exactly what you're telling me. I'm sure she put something in your drink. All the drugs exhibit pretty much the same symptoms. Blacking out, then a headache in the morning. Sound familiar?"

John nodded, rubbing his head at the memory.

"That's what makes it the perfect crime. You drink a shit-ton of alcohol, then you wake up with a chunk of night missing and a pounding skull. But you can't blame yourself. Your girl could've used Ambien, Xanax . . . maybe Ativan. If she went classic, she used Rohypnol or ketamine or GHB. No matter the cocktail, your memory's gonna be fucked. And we can't take a word she says at face value. What happened after London? Any physical contact?"

"I thought I saw her a couple of places around town, but I still can't be sure if that was just my imagination."

"Uh-huh." Danny turned back around. The waitress was nowhere. He looked like he was about to get out of their booth and hunt her down, but he returned his attention to John instead. "We might need to retrace those steps later. Right now, I want to know how you let her in."

"Let her in?"

"Right. Your girl is a vampire. She can only come in if invited. So how did you invite her in?"

"Please . . . stop calling her 'my girl.' And I guess you're saying that I shouldn't have engaged her at all."

Danny shook his head. "How have you not accidentally swallowed a bottle of bleach?"

John wasn't sure exactly what that meant, but it was definitely an insult. "We had phone sex in my hotel."

Danny nodded slowly, as if encouraging a dumb dog. "Yeah, the phone sex. And she said that's recorded?"

"Yes."

"You believe her?"

John shrugged.

"And then . . ."

"We had sex in the laundry room."

Danny's face found another shape, this one of a disapproving teacher. "With your wife home? And your daughters?"

John refused to break his stare. "Yes."

Danny nodded, processing. Finally, he said, "Assuming she was in Connecticut during that call, we could be looking at nailing her for recording your voice without consent. It's illegal in that state. And with everything you said so far, that sounds like our best avenue."

"How do we know she was in Connecticut? She could have called from anywhere — and you're suggesting we go to the *cops?*" John shook his head, tried to reset. "I could've done that myself. I thought talking to you might lead to a more . . . aggressive solution."

Danny laughed. "A more *aggressive* solution? Ha. Go ahead and try calling the cops yourself. See how that goes."

"That's not what I'm suggesting."

"Literally what you just said."

"I'm just saying that this girl seems dangerous." John paused, lowered his voice. "Maybe I'm not explaining it right. I think she's crazy."

"Of course she's crazy! She flew across an ocean to 'bump into you.'"

"She's going to ruin my family. And —"

"Trust me, and everything will be fine. You think you're the first man to get his mayo on the wrong bread? This is as easy as it gets, my friend."

John sighed. "Look, I'll do anything you tell me to . . . but I don't want to go to the police if we can help it. This has to stay quiet. Because if it gets out — if I have to take legal action to get rid of this woman — then everyone will know what really happened. And I'll lose everything. My family. My livelihood. We write together, my wife and I. It's our partnership paying the bills these days. You understand what I'm going through, right?"

"I don't do marriage. Hell, I don't even do relationships. But I get where you're coming from. We're going to do everything we can to shove Jeannie back into her bottle. But let me give you some advice. If this doesn't work out, you should keep your future feminine interests short-term, and learn how to find women who are amenable to such a setup. And rotate. Last thing you need is a clingy woman."

"Sounds romantic."

"Hey, I'm not the one calling *me*." Danny looked back behind him, saw nothing, then turned back to John.

"You've gotta be fucking kidding me. I bet you it's easier to get a blowjob in this place than it is to place a mother-fucking order. Half my riches for a goddamn cup of coffee. Anyway, you said she drives, right?"

"Pink VW Beetle. I want to punch in a window whenever I walk by it."

"Restrain yourself. I'm assuming she keeps her registration in the glove compartment. You need to get that for me."

"What if it's not in there?"

"What if a giant asteroid hadn't wiped out the dinosaurs? Were there really ancient aliens? What if gravity wasn't a thing? Concern yourself with the important questions, John. If it's not there, it's not there. We'll deal with it then. But I'll bet even Crazy keeps her registration in the car."

"Okay. I'll send it to you as soon as I get it. Anything else?"

"I'm going to send a buddy of mine over to sit on your place. He'll take a look around her room when the place is empty."

John nodded. "Sounds good."

The waitress finally appeared looking bubbly, as if she hadn't been keeping them waiting forever. "Morning, boys. Can I get you anything?"

"Not anymore," Danny said, slipping out of the booth.

He left without a wave.

John stayed, eating his two pancakes and sipping his coffee alone. Then he drove home, thinking about Lottie's Beetle and the prize inside it, surprised to find himself smiling.

Chapter Twenty-Nine

John parked nine blocks away from his house — just far enough to be reasonably sure that no one would recognize him — then ran around the block three times at full speed. Winded and sweaty, he got back in his car and drove the rest of the way home.

At the second red light, he glanced at the pink box on the passenger seat. It was maybe the first time in his life he'd bought donuts from Hot Cross Buns without desperately wanting one. Pancakes would do that. But John couldn't eat one even if he wanted to, because Vicky wouldn't believe that he would go out for a run and then scarf down on fried bread and sugar. She *would* believe that he'd pick up a dozen for her — and their resident Help. He lifted the box, just for a peek. The arrangement looked more like a magazine spread than a pile of empty carbs.

The light turned green and he stepped on the gas.

A few minutes later, John pulled into his driveway and parked beside Lottie. The sight of her Beetle again made him want to send his fist through the glass. *Restrain yourself.*

He grabbed the box and got out of the car. Looking

over his shoulder the entire time, he tried the passenger door and then the driver's side. Both locked, with no other way inside. It wasn't like he expected to simply open it, but his meeting with Danny had left him surprisingly optimistic.

That feeling was gone as soon as he opened the front door. Because Vicky was crying.

John said nothing. Invisibility was best if he wanted to hear what was being said.

He set the box down in the kitchen and crept forward, into the living room, walking on the sides of his feet to stay silent. Her crying seemed to swell and crest. There was a deep heave, then things seemed to settle.

John froze as Vicky started crying again.

This was truly terrible, whatever it was. Vicky could get emotional — he'd seen her cry at a Wendy's commercial once. But this was coming from a deep place that rattled his core. And with Lottie in the house, John had little doubt as to what it could be.

He would be sleeping somewhere else tonight. And then forever. Vicky would never forgive him. Neither would Dakota. Evie would grow up to think that her father was a selfish monster who cared only about himself.

John stopped outside the living room and peeked in.

Vicky was sobbing, but it was softer now. Unbelievably, she was crying on Lottie's shoulder. She lifted her head. He could imagine her looking into Lottie's eyes, but all he could see was the back of Vicky's silky black hair. Whatever this was, she didn't seem angry at Lottie.

Vicky spoke, but it was soft, and John couldn't hear what she was saying. He didn't dare take a step. Or move a muscle.

What could Lottie have told her? And how was he going to play this?

Maybe he should call Danny. Or Sam.

No. He needed to know more. But how?

And he couldn't just stand there.

He turned to go.

"Mr. Treadwell."

John stopped, turned back around, and smiled. "Is everything okay?"

The Devil smiled in Lottie's eyes. "Victoria has had a difficult morning. We're processing."

"What does that mean?" John asked, coming up to Vicky and wrapping his arms around her, hoping she didn't slap him.

She turned around and fell into his embrace. "I'm so sorry," Vicky managed before the sobs took over.

"It's okay," he said, relieved. This wasn't about him. "Just tell me what happened."

She pulled away and looked into his eyes.

"It came out of nowhere, I swear it. Everything was feeling great. Like it's supposed to. But you know how this is. It's like being stuck behind the wheel of an out-of-control car after some asshole's cut the brake line."

She paused and choked and almost caught her breath.

"What happened, Vicky?"

"I . . . "I slapped Evie."

The sobbing claimed her again.

Vicky's face stayed buried in his chest as she shuddered. John stared over her head into Lottie's unflinching eyes. A smile cracked the corners of her mouth. Even standing still, her expression appeared to be dancing.

"It's okay," John finally said once Vicky's cries had subsided. "Everything will be fine. You know we've got this. Just tell me what happened."

She swallowed and nodded. "I was trying to get the first chapter written. And I know, I know, starting the book is your job and I'm supposed to stick to outlines and sex scenes. But you're always complaining about how hard it is to start, and I wanted to surprise you. Maybe you'd hate it and that would be fine, but I thought it was at least worth trying. What if it worked? Then I could take that part off your plate. More stories in less time. And we're both happier."

She'd never looked more pitiful.

"But you're right, it's hard. Even though I knew I could come back and clean it all up, I just couldn't figure out where to take that first page. Or the first paragraph. Hell, the first *word*! I was frustrated, and Evie kept calling for me. So Becca brought her into the office, just for a few minutes. But then I got an idea — I knew exactly how I was going to start the book. So I went to the keyboard, but she started whining. I told her to stop, that I'd only be a second. Then she started crying. I was trying to get the paragraph out, and I swear, John, it really was perfect, and then Evie started screaming. I totally forgot whatever it was. I got mad, like really mad. I could feel it coming on but I couldn't stop it. You know . . . the speeding car."

Vicky stopped and took a moment to breathe.

"So I tried to think. I really didn't want to lose it. But as I stood there staring at the page, Evie just kept screaming louder."

"I wish I'd heard her," Lottie said. "But Victoria said that we could plant some herbs outside and I was looking around to see where the garden might go."

"It wasn't your fault, sweetie," Vicky said. "She wanted food, so I took her into the kitchen. But she was still just screaming and screaming and it was like someone was stabbing my skull. I gave her some cereal, but as soon as I put it in front of her, she picked it up and threw it at me . . . and that's when I slapped her."

More tears until Vicky collected herself. John made slow, soft circles on her back while Lottie stood there watching them both.

"I didn't think it was possible for Evie to cry so hard."

"That's when I heard," Lottie added.

"Becca came in and I'm just standing there, staring at our screaming daughter, doing nothing to soothe her. She couldn't even catch her breath . . . I don't even remember what happened next."

Her voice helpful, Lottie said, "You kept whispering 'I didn't mean it' over and over."

Vicky swallowed, stuttered, then managed, "I could see my handprint on her face, John. My hand . . . How is she ever going to trust me again?"

He hugged her tight, glaring at Lottie. "Everything will be okay. Evie will never remember. I'm just sorry I wasn't here."

"Oh, that's okay. Becca was." A glance to Lottie, then back at John. "She's a godsend. First she took care of Evie, then she took care of me. Once Evie was playing — and laughing, if you can believe it — Becca came into the kitchen and helped to reset me. Really" — again she turned to Lottie — "you should be a therapist."

"I used to want to be one when I grew up. But then I decided that life would be better around children. You know, endless imaginations instead of real-world problems." Lottie laughed.

Vicky took John's hands. "What if I've damaged my relationship with Evie forever?"

"We all make mistakes," John said, turning his hands so that hers fell into his. He tried not to choke on his next words. "You heard Becca — Evie is already laughing and playing. You remember how it was with Dakota."

"I know. Becca's been telling me the same thing for the

last hour. I'll get over it, I'm sure." She smiled, but it looked like she was trying to close an overstuffed trunk. She pulled away from John and wrapped her arms around Lottie. "Thank you."

"Thank you for having me." Her smile traveled from Vicky to John. "You too, Mr. Treadwell."

John stood there, seething, helpless, staring at Lottie, unable to say a word.

He'd bet anything that Lottie wound Evie up before sending her into Vicky's office. Waited until Evie's screams pushed Vicky to lose her temper. So she could swoop in and save the day.

Danny was right. This woman was a vampire, and they had invited her inside.

John moved his body so that he was slightly — but not impolitely — blocking Lottie. To Vicky, he said, "Remember that time when you got a flat on your way to pick up Dakota from dance? Adrianna had to bring her home, and then you drove over a broken bottle and got another flat halfway home."

"Of course." Vicky laughed, because eight years later, what else could you do?

"What was the one thing that made that better?"

She smiled. "Donuts from Buns."

"Exactly. You didn't think I was suddenly interested in running for even a minute longer than I absolutely had to, did you? I wanted to bring home donuts. And there's a strawberry in the dozen. First of the season."

Vicky brightened. "A whole dozen?"

"A whole dozen." John jerked his thumb toward the kitchen. "I'm going to check on Evie. You girls enjoy the donuts. Hey, Becca?"

Her eyes on John, suspicious. "Yes?"

"Have you ever had Hot Cross Buns?"

She shook her head. John turned to Vicky. "Don't let her leave this kitchen until she's tried at least a bite of them all."

Vicky laughed and said to Lottie, "You don't know what you're in for."

John left the kitchen, quickly kissed Evie on her forehead, then went straight outside toward the garage and up to Lottie's room. The garage was separate, and it might have been easier to sneak in before coming inside the house, but he hadn't known if Lottie was up there.

He wasn't sure what he expected to see. Half of him imagined that her room would practically sparkle. The rest of him pictured a pigsty, with piles of garbage atop mountains of soiled clothes. But the room was tidy, though far from obsessively so. The bed was made, but the comforter was slightly askew. There was a lone sock on the floor and a thin pile of papers on the desk, next to a tablet. The normality of it made it worse, because none of it screamed "crazy."

John went to the desk and picked up the papers. Impressive pencil sketches with sharp lines and a surprising amount of detail . . . and soul, he was surprised to discover. The first were of inanimate objects — clothing, pieces of furniture, and children's toys from a bygone era long before iPhones and video games. The art had an almost photorealistic effect, with varying degrees of pressure and spacing used in the crosshatching, creating realistic shadows, folds, and textures. These could easily be framed in a gallery.

But the drawings of people were . . . odd. While their bodies, clothes, and even hairstyles were done to the same level of detail, the faces were all blank, as if the people were born with no noses, mouths, or eyes. John couldn't believe that Lottie was unable to draw facial features, so perhaps she was going for a surreal look. Maybe it was some sort of statement in her work. What it meant, he didn't know. But John found himself drawn to the sketches. And that in itself seemed somehow inappropriate. He should want to burn them, not admire them.

He started. He'd spent more time looking at the drawings than doing what he needed to do. And Lottie could excuse herself from the donut tasting to come looking for him at any moment.

He went to the closet. Her suitcases and clothes were inside, but no purse.

Next, he went to the bathroom. He lifted the top of the toilet tank from its base, looked down, and smiled.

Fuck you, Lottie.

John unzipped the gallon-sized freezer bag and removed her purse. Then he dug inside, hoping for a wallet, or any sort of ID. He found a small baggie filled with safety pins, a pack of tissues, a tin of Altoids, another small baggie filled with naked earring backs, and, mercifully, three keys on a ring, one of them emblazoned with a giant VW.

John dropped her keys in his pocket, put the bag back into the tank, then returned the top.

He slipped back into the living room and sat down beside Evie just as Lottie and Vicky entered the room.

Evie giggled. Lottie looked at John suspiciously. He smiled at her, the *fuck you* twinkling in his eyes.

"So, how were the donuts?" he asked.

"There's plenty left," Vicky said. "We just wanted to taste."

"Did you try them all?"

"Yes," Lottie chimed in. "Thanks so much, Mr. Treadwell. *You* should have one now."

"I ran this morning." He patted his tummy. "That's the last thing I should do."

Vicky said, "Oh, John, you can have a bite of blueberry fritter. And if you can't, shame on you."

Lottie laughed. "Yeah, *shame* on you, Mr. Treadwell."

"Please, Becca — call me John. And you're right. You only live once." John walked toward the kitchen, but then stopped and turned back around. "Except . . . I just told Evie that I'd take her to the park."

"You could just grab a bite first," Lottie suggested.

John shook his head and started walking toward Evie. "Nah, I'll just take her now. If I'm going to break down and have a donut, then I want to savor it. Maybe even pour myself a glass of milk."

"Becca will take her," Vicky said. "That's why she's here. You go have a donut, and take your time." She turned toward Lottie with an encouraging nod.

Without missing a beat, Lottie scooped Evie into her arms, and once Vicky's back was turned, gave John a withering expression. "Come on, kiddo. We're going to the park."

Five minutes later — the minimum amount of time that John could claim he'd *savored* the donut — he left the kitchen and dipped into the office. "Hey, honey."

Vicky looked over. "That was fast."

He patted his stomach again. "I finished off that fritter, but I ran too hard this morning for anything more than that. Really, I just thought you could use some work time to yourself — no interruptions. I'll make sure you're not disturbed when Becca gets back."

"Thank you for taking such great care of me."

"Of course," John said.

He closed the door and went outside. He took a moment to look up and down the street, waited for a woman to walk by with her terrier — as if her witnessing his crime would mean anything at all — then shoved the key into its hole and opened the Beetle's passenger side door.

He went for the glovebox first — and sure enough, the registration was there. Except it belonged to someone named Myrella Engles.

Got you.

John took out his phone and snapped several pictures. No time to waste, he slammed and locked the door, then jetted upstairs to Lottie's and back to the toilet. Keys returned to the purse and the purse wrapped in plastic. In the tank, then back outside.

John was rounding the garage, technically still in Lottie's space, when she came walking up the drive with a screaming Evie.

"Going for a walk to work off that extra donut?" she said, before John could even open his mouth.

Evie cried louder. The front door opened and Vicky stepped out onto the porch. "Everything okay?"

"Of course, Victoria. I just think Mr. Treadwell might have misdiagnosed your daughter." She laughed and slapped him playfully on the arm. "She definitely didn't want to go to the park."

"Evie *always* wants to go to the park. Maybe she's upset because I had promised I'd take her. She'll probably want her mommy now."

John walked over to Vicky, kissed her on the lips, then went back inside the house, hoping she wouldn't ask him why he was even out there and feeling the flames of Lottie's rage singeing his back.

Chapter Thirty

John was back at The Kitchen Sink the next morning, but this time Danny had beaten him there and was sitting with a full breakfast already on the table. A stack of pancakes, sausage and eggs, a mug of steaming coffee, and a full carafe ready for refills.

"Help yourself." Danny pointed to the carafe as John sat. He looked down at his plate. "This, too. I'm not gonna eat it all."

"Thanks." John waited for Danny to speak, but he just kept chewing. He watched one sausage and half a pancake disappear before he finally said, "So, any movement on the stuff I sent you yesterday?"

Danny took a long drink of his coffee. John wasn't sure if he really needed the caffeine, or if he was a fan of John's squirming. Danny finally set down his mug, wiped his mouth, pushed the plate forward, and gave John his full attention.

"Plenty. Your girl isn't Myrella. That's the name of her roommate in New Haven, where she does really live. Apparently, Myrella's a rich kid with two cars, so she's not even missing the Beetle. It also looks like Becca *is* her real name, so we can't get her on falsifying information. But we can still hit her hard with the audio. And we should."

"That sounds promising."

"There's more."

John smiled. "There always is."

"I found plenty on your girl's father. There are rumors that she went nuts and got into some trouble, but the records are sealed."

"Sealed?"

Danny shrugged. "She was a juvenile at the time."

"Does that matter . . . that her records are sealed?"

"You'd think so, but fortunately she's enough of a talker that a full day gave us plenty of time to assemble a loose narrative. Your girl talked to Myrella, her shrink, her mom, a girlfriend, and an ex. And we may or may not have installed the tech to hear every word." A wink. "She's smarter than your average cub, but that doesn't mean she's not leaving her tracks all over the woods."

"Is that your fixer's way of saying you have something?"

"Seems boredom is her kryptonite, and you're the spark of her most current interest. But the good news is that it doesn't seem like she's ever finished a thing in her life, so this could all blow over soon. Your girl didn't even finish high school."

This was a genuine surprise. "Really?"

"She dropped out, then got a GED. There were some discipline issues at her fancy-pants private school, but nothing I could nail down. She dabbled in college classes. And not the community shit. Daddy pulled strings. She went to Wesleyan and Trinity, audited classes from gender studies to particle physics — no shit. Like I said, your girl isn't dumb. But she doesn't have a degree, and I need both hands and feet to count the jobs she's quit. I'm sure Rebecca Dawson is the kind of girl that went through her entire life with every teacher telling her that she had 'so much potential' if she would only just 'apply herself,' but she never actually did."

"What about her father? You said there was trouble?"

"The girl is a hell-raiser for sure." Danny chuckled. "And she really loved sticking it to her parents. You know the type. They look perfect to the public, but their private lives are locked doors and leaking libidos — ask me how I know. I haven't dug too deep yet, but her old man looks like a classic politician, glad-handing in every photo I can find . . ."

Danny took a moment to pick, chew, swallow, and sip. Then he continued.

"I'm thinking that while Daddy was kissing babies and making big promises, Daddy was coming into his little girl's room at night and giving her some extra special attention during her extra special years. It was their little secret, and it made Rebecca feel as special as she'd always believed she was. Mommy didn't know, because this was something Daddy only did with *her*. But then the fairytale crumbled, somewhere around the time she was old enough for real men to start looking her way. The truth broke her heart, and the distance broke it harder. Warped love turned to something like hate. She began acting out — cutting herself, destroying things in their house, drinking too much."

Danny noticed John's dumb stare and added, "Granted, it's only a theory, but I've enough anecdotal evidence and unintentional confessions to connect a lot of the dots. She had her stomach pumped twice before her twenty-first birthday."

"Do you think she's dangerous?" John asked, his heart

beating loud enough for him to hear. "You know, besides just telling Vicky everything?"

Danny shrugged. "I can't tell you anything a hundred percent, but I don't like what I'm seeing, and I think we need to move fast. I've never found a politician I couldn't find shit on, but digging ain't cheap. And in this case, it isn't necessary. I don't want to threaten him with what he's done, I want to threaten him with what his *daughter* has done — or might do. William Dawson is up for re-election in the fall, so a public embarrassment could sour his chances. He's been reining her in for fifteen years and he might be our best shot now."

"What are you going to do?"

"I have a few ideas."

"What do you need from me?"

"Permission to execute those ideas."

"Should I know what they are?"

"You ever heard the words, *plausible deniability*?"

"You think this is what's best?" John asked.

"I do." Danny nodded. "I want you to go home and play nice. But don't be sweet. You don't want her suspicious, you want her out of there. Do as I say and she will be. Got it?"

John nodded. "Got it."

"Get her out of the house. She's going to do everything she can to stay the weekend, regardless of what she and your wife have agreed on. It's now or never for your girl and she knows it. So I'm sure she has a plan. You need to derail it. You now have a time bomb in your house, set to detonate sometime between Friday night and Monday morning. You get clear and I'll take care of the rest."

"What does that mean?"

Danny sipped his coffee. "I've got a guy on her. He'll take care of everything as soon as she leaves your place."

John leaned forward and whispered, "You're not going to . . . *kill her* or anything . . . are you?"

"How much do you think you're paying me?" Danny laughed. "No. We're not gonna whack her. Nothing easy about that. We just need to make sure she understands that there are consequences for her actions. Girls like this, they get carried away. Sure, she likes the drama, and she'll take it as far as she can. But she'll also know when the ride's over, and be smart enough to get off the train."

"And if she doesn't?"

"Then we figure something else out. But I'm telling you, Rebecca Dawson won't want to face the consequences. She'll take the easy exit, then find something or someone else to play with." He pointed to his mostly empty plate. "You sure you don't want any of this?"

John looked down at Danny's culinary graveyard and shook his head. "No thanks."

"Suit yourself. I'm having another cup. Me and the waitress made nice. She's getting off in a bit."

John looked at Danny.

Who is this guy?

Chapter Thirty-One

John got through the rest of his afternoon by pretending the whole thing was a game that he was determined to win. He was the protagonist, the hero of his own story, and he had control of the plot.

He was perfectly nice, and displayed his professional affection for "Becca" at every opportunity. But he never allowed her to catch him alone. She tried it in every room she could, and in a variety of clever ways, including scrubbing the tub with the shower curtain drawn so she could catch him when he went into the bathroom. But Satan must have a scent, because he marched right over, yanked the curtain aside, and looked down at *Becca* smiling up at him while batting her lashes.

"Oh, Mr. Treadwell," she cooed.

John was out of the bathroom before she could finish the rest of her sentence.

The most difficult part of the day was during his usual writing block with Vicky. He wanted to work together, but she was still "sorting things out" and eager to finish that first chapter of *Worse Than Murder* without him around.

Dakota came home at 4:20, made a joke about the time, then straight-up asked Becca if she'd ever smoked. John's ears perked up.

Without breaking her gaze for so much as a second, she responded, "I really hope your parents won't kill me for saying this, because I'm just not the kind of girl who can be dishonest. But you asked me a straight question, and at fifteen, you deserve a straight answer. Yes, I've smoked pot, Dakota. Quite a few times, though I haven't in a while — and I certainly never would while on duty."

Before continuing, she glanced over at John and Vicky on the other side of the living room together. Evie played at her feet. Dakota stared, hanging on her every word.

"Marijuana can reverse the effects of tobacco and improve lost lung function, though I don't care about that. I've never smoked cigarettes. Well, once, but I thought it was super gross. I've also never had a seizure, but cannabis can help prevent them. I had a lot of anxiety during my freshman year of college. So yeah, I smoked a little. And it's great for older people, helps with arthritis, blah blah blah. I could go on and on, but I won't. I did my home-work before I did it. *And* I was much older than you, Dakota. Personally, I think THC is good for the brain, but yours is still developing and I think it would be a big mistake to mess with it." Becca spread her hands wide to show the size of Dakota's potential mistake, then she turned to John and Vicky. "I hope that was okay?"

"Of course it was," said Vicky, practically glowing.

John wasn't even bothered. Becca was leaving in half an hour, and all of this would be over shortly after that.

Still, that half hour may as well have been half a day. Becca managed to grab at his cock while passing with a whisper: *"Don't pretend that you don't like it when I touch you."*

She nailed a complicated paella for dinner that Vicky

swore no one could duplicate and should have taken at least twice as long. Yet his wife couldn't have smiled wider. It didn't make any sense. This woman was encroaching on all of the household duties that Vicky was best at, and instead of feeling envy like she had in the past, she was embracing the parasite with every suckle of blood.

Still, John didn't care. Because Becca was leaving at five. He stood by the door, waiting while trying to look like he wasn't, feeling like a little kid anxious for Santa. Becca probably thought she'd have all weekend to plan and plot and picture the many terrible things she could still do to John and his family — but it was already over. Soon she'd be forced to stay the fuck away from them forever.

Danny was right. Becca had been angling to stay all afternoon. That was surely why she'd made the paella. How could Vicky turn her down after that?

"It's her job to be here Monday through Friday, not the weekend. She is not moving in full-time," John said when Vicky suggested that she stay.

Becca had also mentioned the length of her drive, that it was a "wallop to her body after such a long week!"

The breadcrumbs were clear. She even told a story about one of her friends who had a really long drive across state lines and ended up driving off the side of a bridge. But none of it mattered, because it hadn't gotten her anywhere. With only a few minutes until five, Becca was sitting on the living room floor with Evie, working hard to make herself indispensable.

John remained adamant. It was over for Becca.

Until Dakota came in at 4:57 and ruined everything.

"How am I supposed to do this?" she asked.

"Do what?" John asked.

Dakota shook a small stack of papers in front of his face. "This."

John took the papers, but they may as well have been written in a different language. He looked at Dakota. "What is this?"

"Chemistry. And I don't understand it at all."

Becca looked up from the living room floor. "Oh, I *love* chemistry!"

"It's the weekend," John said. "What other homework do you have?"

"Nothing, really. But I've been putting my chem pack aside all week because I didn't understand it, and we have this big test on Monday. I figured I'd study, but I seriously don't get any of it, and now there's like six hours of work that I don't understand."

Dakota looked over at Becca.

John stepped between them. "Tell you what. Let's say goodbye to Becca, then we can hunker down and figure this out together."

"Can't she help me? She just said she loves chemistry."

Dakota looked from her father to Becca.

"I *do* love chemistry," Becca confirmed. "Can I see it?"

Dakota took the pages from her father and gave them to Becca.

She studied them, smiling. Then Becca handed them back and said, "Easy. We could get all of this done in maybe two hours. Give me another two hours after that and you'll ace the test on Monday, too."

"Thank you so much!" Dakota threw her arms around Becca.

"Sorry, sweetie," John said, "but Becca has to go home for the weekend. So it looks like you're stuck with me."

"I don't mind at all! In fact, I'm happy to skip out on all the traffic. If I leave now, I'll just be sitting on the highway. I didn't mention that earlier because I didn't want to interfere with your family time, but if Dakota needs help anyway . . ."

John responded with his kindest voice. "We really appreciate that, Becca, but it's been a long week, and I think we all just need to enjoy the weekend together . . . as a *family*."

"But Dad, Becca *is* family."

That was a punch in the gut.

"*I* can help you," John reiterated.

"Help her with what?" Vicky asked, walking into the room.

"No, you can't." Dakota turned from Dad to Mom. "Mrs. Farrow is giving us a big chem test on Monday, and I have this giant chem packet to finish. Dad doesn't know how to do any of it, and Becca does. She offered to help, but Dad wants to watch TV."

"A movie," he corrected. "Because it's movie night."

"I'm sure that Becca just wants to go home," Vicky said.

"I was just telling Mr. Treadwell," Becca chimed in, "that if I leave right now I'll have to sit in traffic, so there's no reason I can't stay for a little while and at least get her started."

John said, "You do know I graduated at the top of my class in high school, right?"

"Like a hundred years ago," Dakota said, rolling her eyes.

"Twenty-six. And what difference does that make?"

Becca, still studying the pages, shook her head and turned to John. "Don't take it personally. This stuff is hard. I was just always sort of a natural. Now *English*, that's a different story. Half the time I can't even get the difference between desert and dessert right!"

John took a deep breath. He tried again. "That's really

nice of you to offer, Becca, but we have a tradition, and I've been looking forward to it all week. How about —"

"Why are you acting like this, Dad? What's the big deal? Becca just said that if she leaves now she'll be in traffic. So why can't I just get a little help? Who cares if we start movie night an hour later?"

Dakota's voice was getting louder. And more upset. Before John could furnish a logical answer, Evie started crying.

Becca scooped her up and the wailing stopped immediately.

The room was silent, all eyes on John. He was the only one pressing what to everyone else in the room must surely seem like an absurd level of obstinacy. It didn't make sense, the way he would be shoving their new nanny out the door, after she'd offered to help their eldest with homework that neither he nor Vicky were capable of deciphering.

To Dakota he said, "I'm not trying to be a jerk or anything. It's just been a long week and I really miss my family. But you're right, I am being silly. You need help and it doesn't make sense for you to wait on me to figure this out." Then to Becca, in his robotic voice: "Thank you so much for always being so willing to go the extra mile."

They traded a barely-there glare, then Becca smiled. "Thank you for saving me from an extra hour of traffic, Mr. Treadwell!"

"Come on, sweetie," John said, giving Vicky a look: *Follow me.*

But she didn't. As if the entire situation wasn't already infuriating, his wife was now either missing the signals they'd been trading for years, or deliberately ignoring them.

He took Evie to her room, got her situated on the floor

in front of a pile of toys, then closed the doors and started to pace.

Should he call Sam? Danny?

John didn't quite trust himself to deal with this alone. He'd failed so far. It was almost a quarter after five and the bitch was still here — if anything, it felt like Becca was settling in for the long haul. He needed to make just the right moves, or she'd outmaneuver him again and end up staying "just for the movie." Then, of course, she'd wind up in her witch's den above the garage for the night, because what sort of monsters would make her take such a long drive so late at night?

And come Saturday, it would be all, *Why drive back home for just one day?* Becca would worm her way into the rest of his weekend. Danny wouldn't be able to execute his plan. And by Sunday night, she will have likely ruined his life, rather than leaving it forever.

Vicky had ignored him. Well, to hell with that. He needed to be as straight with Vicky as circumstances allowed.

"I'll be back, sweetie," he said, stationing Evie in her crib.

He closed the door behind him, listening. He wasn't sure where Dakota and Becca were working. It could be the living room, or Dakota's bedroom. But John also let Dakota use the office on the weekends because she insisted that it was the "best creative space in the house." She might be in there now.

He pressed his ear to Dakota's door. *Nothing.*

He went downstairs and peeked in the kitchen. *Nothing.*

He looked in the living room. *Nothing.*

Becca sneaked up behind John and tapped him on the shoulder. "Hi, there."

It was a miracle that he didn't scream. But he did

growl, and grabbed her by the arm, hard. "What the hell do you think you're doing?"

"Me? You're the one working overtime to get me out of here. It's almost like you don't care about your daughter's grades."

"I don't need *you* to help her."

"Yeah, I'm sure *you* can figure it all out by yourself." Becca laughed and gave him another playful slap, as if they were good friends and he didn't hate everything about her. "Just let me help her. And Victoria. Let me help *you*, John. You're the one I want to help most of all. You're the reason I'm here. Remember?"

She grabbed his crotch. He pulled away.

"Why do you want me to go? We've already had so much fun . . . don't you want to have more? It could be our little secret. I could live upstairs and you could have me whenever you want me. You can text me things like, *Meet me in the bathroom with your panties around your ankles in five minutes.* I'll be there, John. I promise. I'll *always* be here for you."

"You're crazy. You'll get me divorced. You're going to destroy my family."

"Would that be so bad? Come on, John. How many of your friends are divorced? Isn't the first marriage *supposed* to be practice? The second one is for fun. I could be the fun one."

John looked at Becca as if seriously considering her offer, his wheels spinning for a way to gain control over this situation. "You'd really let me do . . . *whatever* I wanted?"

The Devil reclaimed her smile. "*Anything.*"

He whispered, his voice kind, "You know how dangerous this is, don't you?"

She licked her lips. "That's what makes it fun."

"We have to be careful."

"Now why wouldn't I want to be careful? Do you think that *I* want this to end?" She studied him. "What's the catch?"

"No catch. Just promise that no matter what, you won't get me in trouble. That's all I want. Dakota is in a fragile place. You pretty much said it yourself — I wouldn't be with Vicky if it wasn't for Dakota. It's basically an empty marriage, so I might as well have fun, right? But we *must* protect Dakota. If you can't promise me that, then we have to end this now."

Becca smiled, her eyes hopeful. "I promise, John!" She held out her pinky.

He wrapped his around it, slow and sensual. Then he continued, desperate to believe that this would work. "And even if Vicky finds out someday . . . we can't hurt her, either."

"Wanna feel how wet I am?"

John looked around the living room. "Where are Vicky and Dakota?"

"In your office. I told them I was going to get my iPad to see if I could find my old chemistry notes. But I was really waiting here for you. I knew you'd come back out here and try some other way to get rid of me." She laughed. "So . . . you wanna?"

"Not now," he said, taking a slow moment, as though he were seriously considering it. "Tonight. After everyone is sleeping. It's too quiet, and you've probably been gone too long already."

As if on cue, John heard his office door open and close. Vicky's voice followed a moment later, growing louder as she entered the living room. "Becca? Any luck?"

"A ton," Becca said, then frowned. "But I can't believe I left my iPad in my room. I'll be right back."

The moment Becca was gone, John approached Vicky.

"Look, honey, I'm sorry."

"For what?" She looked at him as if expecting a list. So he gave her one.

"For all the stuff with Becca, for pushing her out. I do trust your instincts. If it had happened at any other time, I wouldn't have this reaction. It's not that I don't want to share my family, or that I want her gone. It's that I don't want to share my family *this weekend*, and I want her gone *tonight*. Christ, Vick. I had to bury my father this week and I came home to a seismic change in our household. You have to admit, that's a big deal. Please, I need you to support me here, tell me you understand where I'm coming from, and that I'm not being unreasonable."

Vicky's expression did a one-eighty. He'd won her over with the mention of his father. "Of course . . . I'm sorry, I —"

"I just . . . I need you. And Dakota. And Evie. Just our family this weekend. Please?"

Vicky didn't even flinch. She nodded and said, "Of course."

Dakota's "six hours" of homework were handled in ninety minutes. Becca and Dakota emerged from the office just before seven, glowing from their accomplishment and starving for dinner. Vicky insisted that Becca stay for the meal, because she had made it and helped their daughter with her chemistry, but agreed that she had to go before the movie started, because there was no way they could put her on the road after that.

John couldn't tell if Becca was furious and hiding it well, or so willing to believe he was now playing her game that her smile was true. Either way, she sounded genuinely happy when she said, "See you guys on Monday!"

But if everything went according to plan, John would never see Becca again.

Chapter Thirty-Two

It was one of those nights.

John was desperate for sleep. He deserved the shuteye after finally getting Becca out of his house. But his brain couldn't relax. He wasn't exactly sure of Danny's plan, whether his guy was really going to follow her from his house, or meet Becca at her home address, or what. He barely remembered the movie they'd watched. Probably because he spent most of it stealing glances at his phone, convinced that at any moment the texts from Becca would start to rain down.

Now, in bed with Vicky snoring beside him, he'd still not heard a peep from Danny. Or Becca. Vicky had fallen immediately to sleep. That wasn't good for John. He had a lot of energy inside him, and he'd just won victory over this whole fucking nightmare — he needed to fuck. He looked at her body, rising and falling as he considered his options.

Despite her heavy breathing, she would definitely wake up if he took care of himself. But he was pipe-hard, and that wasn't going away unless he took matters into his own hands.

John got out of bed as quietly as he could, then crept into the bathroom. He closed the door and started to stroke himself, keeping his mind on Vicky. But John was desperate to finish and get back into bed, frustrated that nothing was coming. And so he let his imagination travel to where he knew it shouldn't, hating himself for the trip. But there she was, anyway. Becca in London, prancing through the Airbnb in her pink panties, begging for him.

Becca on the phone, her breath matching his, begging for him.

Becca in the laundry room, ripping her blouse and showing him her pussy, begging for him.

I want you to taste me, John. Then I want you to fuck me. And when you're done doing everything to me that you can never do to her, you can order me onto my knees, and that's where I'll prove that I can be the fuck-toy you've always deserved.

When it was over, John pushed through the self-loathing and quickly cleaned himself, waited for his breathing to recede, then sneaked back into bed.

He was sleeping in seconds.

The next morning, his eyes weren't even open before he was fumbling on the nightstand for his phone. He grabbed it and saw nothing from Becca. John didn't know if that was good or bad. Mostly, he was just waiting to exhale.

Vicky still slept, and probably would for another hour or so.

John got out of bed and went downstairs to the kitchen. He started coffee, grateful for silence and a house to himself, hopeful that the worst episode of his life might be drawing to a close.

The first cup of coffee helped. So did his early

morning walk, despite the chill and his lack of a jacket. John was feeling so much better after breakfast that he disappeared into the office for three hours and came back out with a full short story. It wasn't great, but it was a solid rough draft.

"You haven't done that in years," Vicky said, glancing over the story. "I'm impressed."

"Don't be impressed until you read it," John said, downplaying the accomplishment, even though he'd written faster than he had in ages, with a draft that he felt was above par. "It's probably shit."

After lunch, they all walked to the park together. Dakota held Evie's hand and John held Vicky's. With his other hand he held Valentine's leash, and because it was the weekend they stopped to let her sniff every patch of grass that grabbed her. Evie laughed and giggled and made a lot of nonsense sounds — on the swings, down the slide, and in the sand. Just before they were all about to leave, she delighted them with her very first word.

"Dog!"

That was cause for celebration, so they all stopped at The Inside Scoop for ice cream. Vicky even let Evie have a few more licks than usual, one for every repeated "Dog!" after she would have normally stopped.

John didn't check his phone even once during their afternoon adventure, wanting both to be present with his family and to prove to himself that he could. But he was physically itching by the time Valentine was pawing the grass a half block from home.

"I have to go to the bathroom," John said as soon as they were inside.

He checked his phone the second he was alone.

Still nothing.

Not from Becca, not from Danny, not even from Sam.

He dared to feel optimistic. He wanted to call Danny, just to close the loop. But he didn't want to be needy. The fixer had promised to do his job, and he sure as hell didn't need John checking up on him. Danny would call when it was time.

But still, the wait was excruciating, and John was stuck onstage, performing his role in a play that no one else in his family even knew they were attending. The guilt was making him silly, and he knew it. He was saying and doing things that were out of character. Never before had John gone into Dakota's room and just sat at the edge of her bed with nothing to say, no reason to be there.

"Did you need anything?" Dakota asked.

"No . . . not really. I just thought you might want to talk."

"About what?"

"I don't know." John shrugged. "How are things going at school?"

Dakota was too busy squinting at her father to answer immediately. She finally said, "You or Mom ask me that every day when I get home. Yesterday it was both of you. Do you want a different answer than the one I gave you then? Since, you know, it's Saturday?"

John laughed, so that Dakota could see that he knew how dumb he was being. "No, of course not . . . is your homework all done? Do you need help with anything — besides that evil chemistry?"

"Nope. Everything is great. All finished."

"Nothing for English? The difference between desert and dessert?"

She laughed. "Nope. Nothing for English."

John glanced over at Dakota's bookshelf, hoping there might be something to start a conversation. His eyes hit the fourth row when his phone buzzed. He reached into his pocket and looked at the screen. *Danny.*

"I've gotta take this."

John left the room and was already outside the house before the third buzz. "Hello?"

"Your girl is all taken care of," Danny said without preamble.

"Great. Does that mean we can finally stop calling her that? What happened?"

"Just what I said. My guy took care of it."

"I got that, but what does 'taking care of it' mean?"

"It means you can flush without worrying about whether or not your shit will float back up. It's done."

John didn't know the protocol, and had no idea how hard he could push this guy, but it didn't seem right settling for scraps when he wanted the meal. And it was more than idle curiosity. Becca was dangerous — the more John knew, the better he could inoculate his family from her insanity.

"But —"

"Look, I get that you want details, but that's not really how this works. My guy had a talk with your girl. The job is done, and that's all you need to know. He made sure that she knew it was in her best interests to quit, leave you and your family alone, and never talk to you again. You're safe. Your problems are over. You're welcome."

"What happens if she comes back?"

"She won't."

"What if she does?"

"Then you call me immediately. But if my guy says it's taken care of and that's enough for me, it should be enough for you. Celebrate. Go fuck your *wife* for a change."

John ignored that.

Danny sighed. "You writers always need to know the details."

"It's not that," John said. "You've never seen this girl. She's totally nuts. Do you have any idea how many times she's looked me right in the eye and told me she'll be gone, and then there she is, smiling at me like we never had the conversation? I want to believe you, but man, Lottie or Becca or whoever she is . . . the woman is scary."

"I hear you, but you've gotta understand that there's a difference between batshit and dangerous. Your girl is batshit, for sure. But that doesn't make her dangerous. Few people are willing to deal with the consequences of their actions, and they'll go through just about anything to avoid them. Don't your characters do stupid shit all the time, just to avoid the inevitable?"

John thought about it, even grinned to himself. "That they do."

"This is no different. You're having a hard time seeing the way out because you're still in the thick of it. But the plates are cleared and dessert's on its way."

"So she's just supposed to not show up? My wife'll go crazy wondering. She won't give up. She'll just keep calling her."

"Your girl is supposed to change her number — that's part of the deal. And she gave your wife a fake address, even though she does live in New Haven. It'll be a helluva lot of work for what will seem like someone who's lost interest in the job."

"She'll blame me."

"Probably. But better that than the other options."

"And my daughter. *She'll* blame me, too."

"You want I should make things like they were?"

"No," John said. "Of course not. I'm sorry."

"The nerves will pass. I'll check in with you again tomorrow. Cool?"

"Yeah, cool. And thanks."

Danny killed the line.

John walked back inside and inhaled the silence.

His house was once again a home, and his family was safe.

So why was something inside him still screaming?

Chapter Thirty-Three

John hadn't known it was possible to feel so good. He couldn't remember the last time the air tasted so sweet. He felt like a new man.

After going inside and checking in with his girls — he'd never been so happy to see them and gave all three of them big wet kisses — John texted Sam to let him know that everything had worked out, and to tell him that he was right, that everyone should know someone who knows someone who knows a fixer.

Sam texted back. *That was fast. No surprise. I'm sure Lottie was a quickie.*

Five minutes after that he texted a second time, now with a change of subject. *Just heard from Harold. He loves the series. Netflix has the treatment now and it looks like we're a GO. More soon.*

Then John: *Should I tell Vicky?*

Not yet. Give it another day or two. We don't want to take it away from her if it doesn't happen. But I'm optimistic.

That sent John's buoyant mood through the roof. He didn't need to tell Vicky. She didn't know about Becca and never would, but he could tell her this in a couple of days. He still didn't feel *true relief*, but he also didn't think that was even possible without a few days of distance between looming disaster and lucky escape. He'd been a big ball of pressure for so long now, it was only natural that it'd take a while to decompress.

"Want to go out for dinner?" John suggested during lunch. "We could go to Antonio's."

"Did I not make enough?" Vicky laughed and cast her eyes across the table. She'd emptied the fridge for a Saturday afternoon buffet — everything except for last night's paella, which she was planning for tonight's dinner.

John laughed back. "Plenty. But it's Saturday night and I thought it might be nice to go out as a family."

"I love your devotion to family time, honey. But you said it — it's Saturday night. Do you really want to deal with the crowds? Especially with Evie? And at Antonio's? It's always busy on the weekend, and she always cries. If it's family time, then shouldn't we enjoy it together at home, away from the crowds? Besides, we still have the paella. And you know it's always better the second day."

Sure, the paella was always better the second day, but John would have been plenty happy without it, or any other reminder of Becca.

Even on Sunday, John couldn't escape her. Vicky kept bringing her up during the day. She wondered if Becca was okay after such a long drive. *"She must have just collapsed when she got home!"* That was at least reasonable.

But then Dakota asked if they thought *Evie* was missing her.

John hated to realize that yes, she probably did. But then he felt the deep comfort of knowing that in a few days she would probably stop thinking about Becca altogether, and then his youngest daughter would never remember that monster in makeup again.

Danny had checked in as promised — over the phone this time, not at the diner. Maybe things had gone sour between him and the waitress. But neither he nor John had anything new to report.

"Wanna play *Monopoly*?" Vicky suggested just before swallowing her final bite of dinner.

John was grateful for the suggestion.

"If we can pick a game that doesn't take one hundred years, I'm in," Dakota said.

They picked *The Five-Second Rule*, a game that had been one of Dakota's favorites ever since she got it for her ninth birthday. She loved the pressure of the countdown, and the ridiculous answers. Mostly she enjoyed the game's speed. And it was loud. Enough that none of them were sure how many times the doorbell had rung when Vicky finally said, "Did you hear that?"

Immediately on high alert, John perked his ears. "What?"

They all fell silent.

The doorbell rang again.

"I'll get it," Vicky said.

"Let me!" John bounded out of his seat.

It was probably nothing. A solicitor, for sure.

Except, what kind of salesman would expect to make any sales on a Sunday night?

By the time he reached the door, John was smiling. It had to be Sam — of course! He'd gotten final word from Harold. Netflix was eager to move forward, and that just wasn't the sort of news you texted.

He opened the door.

His smile vanished.

"Hi, John," Becca said.

"What the fuck are you doing here?"

"Did you really think it would be that easy?" she whispered, then raised her voice. "Victoria . . . ?"

Something happened to Becca's eyes, instant and terrifying — the monster retreated into the darkness, and in its place came something soft.

John could hear Vicky and Dakota approaching from behind.

"Becca," Vicky said. "What are you doing here — is everything okay?"

"Yes, I'm fine . . ." Becca wiped a tear from her cheek that hadn't been there a moment before. "But there's something I have to tell you."

No.

No no no no no.

NOOOOOOOOOOOOO.

"I can't work for you anymore."

Wait . . . what?

Vicky gently nudged herself past John and into the open doorway. "But why? Is it the drive to New Haven?"

"No." Becca shook her head, knocking another tear from its perch. "It's nothing like that. It's family stuff and I . . ." Her voice hitched and she choked, as if swallowing a throatful of tears. "I just don't . . . I *can't* talk about it."

"Is there anything we can do?" Vicky asked.

John looked back at Dakota. She was chewing her bottom lip and looking helplessly up at her father. *Please, Dad. Make her stay.*

Becca dug into her purse and produced her key ring. She pulled off the house key, then the key to her apartment above the garage. She handed them both to Vicky. "I'm so sorry, Victoria. You're my favorite family that I've ever worked for, even though I wasn't even here a whole week. I really thought I would be here forever."

"There must be something we can do . . . some way we can help," Vicky said. "John?"

"I can't imagine what." He shrugged, looking right at Becca. "This sounds like something personal."

"It is," Becca sniffed. "It's very personal. But you don't have to worry. I'm going to make everything right."

"Do you think anything could change?" Vicky asked, taking Becca's hands. "I can't stand the thought of losing you, and I want to know you're okay."

"I'll be fine, and I'm *sure* I'm not finished with your family." Her eyes were on Vicky, though Becca was talking to John. "Unless it happens at the end, it's only a plot twist. Right?"

"Right." Vicky smiled and hugged Becca.

Something seemed to wither inside his wife, although she was feigning strength for the kids. He could imagine her breaking down later, behind their closed bedroom door, only after they were alone and she could confess to missing the thing she never even knew she so desperately needed.

Dakota wiggled her way into the hug. She too was a moment from breaking.

Becca stared out from the tangle of affection, glaring at John, her blue eyes bright and smoldering.

She pulled away and Vicky turned to Dakota. "Can you go and get your sister? She should say goodbye."

"Of course," Dakota said, then went to get Evie.

"Do you need a reference or anything?" Vicky was grasping. "You were with us long enough for us to know that anyone would be lucky to have you. I'd love to tell the world if I can."

"No, but that's very sweet of you, Victoria . . . thank you."

Becca stood there, letting John stew in his discomfort, waiting for Dakota and Evie.

"Would you like to come in?" Vicky asked.

"No, thank you, but I really should be going. I have some things I need to take care of immediately."

"Oh," Vicky said. "That sounds dire."

Deadpan, Becca said, "It is."

Becca allowed the awkwardness to continue, pickling in mutual discomfort until Dakota appeared with Evie for a farewell that she had no way to understand.

After the final goodbyes, John closed the door on their help.

Vicky turned to him and whispered, "I really don't see what your problem with her is."

"I don't have any problem with her."

"Yes, you do, John. Is there something you're not telling me?"

He looked at Vicky like she had three heads and one was turning purple. "Like what?"

"I don't know. You just seem . . . . cold."

"I'm sorry that I'm not as attached to our former nanny as the rest of you are. If you ask me, the whole thing was sudden and weird. Now she's gone. It sucks and I'm sorry for you. Becca shined a light on what our family needs, but she's not exactly irreplaceable."

Vicky glared at him. "Thanks. Your empathy is really bowling me over. It's like I'm falling in love with you all over again."

The rest of their night was somber, with Vicky and Dakota hypothesizing the many things that could have possibly gone wrong in Becca's family, while John worked to feign enough interest to keep their anger and suspicion in check.

But it was hard not to jump up and kick his heels together with joy.

Becca was gone. Sure, she managed to get her final digs in by showing up at his doorstep and trying to unseat him, but she had still handed her keys to Vicky.

But she'd also said she wasn't done with their family yet, which sure as hell sounded like a threat. What could she be planning? What could she possibly do? If she was going to spill the beans, wouldn't she have done it right there on his doorstep?

He would call Sam in the morning. Or maybe Danny. Let them know what happened, and see if there was anything he should be concerned about. Press Danny for details, make sure that Becca was really going to stay away. He should call them right now, tonight, but he didn't want to shake things up any more with Vicky already on edge.

Right now he longed to celebrate, to delight in the fact that she was mostly out of his life.

John found himself thinking about the Father-Daughter Dance, now just three weeks away. He smiled wide, realizing that he was looking forward to the dance even more than an answer on his potential Netflix deal. Really, now that things with Becca were over — not that he had ever wanted them to start in the first place — things with Vicky would probably be better than ever. John had never felt more committed to their relationship. The brush with catastrophe had cemented his feelings better than a year of therapy could have ever hoped to.

It was nice to see Dakota getting along so well with her mother, and he couldn't deny that Becca had helped with that. But *she* wasn't the solution — she had simply made the need for someone in that role clearer than it might otherwise have been. But now they were in this together, and John would get his girls whatever they needed to live their best possible life.

Becca was gone, the Netflix deal was practically in ink, and with the splinter out of his mind, John was no doubt about to ride the wave of his career's creative high.

"Knock knock," he said, opening the door to Dakota's room. Valentine, who was lying at the foot of her bed, looked up and appeared to frown, as if the damn *dog* missed Becca too.

She looked up from her Kindle. "Hey, Dad."

"Just wanted to say goodnight."

"Goodnight."

"Are you okay . . . you know, with everything?"

"You mean with Becca?"

"Yeah, I guess."

Dakota shrugged. "She gave me her email and her Instagram. At least she'll be my friend."

John bristled but tried not to show it. Hopefully Becca was smart enough to give his daughter phony information, or she'd made a decoy account that she'd never post to again.

He went to the edge of her bed and sat. "Can I ask you for a favor?"

"Okay."

"Can you please help your mother as much as you can, until we can replace Becca?"

"What's the big deal? We didn't even *have* her a week ago."

"You didn't have your phone a year ago, either. Want to see if you can live without that?"

Dakota laughed. "What do you want me to do?"

"Just be your best self. Be patient with your mother. Help her when she asks you for help . . . without being a brat."

"I'm *not* a brat."

"No," John said. "You're not. But I have caught you acting the part."

"Okay."

"Can you give me something more than 'okay'?"

"Okay, *Dad*."

"Is that the best I'm going to get?"

"You can try again tomorrow."

"*Okay*," John said, mimicking his daughter. He kissed Dakota on her cheek, told her that he was proud of her, then went to his bedroom.

Vicky was already in bed.

"Wow," John said. "Does this mean that Evie went down without a fight?"

"If she could have asked for her crib, I think she would have."

"And you said goodnight to Dakota."

"Sort of. She barely looked up from her book. I didn't even dare ask her what she was reading — couldn't stand the thought of my daughter rolling her eyes at me yet again."

John stopped on his way to the bathroom. "I'm sorry about Becca. I know she was a big help. But I promise we'll find someone new, Vick."

"I know. But she really was perfect."

"Becca showed us what we need. Now we can be precise in our next ad."

"I still don't see what your deal with her was. Is it because she was pretty?" Vicky gave John a sly smile. "Were you worried about being around such a hot twenty-something all the time?"

"No," John said, perhaps too fast. "But I thought *you* might be. I guess maybe that might have added to my discomfort, subconsciously anyway."

"Oh please. It's not like I'm crazy. That whole Aubrey thing was a long time ago. I deserve more credit than that . . . if that's what your whole deal with Becca was really all about."

"I didn't have a problem with her, Vicky."

"Whatever you say, John."

"I didn't. But I came home from an emotionally exhausting trip, and didn't have any time to decompress with my family."

"You're right," she said. "I'm sorry. Now can we go to bed?"

"I'd love to."

Nothing would make him happier, in fact. John was exhausted. Becca was probably out of his life, but it hadn't sunk in yet. A part of him still half-expected his phone to buzz with another text from her.

He brushed his teeth, changed into an old pair of sweats and a newish T-shirt, and slipped into bed, wondering if Vicky would want to keep reading, watch something together, have sex, or turn off the lights and go right to sleep. Whatever it was, he didn't want to ask.

Vicky kissed him. "Goodnight."

"Goodnight."

The lights died and John was alone with his thoughts.

Tomorrow was the first day of the rest of his life, and a fresh chance with Vicky. He really did love her, and they had so much good between them. So much history, so much chemistry, so much storytelling potential.

Things were back to normal, and John could finally bury whatever repressed urge led him to start flirting with Becca in the first place.

Yes, everything was finally going to be fine.

Chapter Thirty-Four

Life was better than fine.

Though he obsessively checked his phone all that Monday, expecting a text or an email or an angry manic voicemail, John heard nothing from Becca. By Tuesday, Vicky already had a call out on LiveLyfe for new interviews, and she seemed happy with her new prospects. On Wednesday, she finished the first chapter of *Worse Than Murder*, and John had to admit it was excellent. He changed a character name, moved a few paragraphs around, and sharpened some of the lines, but it was as good as if he'd written it himself. They celebrated their best collaborative week ever by fucking twice in a row during Evie's nap time.

"I didn't know you still had that in you," Vicky said.

"Neither did I," John said, laughing and thinking for the first time that maybe this whole thing with Becca had been a godsend.

Every day John would text Sam and ask for any updates on the Netflix deal, and every day Sam would say that news should be coming soon and to hang tight. On

Friday evening, just as John was planning to turn off his phone and shut down for the weekend, Sam texted.

It looks like next week for sure. Get ready for the rain.

That text made Saturday and Sunday feel like a month. On Monday, just before dinner, John finally ran out of patience. He hated feeling needy, but texted Sam anyway.

Any word?

Sorry, cowboy. Soon.

Nothing the next day, either.

But John was comforted by how well things were going with Dakota. Boosted by Becca's initial aid, she'd started going in to get extra help with chemistry during zero period. It had only been a week, but Dakota announced she already felt "reasonably confident" that she would pull her hard-won B- to a relatively simple-to-maintain B+, "or an A-minus if I'm lucky!"

Two weeks after John closed the door on Becca, he finally got the text from Sam.

Get the champagne. I'm coming over.

Vicky screamed with pure delight when Sam told her.

Dakota said, "None of my friends are going to believe it! Are we famous now?"

John just kept thinking how lucky he was to have dodged such a dangerous bullet.

"So it's a done deal then?" he asked Sam, refilling their glasses.

"This is as close to 'done deal' as we can get without signing, but Netflix is definitely in. They love the project and trust Fable. They do still want to meet you, but that conversation is more about everyone getting to know each other than it is about earning a 'yes.'"

"How many seasons?" Vicky asked. "Are they just starting with one?"

Sam nodded. "One season to start. But we have strong material here. I'm sure the only obstacle to a second season is getting the first one in the can. And if everything goes well next Tuesday, we can be in pre-production on *Worse Than Murder* by the end of the month."

They toasted, they drank, they got a bit tipsy. John and Vicky had great sex after Sam left, then woke up in the morning laughing. Life was so good, John could barely believe it.

The next half a week took forever for everyone except Evie. Vicky was so excited, she swore she was "one thousand percent positive" that she wouldn't have any problem making the trip to California, though she did insist on making it a family affair, all four of them. They had yet to replace Becca and Vicky didn't want to worry about who Dakota and Evie would be staying with. Dakota was thrilled to be taking a two-day vacation from school, even though she had to take a chemistry packet to the opposite coast to maintain that B+.

Life was perfect and still getting better.

Right up until Monday afternoon — an hour or so before Dakota was due home from school, and three hours before their flight.

Vicky was just finishing up a few loose ends in her office with Evie at her feet. The car was packed and ready. But then John's phone buzzed and ruined everything. *Sam.*

"Let me guess," John answered. "They want to go ahead and greenlight the second season now."

"Are you near a computer?" Sam asked, sounding thoroughly sober.

"I can be," John said, suddenly very nervous. "But I also have my —"

"I'll wait. You shouldn't do this on the phone. We'll need to talk."

It barely sounded like Sam. Whatever this was, it wasn't good. "Is everything okay?"

"Just get to a computer, John."

John swallowed, his heart now pounding. He was halfway to his office when Sam said, "And you shouldn't be anywhere around Vicky."

He stopped. "Well, shit. What am I supposed to do? My laptop and desktop are both in the office."

"Your iPad?"

John thought. His brain was already muddled. Was this Becca? It had to be.

"I'm pretty sure that's in my office, too."

"Does Dakota have anything you can use?"

"Not sure, but I'll find out." John started toward her room. "You're making me really nervous, Sam."

"I'm not trying to make you nervous, but . . . you should be."

"Now you're scaring me."

"Find a computer, John."

He closed Dakota's door behind him. Dammit, this place was a mess. She had promised to clean it up before the trip, but if anything it looked like his daughter had started pulling drawers at random and turning them over onto the floor. He scanned the room, saw nothing, then scanned it again and saw the charger plugged into the wall above her nightstand. He followed the white line to the pink edge of her iPad case sticking out from under a pillow, then picked it up and turned it on.

"I can't get in here without a passcode."

"Try."

He tried her birthday, his and Vicky's anniversary, and several other dates before he was about to tell Sam that he didn't know what to do. But then he tried a Hail Mary. "Hold on," he said, then used his phone to check the school district calendar for the last day of school. He entered the digits into the iPad and it unlocked. "Got it!"

"Good man. Now go to the Bitches Love Drama site."

"What's that?" John asked.

"And *this* is why you can never go indie. Bitches Love Drama is currently the biggest romance blog in the world, or a trashy tabloid site, depending on who you ask. I imagine you'll see it as more of the second."

The page came up. The site was gorgeous. All black and pink, with rich pictures in the header and sidebar. The typography was sharp enough to draw blood.

"You see it?" Sam asked.

And then he did.

But John was speechless.

His throat tightened, constricted.

He tried to swallow but couldn't.

He tried to speak but could only choke.

Rebecca Dawson was on the homepage. She looked gorgeous, in what had to be a photo from a professional shoot. The headline read, *Bitches Love Drama Exclusive Interview with John Treadwell's Mistress: YOU WON'T BELIEVE THE THINGS HE MADE HER DO!*

"What am I looking at?" John finally managed. "And how bad is this?"

"You need to read it."

So he did.

The article was as twisted as Becca.

She claimed that he took her to London after leaving his wife at home, and that they'd had a constant sex romp during his three days at the book fair. The blog had pictures to prove it. John had never seen any of them before. They were candid and — he had to admit — brilliant. Because while he hadn't even known the pictures were being taken, Becca clearly had. There were three total. One just outside the steps of the main hall, one spilling out of a session, and a third in the pub. All staged in a way he could never hope to disprove.

According to Becca, John became so infatuated with her that he insisted they continue to see each other back in the States. But their occasional hookups just weren't enough. John was too greedy for that, and he had no respect for his family, actually got off on flaunting his conquest in broad daylight. So he had her move in as the nanny, telling her how and when to apply, and even what to put on her application so that his wife would love it.

John Treadwell brought a naïve girl close to his daughters and made his wife feel indebted to her only so that he could continue to take advantage of her and use his position of authority to objectify her, going so far as to tell the innocent Rebecca Dawson that he could get her a book deal, *if she continued to be his special friend.*

John felt sick. He was seconds from hurling.

"I'm halfway through. Do I need to finish?"

"Yes."

It got worse from there. Rebecca Dawson also claimed that John was abusive, and that he would regularly get her alone and demean her, choke her, order her to do things that she didn't want to do.

So far, it was all things that happened between John and Becca, and though he hated her to his core, he couldn't say he was too surprised that she went nuclear.

But then she got personal.

The interviewer asked Becca how long she stayed with the Treadwells.

RD: I was able to escape that first weekend.

BLD: Escape? That's a big word.

RD: That's what it felt like. I was under his spell, and he could get . . . violent. We agreed that I could go home for the weekend, but I knew that once I left I just couldn't go back. I loved both of those girls. The Treadwells really do have the sweetest children. But Victoria and John are terrible people. And this is coming from someone who loves pretty much everyone. I hate to say this, but . . .

BLD: Go on, Rebecca. You're safe now.

RD: There's something wrong with Victoria. I don't want to say that she has mental problems, because that's not really my place to determine, but . . . she doesn't seem . . . balanced. She's excited and happy one second, and then she'll be screaming just a couple of minutes later, you know, totally ranting and raving.

BLD: These are big accusations. Do you have any proof?

And of course, Becca did. Below the interview, there was an audio file, and below that . . . a video. Just above that, there was a disclaimer: the following clips were of an adult nature, and the video was especially disturbing to watch.

"What's on these clips, Sam?"

"If you're at the clips, then you don't need to play them. You've got the gist. They exist to prove everything else Becca is saying."

"But it's all a lie!"

"Do you really think that matters? The best lies are shot through with truths. She wrote a story that's as good as anything you've ever done. Our job is now damage control."

John paced Dakota's room. He tripped on a pile of her crap and growled.

"What's on the clips?" he asked again.

"The first one is you and her having phone sex. It's rough. You say some things that don't make you look good. But the video is worse."

"Did she get us in the laundry room?"

"You better hope not, though I wouldn't be surprised if this girl's holding something back for round two. But no, the audio takes a shot at you. The video is a direct hit on Vicky."

"On *Vicky*?"

"It shows Evie throwing a bowl and then Vicky slapping her."

"Oh my God . . . you know that was —"

"It's okay, John. You don't have to explain it to me. I understand. I know you, and I know Vicky. But this is about public perception."

"What can we do? Can we get them to retract this thing before Vicky sees it?"

A sigh. "Come on, John. You know that's not how the internet works. Even if you were to get Bitches to take it down, the story is everywhere by now. You have to assume that Dakota is going to know about this, too. We have two jobs. First, we need to control how Vicky finds out. That means you need to tell her. I'll worry about Netflix."

"Netflix? Why do you need to worry about Netflix?"

"Because they don't like controversy, and that's exactly what this is."

"It's a lying stalker making things up about me and my family!"

"It's a young woman claiming that you abused your position of authority, with documented proof of you cheating on your wife — and your creative partner, which, if you recall, is one of the things that Netflix is most interested in. She also has video evidence of your wife slapping her infant daughter. I'm not sure you appreciate the gravity of our situation, John."

Now his tone was admonishing. Disappointed.

"Like I said, you take care of Vicky. I've got Netflix. And don't wait, John. You hang up with me, and I don't care that it's the hardest thing you've ever done, you need to tell her *now*. Got it?"

"I'm on my way."

John hung up. His hands wouldn't stop shaking. His brow was beaded with sweat. He tasted blood, and realized he'd been chewing his lip.

John walked toward the office.

He had no idea how he was going to tell her.

But just outside the door, John knew he wouldn't have to.

Because Vicky was already screaming.

Chapter Thirty-Five

John stood frozen outside their office door, listening to Vicky's screams.

He was paralyzed, no idea what to do. In his career as a writer, he had written immobilized characters many times. Most readers accepted it just like chlorine in their water, but he'd never really believed it. Because how could emotion pour cement into your body? Surely even in the darkest circumstances, a person could move if they really wanted to.

But John was a block of ice.

Vicky threw open the door. And there he was, staring into her eyes, two green marbles on fire. She seemed startled to see him. The fire raged and she shoved him.

His paralysis broke and he stumbled several steps back. It had been a hard push, but the second one came harder.

Evie toddled out behind her.

He fell to the floor and she was on top of him, first slapping his face, then punching every part of his upper body with her flailing arms. None of the blows particularly hurt — they were too wild — but Vicky was relentless. He couldn't find the strength to push her away, despite her weighing nearly sixty pounds less than he did.

He lay there and took it. Just like he deserved.

"How could you?"

Slap. Punch. Punch. Punch.

"I can't believe you would do this to me!"

Punch. Slap.

"I can't believe you would do this to *us!*"

Punch. Punch. Slap. Slap.

"I HATE you!"

Slap. Slap. Punch. Slap.

John didn't try to defend himself. It would be better if he didn't. The sooner she wore herself out, the sooner they could talk about this. He had no idea what she knew. How far into the article had she read before the screaming started?

The pictures from London would have been enough. They said everything, "proving" so many things that weren't even true.

Vicky climbed off of his body and kicked him, hard. Her foot landed somewhere between John's ribs and his stomach. He doubled over and grunted. Then he swallowed his vomit and rolled onto his back and choked, "I'm sorry."

Evie was watching the whole thing, crying. Valentine began to bark.

Vicky pointed toward nowhere in particular. "Get out."

He got up, saying, "We need to talk."

"GET OUT!"

John looked at Evie, then at Vicky. He shook his head. "I can't go. Not until we talk."

Vicky charged. She shoved him again. Even though he was expecting the strike, it was still hard enough to buckle his knees and send him wobbling backward. She shoved him yet again. John fell on his ass.

"I hate you." Her rage was now frost. "Get out of my house."

"It's our —"

"Don't you *dare*."

Crying louder, Evie started toddling toward John, hands outstretched for him to pick her up.

John scooped her up into his arms and stood back up. She kept crying, but something hitched in her voice and she lowered her head onto his shoulder. Valentine barked louder, more relentless. John worried the dog might bite one or both of them, thinking she was protecting Evie.

"Put her down."

"She's upset. You're upset. Let's just —"

"*Put my daughter down!*"

John swallowed and nodded. He lowered himself to one knee and gingerly planted Evie's feet on the floor. "Everything is okay," he whispered in his most soothing voice.

"Don't you act like I'm the problem! Get the fuck out of my house, *right now!*"

He said nothing. Evie had stopped crying, as if she was too scared to continue. The room was throbbing with the beat of Vicky's heavy breath and John's pounding heart.

The front door slammed.

John and Vicky eyed each other like gunslingers with Evie and the barking dog between them.

Thirty pregnant seconds, then Dakota entered the room. John heard her before he saw her.

"What's going on in here?" She circled around them, surveying the room, then repeated, "What's going on?"

Vicky stared at her daughter long enough to make

Dakota visibly shudder, then she said, "Why don't you ask your father?"

Dakota turned to John. "Dad?"

"Let's all go to the dinner table. We should sit down. Talk about this."

"Get out, John."

"Why does he have to get out?" Dakota asked. "Will someone *please* tell me what's happening?"

"I made a really big mistake."

"A *mistake?* You asshole!"

"Was it Netflix?" Dakota turned to her father. "Did you screw up the treatment? Is this because it's too much like *First Degree?*"

John shook his head. "No, Dakota."

She looked at him helplessly, her eyes saying, *Please tell me.*

Vicky spat, "He screwed something, all right."

Dakota's eyes went wide, dilating with a sudden, certain sorrow. She pursed her lips and swallowed. Took a breath. "Dad . . .?"

"Tell her what you did, asshole. Tell her what you did with Becca!"

"*Dad?*"

"Tell her what you did with our *underage nanny!*"

"She's not underage."

"*FUCK YOU!*"

Evie finally found the courage to cry, and more than made up for her earlier silence. Impossibly, Valentine found another octave.

Dakota had to shout to be heard. "Dad, tell me what's happening!"

"I did something wrong. Something terrible. Something there's no excuse for. But I didn't do what your mother thinks I did. Lottie is setting me up. This whole thing —"

"Wait," Dakota said. "Who's Lottie?"

"Who's Lottie?" Vicky asked.

"That's her real name. She's not who you —"

"No, you don't!" Vicky screamed. "You do not get to make up a story right now. Fuck you! Get out."

"I want to know what happened," Dakota said.

"Just let me —"

"*GET — OUT!*"

Evie and Valentine continued to battle for supremacy over the background noise.

To Dakota, John said, "Can you please get your sister?"

Dakota nodded and went to retrieve her.

"Get out, John. I will call the police right now."

"And tell them what, Vicky? I haven't hit you, and I'm not the one who's out of control."

"DON'T TELL ME I'M OUT OF CONTROL, YOU FUCKING ASSHOLE!"

Evie's body rattled against Dakota's chest. "Please," she said. "Someone tell me what happened."

"I —"

"You don't get to say anything!"

"Mom!" Dakota glared at her mother. "You can be mad at him, and it sounds like I'm going to be really mad at him too. But not yet. I have to catch up. You may not think he deserves to tell me his side of the story, and maybe you're right, but *I* deserve to hear it."

Vicky stared at John, fuming. Nostrils actually flaring. Knuckles white. Leaning slightly forward. A bull gnashing at a flag. "Fine."

Dakota turned to John, and he spoke.

"When I first met Becca, she was using a fake name. Lottie. She —"

"Wait." Vicky cut him off. "You just said that her *real* name was Lottie."

"She's right, Dad. You just said that."

"That's not what I meant. I just meant that when I saw her here, after you had already hired her, I knew her as Lottie. So Becca was the fake name, from where I was coming from."

"Right," Vicky said. "From where you were coming from."

"I met her in London."

"In London?" Dakota repeated.

"In *London*," Vicky confirmed.

A single tear spilled down Dakota's cheek.

"Honey," John said, moving to wipe it.

"Don't," Dakota snarled, pulling away. "Mom's right. You need to go." He reached for Evie and she pulled back farther.

Vicky said, "Go. Nobody wants you here. And when your littlest girl is old enough to know better, *she* won't want you here either."

Vicky turned away from John, plucked Evie from Dakota's arms, and calmly walked out of the room.

Dakota stared at her father for another long moment, her mouth half-open. He kept expecting her to say something, to yell at him, curse him out, say all the things he deserved to hear.

But instead she just stared.

When she finally had to start blinking to keep the tears inside her eyes, she shook her head and gave him a final look of rotting sorrow and crumbling trust.

She left without a word.

And then John was alone — except for the dog, who was still barking at him as if he were an intruder in his own home.

Chapter Thirty-Six

John was lost.

Not just spiritually and emotionally, but actually lost. He didn't know where he was going and he wasn't sure where he was. He had no destination or timeline. Who needed a compass when your only direction was down? He might as well stay aimless until his arrival on the bottom floor of Hell.

He needed to talk to Sam, but he didn't want to do that while driving around. He would obviously need a bed to sleep in, but even that felt like a landmine. He wanted to stay close to home, but he only knew a couple of places — and both were expensive, more like executive suites meant for people to stay for months at a time. He should be suffering, not living it up with fully furnished rooms and a trio of pools to choose from.

Finally, John found a semi-shabby motel that he'd never noticed before, though he must have passed it a thousand times. He parked in one of the empty spots, all the way at the end, then walked into the lobby of the Tidy Motel.

The girl behind the counter was surprisingly young. Not underage, but young enough that John wondered why she was working at a seedy motel rather than a restaurant or somewhere she could make some good tip money.

"Can I help you?"

She studied him as he entered. John wondered if the girl was naturally curious, or if there was something about him worthy of scrutiny. She had long black hair and razor-straight bangs. Her big eyes were black and serious, but her lips suggested that she witnessed the world with a smile. Her nametag said Carrie.

Carrie Lansing was always quiet — the family therapist called her an introvert. Maybe that was why people thought she was stuck-up sometimes. She wasn't; she just didn't blather on and on like most other girls, who seemed to talk endlessly about nothing but clothes and what guy looked at them. Carrie preferred her thoughts to go deep, and she —

"Sir?"

"Sorry. I need a room, please."

"We're full."

John looked behind him, out the window and into the empty parking lot.

"Kidding," she said. "I think this place was full once in the nineties. How long are you staying?"

After a second, he said, "I don't know."

"Okay. Like a day? A week? Rates are different, depending."

"I don't know."

"You don't know whether it might be more like a day or more like a week? It's a big difference. Reason I —" She stopped, seemed to study him again, then said, "Oh. It's a thing with your wife, right?"

John just stared at the girl, unsure of whether he felt violated or impressed. "I just need a room."

"Okay," she said, giving him a wink with her smile. "We'll leave this one open-ended."

She made him a keycard and drew him a map. "You'll probably want to pull around if your luggage is heavy."

John didn't want to admit that he had only the clothes he was wearing.

His room was dingy, but not dirty. He collapsed on the shitty bed and dialed Sam.

"I can't imagine that went well," his agent said.

He grunted in affirmation. "I'm in a motel a couple of miles from home."

"Why didn't you come here? You know I would have put you up."

"No offense, but I'm barely gonna make it through this phone call with you."

"Wanna tell me what happened?"

"No. But I suppose I probably should."

John told him everything, hating himself more than ever by the time he was finished.

"Shit," Sam said.

"So what's next?"

"I have some news."

"I could use it."

"Not that kind, John." A cleared throat, then, "Netflix has pulled out of talks."

"Awesome."

"I'm sorry."

They shared a long silence, then John repeated his question. "So what's next?"

"We call Danny."

John sighed. "Just when I was starting to miss the guy."

Sam dialed and put them together.

"Looks like I underestimated your girl," Danny said.

"That's *all* you have to say?" John felt the anger well

back up. Here was somewhere to focus his rage. "I asked if you were sure. You said the plates were cleared and dessert was on its fucking way."

"I know, and you can yell at me if you want to. But that isn't going to solve your problem. If you want a solution, then you and me should work on getting there. I'm sorry for your loss. Now let's make some lemonade."

"How do we do that?"

"By deferring to someone who knows better."

"It seems like a lot of your job is outsourcing," John said.

"What do you think my job is? Sam, you know I have a one-asshole-at-a-time policy, and you already have one client filling that spot. You don't get two." A pause. "We could press charges, but the damage is done and I'm not sure of our best route. That's why we're going to call my lawyerish."

"What does that mean?"

"It's my lawyer*ish*. No actual law degree, but I don't need that for this purpose. I need someone who knows their shit and will pick up the phone no matter what time I call. Give me a second."

There was a click and silence from Danny's end. Sam remained silent until Danny came back on the line. "Marmaduke?" he said, in a voice that wasn't quite like any of the other ones that John had heard him use so far.

A woman's voice: "I hate it when you call me that."

"You want I should use your real name? Listen, I got questions and you got answers. That's the deal, right?"

"What do you need, Farmer?"

Danny — or Farmer — crammed John's entire story into a few compact sentences, then waited for the lawyer-ish's response. John couldn't help thinking that the man would be brilliant at loglines.

Finally, Marmaduke spoke. "Whatever happens, the wife is your starting point. You need to get her on your side before going after this woman."

"That isn't going to happen," John said.

"It has to," Marmaduke said. "That's the biggest chink in the armor. Your most vulnerable soft spot. If she can't get to the wife, then she can't really get to you. United front."

"There *is* no united front. My wife hates me right now."

"I'm sure she will for a while. But getting through to her is your only choice. You're a writer and you've been married for a while. Write a script that you can believe, then play it out as best you can."

"You think I haven't tried that before? This isn't a fucking story, it's my *life*."

"Do what you can. Take your lumps. But make sure that your wife understands that she can hate you while also protecting herself and your family from this woman. You need to shut her up immediately. And you need to get on the same side." A second of silence. "Is that it?"

John wasn't sure if she was asking him or Danny, but then she added, "Can I go?"

"Yes. Thanks, Marmy," Danny said.

The phone clicked and the call went dead. John looked at the phone.

Call failed.

WTF?

He dropped his phone on the mattress. If Sam wanted to call him back, fine. Or not. John was no longer in a hurry for anything. He had some thinking to do, and then some doing to do after that. But for now, he would lie here, thinking about what he had to do and . . .

John woke up in a panic, worried that they would miss

their flight. Then he felt the strange bed beneath him and remembered.

He sat up in bed, his stomach tumbling.

The hours before he'd fallen asleep were a fog. A terrible wall of new and violent emotional realities, made of bricks he had laid himself. And now he had to walk through that fog and scale that wall, then descend to the other side and, hopefully, redeem himself in front of his family.

He had to tell them what really happened. That was the most important thing in his universe.

He got out of bed and wished for a change of clothes. His shirt was sticking to his skin like a scab.

John left his room and went outside. Reality punched him in the stomach again.

He got in his car, gunned the engine, then killed it and started to walk.

He'd passed a half-dozen stop signs before he finally looked at his watch. 11:34 p.m.

He kept walking, deeper into the residential streets buried behind the boulevard that John usually flew down at over forty miles per hour, and out to the other side. He walked in a loop, and when he found himself staring up into the only lit room in his house, John finally looked at his watch again.

2:14 a.m.

He had to explain everything. Not just for his sake, but for theirs.

Becca was crazy. Dangerous. A menace to society and a cancer in their lives.

Vicky had to know that. Dakota, too.

But how could he explain the truth without it sounding self-serving?

Especially after two in the morning?

The light died and his decision was made.

John turned around and started walking back to his dingy room at the Tidy Motel.

Chapter Thirty-Seven

John stood in front of his house — in daylight this time — holding an especially large pink donut box and feeling like an idiot.

He'd already spent ten minutes on the front porch, knocking. He'd peeked into the windows and tried the back door, too. He finally went to let himself in, but his key no longer worked, and the emergency spare was missing from the roof of Valentine's doghouse.

Now all he could think to do was stand and stare at the front door, hoping that someone — most likely Dakota — would declare mercy on him before another one of his neighbors walked by, staring as they passed. He had been lucky with the first two, but the third would surely ask him if he needed any help.

He walked back up to the porch, shifted the pink box from one arm to the other, then knocked. Three times, hard, with the side of his fist, then a fourth time with his knuckles.

"Vicky, Dakota, will somebody please come to the door? It's important!"

Yes, he wanted to apologize. But he also wanted to warn them. He could hear the lawyer — or whoever "Marmaduke" was — in his head. He needed them to understand, and to be on his side. This was bad, but leaving it alone would be so much worse.

In a way, John was almost grateful for their common enemy. Maybe it gave him a chance. Because as dim as that glimmer of hope might be, John kept thinking that if he could just get the conversation started, soon enough they would start to see things his way.

He'd never meant for any of this to happen. He had cheated, yes, but he wasn't a cheater. That whole thing in the laundry room was manipulation and biology in a head-on collision. He wasn't exactly a victim . . . but he was *something*. An asshole, for certain. But not a cheater. So it had to at least be worth a discussion. His family of more than fifteen years couldn't just wash their hands of him because circumstances that they were far from fully understanding.

"*PLEASE!*" John yelled at the top of his lungs.

But still the house was silent. He took out his phone and dialed the landline. It rang until it clicked over to voicemail, introduced by a recording of Dakota from five years earlier. *Leave a message,* she said, mentioning everyone in the family except for Evie, who wouldn't be born for another several years.

The door would have to open soon. It wasn't like Vicky could just keep Dakota home from school. Eventually she'd have to —

The door opened and Dakota looked out. She glared at her father.

John strode toward the door. But she didn't open it farther.

"Dakota, I —"

"I don't want to hear it, Dad."

He paused on the porch, wondering how this would go down. She looked like a sentinel, filling the doorway with her hunched shoulders.

"I need to talk to you and your mother. It's important."

"So you can tell us how you fucked the nanny?"

"Don't talk to me like that."

"If you didn't want me to talk like that, then you probably shouldn't have fucked the nanny over the phone. Now I know *all* the words, Dad." She narrowed her eyes. "Or is there something I'm misunderstanding?"

"Yes, Dakota. There is. Can I please come inside?"

"No."

John eyed his daughter. He could easily shove his way in, but that would surely make everything worse. He drew a breath and tried again. "Please . . . I'm not saying that what I did wasn't wrong, at all."

"Good for you."

"I accept full responsibility for my actions, and understand that there are consequences. But in the meantime, there is something else we need to talk about."

Dakota turned her head and called out behind her. "Good news, Mom! Dad has something *else* we need to talk about."

From deep inside his house, John heard, "Tell him to fuck off."

Dakota turned back to her father. "Fuck off."

"Please. You already opened the door. There must be a part of you that wants to hear me out . . . right? Otherwise, why would you be standing there?"

"Because," she growled, opening the door all the way.

Then he saw it. A dress in her hands. A two-piece crop top with a high-waisted skirt, simple and in the perfect shade of blush.

John looked from the dress to Dakota, confused. "What is that?"

"What do you mean, 'What is that?' You *know* what it is!"

"Your dress for the Father-Daughter Dance. But why are you holding it?"

"Because, *Father* . . ." She crumpled it up into a ball and hurled it outside, not just onto the ground but into the dirt, right under the rose bushes. "This *daughter* doesn't want to go with you!"

Crying, she slammed the door.

John stood there, staring at the peephole, hoping for mercy and one final chance.

He finally turned around and started to walk up the drive, but then heard the door open behind him. His heart skipped. Dakota was going to listen. Or maybe it was Vicky, finally willing to hear him out.

It was Dakota, just in time to see the blur of something as it flew from her hands.

John caught it with reflexes he didn't know he had, but not without dropping his box on the ground. He studied the object now in his palm: the music box he'd brought back for Evie from London. He looked from the box to Dakota.

"Because she would have thrown that at you if she could have."

Then Dakota slammed the door again.

John opened the music box, listened to the first few notes of "Für Elise," then closed it back up and tucked it into a corner on the front porch.

Crying, he got into his car and drove away.

Chapter Thirty-Eight

Bottles clinked inside their paper bag as John carried it into his Tidy room and closed the door behind him. He poured himself a drink to drown the embarrassment, downed it, then poured himself another.

And so it went until the sun was down and John couldn't make a circle in his room without planting his face in the carpet. He lay on the bed, thinking about all the ways he fucked up, and all the ways he might be able to fix what he'd definitely demolished.

Then, for the first time, John thought: *What if I can't?*

Even when Dakota had slammed the door on him, John had to believe that the future would eventually smile on him again. He had been a good father and husband for fifteen years. He'd made one very big mistake, sure, but he wasn't a bad guy. Surely he would be forgiven . . . someday.

But what if that wasn't true?

What if Vicky really could hate him forever, and teach their daughters to do the same? And what if — even though John was loath to admit it — he really did deserve it?

Another drink. He should probably cut himself off. His stomach was somersaulting all over the place. Fuck it. He took another pull from the bottle.

His phone buzzed. He frantically searched the room, but couldn't pinpoint the sound, pawing his pockets and then the bed before he rolled over to the other side and ran his hands along the floor. The whole room felt like the deck of a ship in a storm.

The buzzing died.

What if it had been Vicky? Or Dakota?

Maybe Sam was calling to tell him that Netflix had reconsidered.

Another buzz, followed by more frantic searching. This time John found it right where he'd left it: sitting next to an impressively-diminished bottle of vodka.

Private Number.

Becca.

John stared at the phone in his palm, at war with himself. He let the buzzing die. But then it started again. He answered just before the fourth buzz ended.

"What do you want?"

"John!" Becca sounded genuinely thrilled to hear his voice.

"What do you want?"

Becca laughed. "How much have you been drinking? I can barely understand you."

John planted his feet firmly on the carpet to steady himself. He cleared his mind, laid his next thoughts in approximate order, then drew a breath and said, "Fuck you! How dare you do that to my wife! How dare you do that to my daughters! My family trusted you, even though you're a lying cunt! They *loved* you, because they couldn't have any way of knowing what a lying fucking snake in the grass you are!"

Stone-cold she said, "You should never call a girl the C-word, John. It's like the N-word for a woman." Then, much softer, "But really, you're looking at this all wrong, and I have to admit I'm a little surprised. You should be thanking me."

"*Thanking* you?"

"Yes. Thanking me, John. Victoria made you miserable. You said so yourself in London. I saw it while I was living at your house. You love your girls, but your marriage was a joke. She was dragging you down, and all three of us know it. That's why she was always flipping out, because she knew she couldn't keep up with your genius. Now you can finally write on your own, and write what you want to. It's time for your name to be on a classic, John. I *know* you can do it."

Becca paused. John said nothing, trying to process this woman's insanity.

"If you need a new writing partner, I'm better than you think. Definitely better than Victoria."

"You're fucking crazy."

A long silence. "That's another C-word, John."

"How about an N-word? You are totally, thoroughly, fucking *nuts*."

"I'm going to hang up now, John. I think it's best we continue this conversation later. You need some time to think, to realize that your life just took a positive leap forward. Get some sleep, John. I'll call you later, when you're ready to talk."

Becca hung up and something new broke inside John.

No matter what, he promised himself, he would never answer a private number again. He had to make sure that every window, door, and skylight into his life was closed and locked. He had to quit with the drinking and *do* something.

So he started that moment, and two weeks later John was living a different life.

It wasn't easy, but he forced himself to stop wallowing. The first two days were spent on long walks that started in the morning, ended in the evening, and looped around the front of his house every forty minutes or so. For three days after that, John didn't leave his room.

No one answered the door at home when he knocked, and no one answered their phone. They hadn't responded to a single text.

The only person he spoke with was Sam, though it was Sam calling him. John still refused to stay with him, though, and didn't really feel much like talking when they spoke.

"She said to fuck me and Netflix, and then to triple-fuck you," Sam told John on the fifth night — or sixth morning, since it was just after 1:00 a.m. when John finally answered his phone.

By the following week, things began to settle.

He started to write.

After staring up at the ceiling for several hours straight, John had reached the obvious conclusion that he'd always sorted through the thickest emotional shit in his life by writing his way through it — why should this be any different? His art had originally been fueled by a sense of discovery, believing that every new story was yet another chance to explain the world to himself. But he had lost that — first to the publishing machine as shepherded by Sam, then to Vicky and her desire to write alongside him and reap the benefits of their more commercial fiction — and he'd eventually swallowed most of his creative instincts, left only with a hollow reminder of what writing *could* be.

He thought of the last five books written with Vicky.

What had he actually managed to say in those narratives?

John was determined to attack the week, and started Monday morning in a brand new story by hitting the words a few minutes after waking up. He didn't have a name for the book, nor did he know a single character or what would happen to them at the end, let alone the first page. He didn't even have a genre. But John didn't care.

There was something freeing about *just writing*. Something he hadn't felt in years, with Vicky dictating a strict plotting technique. He didn't know where he was going, but that didn't matter. The characters didn't exist until he offered them life, and he followed them to wherever they wanted to take him. He listened to their words and heeded their examples. Then, after fifty aimless pages, he thanked them all out loud and started over.

John would design a series to sell. He would pick a pen name and publish his new books without anyone knowing it was The Bastard Cheater. The stuff he was writing now was coming fast, and he was sure he could go even faster. He just had to plan it all out. Once the series was successful, he could go back home, able to provide for his family again, and navigate through the storm of disgrace. Enough time would have passed, and with a new series behind him, Vicky and Dakota would finally be willing to listen. To *hear* him.

But John was overwhelmed by his choices, past and present alike. He couldn't escape the feeling that this was the most important decision of his life. No writing project had ever been this significant, or would so deeply impact the rest of his life. The pressure was a vice at his temples, desperate for *once upon a time* to finally fall in line behind him.

He came up with one idea, and then added five more. Another dozen piled atop them, and soon he was looking at twice that many. John had to ask himself where he wanted to go, who he wanted to be, and what he was most trying to say with the first words that he'd publish after flipping his good life on its head and shaking all of the best bits into a bottomless abyss.

Maybe most importantly, what would be most likely to sell? Because John wasn't too proud to admit that right now, that's what he wanted most. Yes, he longed to write something deep and meaningful, something that touched every person who read it, helped him grow as a human and artist, and proved that he still had *it*. But he also wanted to prove that he wasn't the worthless pile of shit that Vicky and Dakota surely thought he was.

Finally, he had it — science fiction, an infinite canvas. Good sci-fi wasn't just about what might happen tomorrow; it was a reflection on what was already occurring today. The right book could change the way a person thought, and the very nature of science fiction made that easy. The genre existed to give hope for the future and inspiration to the present. And sci-fi had rabid fans. People who would start on one book, then devour the rest of the series without stopping. That was exactly what John needed now. Not the readers who would mull over every page, savoring his sentences as if they were sipping a fine wine. He needed a new series and fresh fans to maybe help him buy back his old life.

Infinite canvas it may be, but John still couldn't get a single idea to work. Every seed germinated into some literary take on a genre convention. John soon found himself stranded more than seven thousand words into a story about an astronaut on a mission to the moon, solo after losing his crew and all communications. He was rambling, had no idea where to go. His main character was alone, with no one to talk to, a quarter million miles from Earth with only his thoughts. John finally realized that not only was he writing shit — and perhaps a subpar *The Martian* on the moon — but he was writing shit that was all about *him*.

Fucking John Treadwell.

He scrapped it. Started again. And this next time . . . he had it:

In the not-too-distant future, a company called Hush becomes the world's biggest databank — a safety deposit box for all the world's information, a place where everyone can safely and confidently keep their secrets. But that's because Hush has only one objective: *to rid the world of all secrets . . . because secrets are what kill us.*

He outlined the entire story, and only after the end of the treatment did John again realize the transparency of his narrative. But this time he kept going regardless. Now he was writing faster than he ever had in his life. For the first time, he forgot everything he'd learned in college, leaving his degree behind and simply telling the story. He focused on the characters and what happened to them, listening to where they wanted to take the story and following their lead without argument. He found himself remembering things Vicky had told him about storytelling and realizing how he could use them to goose the plot along.

In a few days, John had cranked out more than twenty thousand words at the Tidy Motel — the same amount he would be lucky to get in a full month of closed-door diligence at home.

And the words were good; he could feel it. Sure, he'd have plenty to cut, and an awful lot to rewrite. But the story was there. Every minute that he wasn't getting the words down felt like a blade sliding deeper between his ribs, but pouring them onto the page somehow lessened his aching. Made him feel human. A part of him could picture the story finished, and see where that might take him.

It was the only thing that John wanted to think about.

It was the only thing he could *allow* himself to think about.

Because in the story he had total control. Outside it he had none. and that felt like dying. Whenever he wasn't writing about a world where Hush made intimacy illegal, John would get stuck in a loop thinking about Dakota and Vicky, wondering if he would ever manage to win them back.

But he wouldn't call. Not until he could prove himself. And this new series would show Vicky that he knew how to listen. He believed it would happen — he *had* to believe it would happen — and kept pushing himself a word, a sentence, a paragraph, and a page at a time.

For two weeks, while the writing was going well, he didn't take a single drink, and he ignored Becca's every call.

Deny a fire oxygen and it'll eventually burn out. Perhaps his favorite line from *Hush* — that was what he'd decided to call it — that he'd written to date.

Becca kept calling, and he kept denying her oxygen. The girl refused to give up, but John refused to listen. Every time his phone rang with a blocked number he would look at the screen and either growl in uninvited and unvented anger . . . or smile, satisfied that he wasn't weak enough to answer the call.

Because he *did* want to answer. He wanted to pick up the phone and yell at Becca. Verbally destroy her. Ruin her the way she'd ruined him. But John took Sam's advice instead.

Don't talk to her. No matter what. Not now. Not after this is all sorted and solved. Not ever. No good can ever come from talking to her. Got it?

Blocked calls were easy to ignore. And she never left a message.

Until she did. He almost considered deleting it unheard, but he was only human.

Hi there, John . . . it's me. We really need to talk, but you won't answer and I don't know how to get a hold of you. I know this isn't what either of us want. You're probably really sad right now. And lonely. But you don't have to be. I can fix this. WE can fix this. Remember, if it isn't the ending, then it's only a plot twist. This is OUR plot twist, John. The big one, right before the climax, the one we need in order to reach our "happily ever after." Please. Call me. I'll make everything better. I promise.

Then she left her number. John burned with temptation.

He wasn't a fool, he'd managed to refuse the call. But then he made the mistake of listening to Becca's message several times, and then quite accidentally committed it to memory. A day later, those ten digits were like an itch in his brain.

It would be so easy to pick up the phone and scratch that itch.

He could tell her exactly what he thought, get the last word, then change his number and never talk to her again. He could call Vicky after that — he'd even have a reason. They shared two children, and she would need his new number.

But no, John would ignore the siren's song and focus on the one thing he could control: the story.

So he wrote and wrote and wrote and wrote until he finally crashed face-first into a narrative wall. He'd sailed through the first act, with a powerful emotional wind at his back. Hush's sinister plans were known to the reader, but his story had already strayed from his outline a bit too much, and John wasn't sure he could keep plowing forward from brute force alone.

He took a break, and then he took a nap.

When that didn't work, John finally took a drink.

Chapter Thirty-Nine

Apparently, a life of stopping at only one or two drinks was long behind him.

John looked at the bottle and started laughing. A deep, almost bottomless guffaw.

He started to cry, but this time it wasn't from sorrow. It really was hilarious. He wasn't a drinker, and yet here he was alone in his motel room, staring at an empty bottle.

Another empty bottle.

He laughed harder, and cried a little more. He sure as hell couldn't write.

That was a joke, thinking he would be able to get anything down. Hemingway said, "Write drunk. Edit sober." But what did that asshole know? He'd ended up buying a place in Ketchum, Idaho, and eating a faceful of shotgun, after all. Besides, Hemingway would never make it as an indie. And that made him laugh, too. Because Hemingway might have crushed it as an indie. John imagined Ernest changing his name to Yardley — it was unisex, right? — and then he really lost it.

He recovered and looked at the cursor on his laptop,

still blinking at the spot where he stopped typing an hour ago.

He closed the computer and stood. Then he paced his hotel room, hating himself.

He looked out the window, sat, stood, looked out the window again, saw nothing of interest, then went back to pour himself another drink.

But then John got a better idea.

Nodding along with his genius, he picked up the phone. Two taps later, it was ringing.

But still no answer. Because his family hated him.

Dakota's old outgoing message . . . and one final try from her father.

"Hey . . . um, hi. I'm just calling to see if maybe you'll talk to me . . . if you're there, or if you come back later and hear this. There's no excuse for what I did. You should know that I know that. You should also know that Rebecca Dawson was a predator. And that I allowed myself to be her prey. This is all my fault. And I'll do anything to earn your trust back . . ."

John desperately wanted to add that he was trapped, that it didn't mean anything, that it was only biology. That he had never meant to do anything in London, and that the further he got from that night the more convinced he was that he *couldn't* have slept with her.

But none of that would matter to his girls.

"I'm sorry. Really, really sorry. If we could just talk . . . get some closure."

He laughed, because he was thinking about Rachel getting "closure" in *Friends*, and he knew that despite themselves, his wife and daughter would be thinking the same thing.

"Closure . . . maybe I could come by . . ." He was

rambling, sounding like an idiot. "We could have breakfast
. . . I could take Valentine for a walk."

Take Valentine for a walk?

"I miss you, and Evie. She's probably not listening to
this." A wry laugh, doused in alcohol. "She's probably not
allowed."

A long pause. Thirty seconds or so while John stared
out the window.

Then he hung up without saying goodbye.

He stared at the phone, and when despair finally swallowed the last of his will, John tapped to the contact he
should never have added and waited for Becca to ruin the
rest of his life.

Though maybe this time he could ruin some of hers.

"John!"

"Rebecca."

"Oh, you can still call me Lottie if you want to. I'd
like that. It's our special name. How we met. Part of *our*
story. Or maybe we could make up a new name
together."

"How about Annie?"

"I *think* I might like that. I've never known an Annie.
Are you thinking 'Little Orphan' or 'Oakley'? I like Oakley
better."

"Wilkes."

A silence. He could practically hear her thinking.

"Oh! From *Misery!*" Then, "That's not very flattering.
Kathy Bates is frumpy. How about Willow? That's a sexy
name."

"I was considering her character, not her appearance."

A pause. "What are you trying to say, John?"

"Annie Wilkes trapped her favorite writer, didn't she?"

"It isn't a trap if it's what you really want."

"How do you know what I really want, Rebecca?"

"Because you *told* me, silly. We spent the night together in London. Remember? You said a lot of stuff that night."

"No, I don't remember. Because you drugged me."

"Oh, please."

"You're saying you didn't?"

"I did exactly what I had to do to get us where we are right now."

"And where are we, Annie?"

"I don't want you to call me that."

"I don't want you to call me at all."

"*You* called *me*, John."

"Because I have to know why you ruined my life. Why me?"

"You wanted this, John. You said that we could be together. You said that 'happily ever afters' really could happen. You know, *before* you started acting like an asshole. But I forgive you. It's not too late. We could still have a lot of fun. I know it hurts that your family is gone. I did a lot of —"

"Did you drug me or not?" he asked, not expecting a confession. She'd recorded him, so wouldn't it at least occur to her that he might do the same? He wished he'd had the forethought, but then again, John hadn't thought of much before drunkenly dialing her number.

"How else was I supposed to get all this started? We're exactly where we're supposed to be *right now*, but would we have ever gotten here if I hadn't taken the initiative? You're a writer. You should appreciate the effort it took to connect all the dots and make all of this happen. You were too timid to have ever taken the steps on your own. That's not your fault, John. It's just how some guys are. Fortunately, I knew you'd eventually come around, once you could see what our lives could be like together."

"Have you ever thought you were crazy?"

"One time. I was at this bar, talking to some metalhead idiot. He bought me a drink and I was like, why not? But then the next thing I knew I was waking up in his bed with him on top of me. I pushed him off and grabbed a pen from his nightstand. Then I stabbed him in the eye. Over and over and over. I could hear it squishing, but I couldn't stop. I didn't want to. I liked the sound. It was the only thing that kept me from crying. It all happened so fast . . . So, yeah, I thought for a minute that I might be crazy."

"That's not what I —".

"What are you wearing?"

"Jesus — you're fucking nuts, Annie. Absolutely batshit."

"Please don't be mean. Call me when you're not drunk. We have a lot to talk about. A lot of planning to do. I've been really patient with you, John, and I can continue to be patient. But don't call me names. And don't be mean. You can only call me names when you're fucking me." Her last sentence lost its serious edge and ended in a giggle. "You can use both of the C-words when you're fucking me if you want to: *I love coming in your mouth, you crazy cunt!*"

"I'm never going to call you again."

"Don't say that, John."

"I'm going to hang up right now and then I'm going to change my number. You will never hear my voice again, and I am going to spend the rest of my life delighted in the truth that you have no idea where I am or where I am going to be."

"But —"

"Even if I wasn't married, even if you hadn't fucked with my family and destroyed my relationships with my wife and daughters, even if you hadn't so thoroughly sodomized my life and career, I would never, ever, ever be with someone like you. You're a psychopath. Nowhere near the woman my wife is on her worst day. I don't know how you can live with yourself. I hope you have a miserable, lonely life, and that you're never able to feel the love I have for my family — a love that you've now taken away, because you are a horrible wretch of a woman who isn't even capable of knowing the meaning of love. You're —"

The line went dead.

And something inside John knew with a wretched, twisted certainty exactly what Becca was thinking.

I'm going to make him regret every single word.

"Just you try, Becca."

Chapter Forty

John finally won his war against the night around two in the morning.

Then he woke to sunlight that hated him.

He closed the drapes and stumbled into the bathroom.

It took ten minutes of retching before he could step away from the toilet. He looked around the shitty hotel room, remembering last night.

As usual, calling Becca had made his life worse. John was sick to his stomach. She'd only *ended* the call, but it had sounded like a gunshot. He couldn't call her back. Then she'd win and he'd be the loser. The worst thing he could possibly do was encourage her. Becca saw six inches and assumed six hundred miles.

But the fact that she hadn't called back, right then or at any time through the night, was terrifying. John had already fallen into the habit of checking every few minutes. It was so easy, right there by the nightstand . . .

He gathered the bottles and threw them all in the garbage, including the full ones, and chastised himself for not doing that two weeks ago.

Then he started to write.

Or at least he tried to. But he couldn't get a single sentence out that his brain would allow onto the page without deleting it less than a minute later. He second-guessed everything, completely incapable of producing a single syllable that was better than *shit*.

But he stayed at it, determined. After an hour and a half without a legible paragraph, he took a walk, came back, and hit the keys with a grudge. But still, nothing.

His story was dead.

He needed food. John crossed the street to the diner where he'd been eating most of his meals. He ordered pancakes and thought of Danny. The waitress was young and pretty and usually made John feel smart and funny, but when she asked him what was wrong, then told him that it looked like he'd "slept in something sad," he lost his appetite and left.

He sat down again and started typing, but the first sentence was just as stupid as the second and third and all the ones after that. Two hours later, he had a hundred words of dry piss.

He called his sister.

"I thought you died," she said.

"You could have called me."

"It was your turn. We have a deal. Anyway, I don't give a shit if you don't call me, we talk when we talk, but you're a dick for not calling Mom. I know she and Dad weren't exactly whatever, but he's dead, dude, and you're not even phoning it in. See what I did there? Seriously, call her. She wants to brag about her catering business."

"I'm living in a motel."

"Shit. What did you do? Oh, wait . . . what did *she* do? Where's Dakota?" Gasp. "Where's Evie?"

"They're with Vicky. I cheated on her and she kicked me out."

Silence. John took all twenty seconds and was grateful she didn't stretch it to thirty. "Asshole."

"I know."

"Did you tell her, or did you get caught?"

"It wasn't like that."

"Has any guy *ever* said, 'It's exactly what you're thinking'?"

"I'm serious. She was a stalker."

"Oh. That makes sense. Husbands are allowed to cheat as long as it's with a stalker, everyone knows that."

"That's not what I'm saying. She set me up."

"And then you fell into a trap? 'You' meaning your dick and the 'trap' being her pussy?"

"She made me think that she lived in London."

"How did she make you think that? And why would that matter, asshole?"

"Because that's where I met her, and because we went back to her place, or what I thought was her place, and she had an English accent."

"You're making me feel really sorry for you. Oh wait, no I don't."

John sighed. "I don't even remember going back to her place. Like, at all. I woke up there. She drugged me."

Now serious: "Do you know that for a fact?"

"She told me that she did it. I'm telling you, this woman is totally fucking crazy. Vicky kicked me out almost a month ago."

"Shit." He could hear her breathing, processing. "So you don't even know if you slept with her?"

"I slept with her."

"*After* you woke up?"

"No. It was here. I honestly don't know if we had sex

in London, but Vicky hired her as a nanny while I was out in California."

"VICKY HIRED HER AS A NANNY?"

He pulled the phone from his ear, wincing. "Yes. Like I said, the girl is crazy. She was there when I got back from the funeral, and Vicky and Dakota were already in love with her. She was brunette instead of blonde. No accent. I think she might have been following me for a while before that."

"Are you telling me one of your stories right now?"

"Wish I was."

"Shit."

"You already said that."

"What else am I supposed to say?" A pause. "Did you know that Barry accidentally butt-dialed Mom while he was at a strip club?"

"Who let Barry into a strip club?"

"You know how Mom will never laugh at Barry in front of us, or with us when we do? Well, she totally made an exception this time."

John laughed, for the first time in forever. "What did she hear?"

"I'm not exactly sure, because I didn't want to know and I couldn't really tell what Mom was saying because she was laughing so hard, but there was definitely something about baby-talk."

"Gross. Why doesn't that surprise me at all?"

"Because our brother should be in diapers. Seriously, I still can't believe we're related." With a beat so short that John had to wonder if the segue was planned, Sherrie added, "Have you thought about them at all . . . you know, our other family?"

"No." John was surprised to realize that he hadn't. "Not at all."

"I have. I can't stop. I'm wondering if I should look them up. Pay a visit."

"Why would you want to do that?"

"Will you go with me?"

"Why would *I* do that?"

"What else are you going to do? And how long do you expect Vicky to stay mad at you?"

"I don't know. I think it might be for good this time."

"Fuck that. If Mom and Dad could make it through a second fucking family, you and Vicky will be fine. Will you go with me to meet our mysterious sister from our momma's mister?"

"I can't imagine that's a good idea."

"Why not, John? What do we have to lose?"

"You can pick at your open scabs all you want. I prefer to let mine heal."

"This isn't an open scab. You don't know the first thing about these people. They could be really nice. They're our family, even if we didn't know it until recently. It's not their fault our father was an asshole. He's their asshole, too."

"Maybe you should try and ask me when I'm not grieving the loss of my family."

"The *temporary* loss," Sherrie corrected. "They're not dead. And besides, I was offering you a distraction."

"By suggesting the most awkward thing I could possibly think of?"

"What are you going to do? About Vicky, I mean."

"I don't know. Take it one day at a time. I told the stalker off last night. Hopefully that's the end of her."

"I mean, what are you going to do? To get your family back? And your career? You gave up the lit shit to write with her, so what's next?"

John brightened. "I started a new story. Sci-fi."

"Oh yeah?" Sherrie sounded surprised, but pleased. "What's it about?"

"I'm not totally sure yet. It's changing. But it feels good, and I'm writing fast. I'm thinking about using a pen name and self-publishing."

She laughed. "I thought that — how did you put it? 'Self-published authors are ruining literature.'"

"Maybe they are, but *I* know how to write. And I don't need a publisher. I can do this all on my own, and when I do, I'll go back home."

"They don't want you to come home with a winning series, John. They just want you to come home."

"No. They don't."

"When's the last time you tried?"

"Yesterday."

"Try again today."

"I'll think about it."

"You don't mean that."

"You're right," he said.

She sighed. "Call me tomorrow."

"Okay."

"And call Mom."

"Okay."

"You sound like your daughter."

"Okay," he said, smiling even though it hurt.

He was about to hang up, but then Sherrie said, "John?"

"Yeah?"

"Good luck."

"Thanks," he said, then hung up too fast. Maybe Sherrie wanted to say something else.

The phone buzzed in his hand. John answered without even looking. "Sorry, I —"

"Sorry for what?" Becca asked.

Chapter Forty-One

"Sorry for *what?*" she repeated.

"What do you want?"

"I want to know what you're sorry for."

"I'm sorry I ever met you. I'm sorry I went to London. I'm sorry I let you anywhere near my children."

A long silence, then, "Well, I'm sorry to hear that."

"Why are you calling, Becca?"

"I've been thinking about what you said." John waited, unsure of what exactly the psycho was talking about. "At first, I told myself that you didn't really mean it. Because who would say something like that for real? I 'sodomized your career'? You could 'never, ever, ever' be with someone like me? I'm a *psychopath?* I don't know what else you said after hoping that I have a miserable, lonely life, and that I'll never feel a family's love. It was just too much, so I had to hang up. But you gave me plenty to think about, and I appreciate that. Maybe you're right, and I'm nowhere near the woman that Victoria is. Maybe I can't ever really compete with her or your daughters."

Another pause. Surely she expected him to say something, but John was terrified of what might come out of his mouth, or what kind of trigger he would be pulling if he spoke, so he said nothing.

"Are you right, John? Can I really never compete with Victoria or your girls?"

There was something about the way she said *girls*, something about the way she was saying everything. Something . . . off. John wanted to hang up, but right now that seemed like the most reckless move of all. He had to put an end to whatever this was.

"You really hurt me."

"I'm sorry," he said.

"It will be okay . . . after I hurt you."

Fine. Just leave my family alone.

"Or your family."

"Wait, Becca. Just stop. I promise —"

"Your promises mean nothing! You're a liar! You lied to me!"

"When did I lie to you?"

He wanted to call her delusional, but John had no idea where that accusation might take them. Becca was unbalanced, and if she toppled off the edge of whatever beam she was currently — and precariously — balancing on, she would surely grab John and drag him down with her.

"In London. You told me I was the type of woman you could see yourself starting over with."

"I never said that, *Lottie.*"

A click, followed by a voice. It sounded far off, but was unmistakably him, a recording of their encounter.

You're so much fun, he slurred. *Exactly the kind of girl I could start over with.*

Becca, also far away: *I'm too young for you.*

That's exactly what I need. Someone to help me start over. You're fun. And sexy. Then, like he'd just discovered a new kind of physics, *We could have sex every day!*

And you could come in my mouth. She said this like it was already an old joke between them.

He laughed like he'd been doing it for years. *I can come in your mouth!*

And you can bury your face in my pussy.

Say more things like that . . .

You can bury your cock in my pussy.

Becca came back on the line. "You lied to me, John."

"I didn't —"

"You lied to me, and now I'm going to kill your family."

Kill my family?

"You can't be serious. Just —"

The line went dead.

But a split second before it did, John heard music.

"Für Elise."

Becca had Evie's music box.

Chapter Forty-Two

John called 9-1-1, blurted his emergency and home address, then got in his car and peeled into the street. He ran two red lights and made it home in three minutes.

The cops weren't there. John didn't hear a single siren.

He fumbled with his keys before remembering that they wouldn't do any good, then threw his shoulder against the front door for a long minute until it was throbbing and purple under his shirt. He clearly wouldn't be gaining entry that way.

He went around to the back, looked around until he saw a rock big enough that he'd need both of his hands to lift it, then hurled it through a window. Shards rained onto the floor. John waited a moment for the shower to settle, then he ducked inside.

"Vicky! Dakota!" he screamed. "Vicky! Dakota!"

He heard nothing.

Until he reached the living room.

And there he heard a whimper.

John wasn't sure if it came from his daughter or his

wife, but it scraped his insides and sent chills racing down his spine.

His children were nowhere to be seen.

Vicky stood in the living room, gagged, her hands bound in duct tape.

Becca stood behind her, a knife to her neck.

"I applaud your bravery, John. You got here fast. I was hoping that you would come instead of calling the police like a coward."

"I did call them. They're on their way."

"Of course you did. But you came, too. And now you get to see how this ends."

"Don't make this worse than it has to be," John said, not daring to edge a single step forward, knowing that Crazy could do anything it wanted, whenever it wanted, because the rules didn't apply.

"What can the cops do to me? I'll already be dead."

"You don't have to do this," he pleaded.

"I'm afraid that I do." Becca pressed the blade harder against Vicky's throat. A drop of blood kissed the metal. Vicky whimpered through her gag.

"Where are my children?"

Becca gave John the ugliest smile he'd ever seen. "Where do you think they are?"

The sirens started.

"Where are they?" he repeated, his voice breaking. "Tell me they're okay."

"They're dead! Just like she's going to be! None of this is 'okay,' John!"

Vicky screamed around her gag.

Something snapped inside John. Whatever made him human was gone. Because he couldn't be a man if he was going to kill a monster. And that's what this woman was. A demon beast who had stormed into his life, intent on ruining everything that he'd built.

"You lied to me, John. Now your wife and children know it. I wanted them to hear you tell me that we could be together. I thought it was important that that was the last thing they ever heard. Because —"

John rushed Becca and grabbed for her knife.

She pulled back, fast but startled. John had missed.

Vicky's screams were muffled, but the sirens were not. They sounded right on top of them.

John made another grab for the blade.

Becca pulled back again, but this time charged forward with an aggressive swing, blade slicing through the air, then slicing his arm in one long swipe, sending a spray of blood onto both women.

He cried out, though his mind barely registered the pain.

Free from Becca's grip, Vicky scrambled away.

Becca made it three steps before she tripped and toppled onto the floor, the knife slipping from her. She dived toward it.

John charged, screaming, rage fueling his every motion. He landed on top of Becca. She somehow got a hold of the blade and brought it up toward him.

He palmed the blade to prevent it from gutting him and it cut a ribbon of flesh from his right hand, causing him to fall back with a scream.

But not before more blood spilled onto Becca. Into her eyes and open mouth.

As she tried to stand, stumbling blindly and choking, his instincts kicked in and he punched her hard in the chest with his left hand.

Becca lost all her air. She dropped the knife and her hands went to her chest.

John shoved her as hard as he could, then grabbed the knife.

She scrambled backward on the floor, tried to stand, but John pushed her back down. He got on top of her and raised his blade overhead.

"No, John! I didn't —"

His rage was blind. He couldn't hear a word she said, even though he could clearly hear the squelch of the knife as it entered Becca's flesh, over and over and over.

"*You — killed — my — daughters!*" John screamed, punctuating every downward thrust until Becca stopped twitching and lay still.

Her screams stopped just before the sirens did.

The house was silent.

John looked up, hoping to see Vicky.

And he did — standing at the foot of the stairs next to Dakota and Evie.

His girls weren't dead.

They were unharmed and trembling, staring at him in terror, tears spilling down their faces. Even Evie's crying was practically silent.

"Drop the fucking knife!" John heard from somewhere behind him, or around him. Maybe everywhere. "Drop the fucking knife!"

He was surprised to hear himself laughing, because despite all the screaming and blood, despite the corpse on the floor, John knew that he would never have to hear Becca's laugh again.

Even if his family was destroyed, at least they were safe.

Chapter Forty-Three

John finished giving his statement to the officer, and all he could think was, *I couldn't make this shit up.*

For most of the time he was telling his side of the story, John kept thinking that *he* wouldn't have believed him. If this were one of his stories, there were quite a few things that he would have taken out or tweaked to be more believable.

John wondered what Vicky would say to the police. What Dakota would say. Their statements were, in some way, a declaration of how they felt about him. Was Becca the monster and he had come to save them? Or was he the biggest monster of all for inviting her into their lives, intentionally or not?

It didn't matter. As long as they were safe.

When John thanked the officer in charge for her time, she told him to not go too far — they weren't finished with him yet.

He went to his family, the three of them huddled together, still at the base of the stairs, nestled in gray blankets. Becca's body was to his right. Evie couldn't stop staring. Vicky turned Evie to look the other way.

John said, "I'm sorry."

As the words left his mouth, they sounded just as hollow as they were. Because even though John was sorry, nothing could ever make up for what he had done, or for the misery that he'd ushered into his family's lives.

His girls said nothing. Only Evie met his eyes, and her expression was glazed, confused.

"Is there anywhere else you can stay tonight?" the officer asked them. "We're going to need to process the crime scene." She turned to John after Vicky nodded. "You need to go down to the station to give some more details."

He nodded without a word and followed the officer.

Life, as John Treadwell knew it, was officially over.

Chapter Forty-Four

One year later

━━

John stood on his front porch, waiting for the door to open.

Except it wasn't his front porch anymore. It hadn't been for over a year now, since a few weeks before he'd left in the back of a cruiser headed downtown.

It wasn't the first time he'd waited on this porch with his heart at a gallop and sweat beading his brow. But at least this time the door was going to open. Eventually.

When it finally did, Dakota stood on the porch, hair and makeup turning her into someone much older than the little girl she'd been the last time they saw each other in person. She was wearing a beautiful dress, smiling awkwardly at him.

His entire body exhaled.

"Hi, Dad."

"Dakota." Then she gave him a tentative hug. "It's good to see you."

"You always see me."

"It's good to see *you*, not on Skype."

He kissed her on the top of the head before she pulled away. Valentine barked and charged up to the door.

"Back, Valentine!" Then, to John, "She's happy to see you."

"Do you think anyone else will be?" John smiled, but he felt the strain.

Dakota nodded but didn't say anything. She reached down with one hand and grabbed Valentine by the collar, opening the door all the way with the other. "You should probably come in."

John had rehearsed a hundred things he could say to Dakota once they saw each other in person. Still, he led with, "So, how are things?"

Evie ran into the room before he could answer. "I want to play *The Perfect Day*! I want to play *The Perfect Day*! I want to play *The Perfect Day*!" She ran past John, glanced up at him on her way past, and then kept on running, presumably to the kitchen. "I want to play *The Perfect Day*! I want to play *The Perfect Day*!"

"What's *The Perfect Day*?" John asked.

"Her favorite game."

"Sounds like it. How do you play?"

"Oh, we don't play. Only Evie plays. She just rambles for like five minutes at a time about all of her favorite things."

"Sounds delightful."

"Not so much."

A moment of silence. "So —"

"Please, Dad. Don't ask me how things are. I read *Barbados*."

"Oh? The first one?"

"I've read all four. I like them a lot. Each one more

than the last. It's trashy, like the stuff you did with Mom, but it sounds more like you. It's like you got your voice back. I'm really excited for the next project. Big thumbs up from me."

She smiled, but this was the first one that felt more like the sun. "Thanks, Dakota."

"You're a great writer, Dad. You just . . . did a really shitty thing."

Evie ran back through the living room yelling like Tarzan, disappeared down the hallway, then reappeared from the shadows in Vicky's arms. She carried Evie over to John and met his eyes. "Say hello to your father."

"Hi!"

"Hi, Evie," John said, hoping he'd manage not to cry.

"It's good to see you, John," Vicky said.

"Do you mean that?"

"I do." She set Evie back on the floor and gave him a hug. "I'm still ready to start."

"You're really serious about this?"

"Totally. I love what you've done with the *Barbados* series, and I love that you've gone indie. Is Sam giving you shit?"

"He says he's happy for me."

"Do you believe him?"

John laughed. "Only a little."

"You were always the better storyteller. I never felt more alive than when we were doing it together." She looked him in the eyes for the first time in more than a year. "I hate what you did, and it can never be like it was. Nothing will ever change my mind about that. But I do want to do *this*." She pointed toward what John was pleased to realize he still thought of as *their office*.

"I'm excited for this, too. And I can't wait to hear your ideas. Thank you for giving us . . . *this* another chance."

Another nod, kinder than he expected, then Vicky took Evie's hand and led her from the room.

"So," John said to Dakota. "Are you ready?"

"I am."

John held out his arm. She hooked hers through it, and they walked outside to the car together.

A year's changes had washed away the old to make way for the new in ways he could never have imagined. Not just with the insights into his life and craft and the evolution of what family would mean, but with another character added to the cast. Someone he now considered one of his best friends — a brand new sister named Caroline, from his father's secret family.

"When do I get to meet her?" Dakota asked.

"This summer, like I promised."

And now Dakota wanted to be a writer. She had always been so together, but this year had matured her even further. She was getting her thoughts on the page in impressive order. She wasn't *good* yet, but she would be.

After they decided to skip out on their overcooked spaghetti and instead stop for ice cream on the way home, John and Dakota found themselves on the floor at the Father-Daughter Dance, swaying to Springsteen's "When You Need Me."

"I'm sorry," he said.

"Stop it, Dad. It's okay. I don't want you to apologize. You've already done that plenty."

"I thought I could 'never do it enough.'"

"You already have. I'm sorry I said that."

They continued to dance without conversation. The song ended and John followed Dakota back to their seats at the now-empty table.

"I read your book," she said.

"You said that already. I'm glad."

"No." She held his eyes. "The real one."

A moment, then John knew he couldn't hide it. "How did you know?"

"Mom found it. She had no idea. It showed up in the Top 100 and she really liked the cover. She said that something about the pen name 'tickled the back of her brain,' but she didn't think too much about it. You know how Mom is, she has hundreds of books that she'll never read on her stupid Kindle. But something about that *Secrets We Keep* book kept calling to her. She said she knew it was you a paragraph in."

Stunned but hopeful, he said, "Do you know if she liked it?"

"She didn't finish it."

"How much did she read?"

"'Enough' is how she put it. I don't know what that means and she wouldn't tell me."

"I wrote that one for me. Adrian Novak had exactly one book in him, and that one book was never supposed to take off. I just needed a space to explain things . . . to myself."

"Don't you think you were a little obvious? Down to the fixer making the whole thing just disappear?"

John shrugged. "Names were changed to protect the guilty."

"Do you feel bad making so much money off of it? And how long has it stayed in the top one thousand?"

"Six months so far, and no, I have plenty to feel terrible about. That money is all yours and Evie's and your mother's. I'm glad I could make something good from so many mistakes. Is that why your mom wants to write with me again?"

"No, Dad. It's because she misses you. We all miss you.

Evie, too." She looked outside, then back at John. "Wanna go for a walk?"

"Definitely."

Outside, she said, "That story about Becca . . ."

"You mean Anna," he said, reminding her of the name he'd used in his book, a play on Annie Wilkes.

"Yeah, *Anna*. You said in the book that she was obsessed with you because something tragic happened to her as a kid, and she was prone to these obsessive situations where she created a whole other reality in her head. Was that what happened to Becca?"

"I don't know what happened to her."

"It's so hard to think of the Becca we knew versus the one who tried to destroy us. It's like they were two different people. I'd like to think that she couldn't help what happened."

"Maybe she couldn't," John said. "I might have felt pity for her, until she threatened my family. Any sympathy I had for her was gone that second."

"Do . . . do you regret . . . killing her?"

"I'd kill her again in a heartbeat if I thought she was going to harm any of you."

"You don't really think she would've hurt us, do you?"

"I don't know."

John felt tears welling up in his eyes, and he was glad it was dark outside. Killing her had affected him, more than he could ever really understand, let alone share with his daughter. He'd been in a blind rage when he ended her life, believing that she'd murdered his children. But with distance, he realized that she'd *wanted* him to kill her. She couldn't have him. He'd hurt her with his words, and so she did and said the one thing that would get to him.

She wanted to die at his hands. And that terrified him.

Part of him wondered if maybe she wouldn't have

really harmed Vicky. That maybe somebody else, like the cops, could've talked her down before he killed her. But another part of him was glad, if only because he knew she could never threaten his family again.

After the shit show, John's and Vicky's names were cleared in publishing circles. More stories came out about Becca and her family, every one of them tragic. Every one of them making John's version of events more believable.

John and Vicky's books had picked up steam — maybe people hoping to glean something more of the tragedy from their writing. John wasn't sure. There were still some people who thought he was an asshole who deserved everything he got, which was fair enough. There were even a few people who refused to think of Vicky as anything other than an unfit mother. But, for the most part, she had a lot of public sympathy and love, which made him feel at least a little bit better. He hadn't destroyed her career.

Dakota hugged him.

"So is that why you don't hate me? Because of the book?"

"I could never hate you, Dad. But at least now I understand. And I am glad that you wrote it . . . aren't you?"

"I am." John paused, thought, and inhaled the second chance that he still wasn't sure he deserved, feeling more alive than he had in a very long time. "I'm glad I wrote the book because I got all of the poison out from inside me. If I'd done that right when I got home from London, then I'd still have my family."

He took a deep breath. "It's the secrets we keep that kill us, and I'll never murder our future again."

Epilogue

John couldn't stop fidgeting through the entire flight.

But his nerves had nothing to do with being trapped in a metal tube flying high in the sky. And unlike those times when he'd flown a bit more than a year ago, his anxiety had nothing to do with secrets or lies. No deception of any kind.

This was the worst and best sort of angst, the kind that promised to change his life.

He wondered if he'd be attending the meeting alone, or if Vicky would be brave enough to show up.

He shuffled off of the plane, rolled his single piece of luggage through John Wayne Airport, and rode the escalator to the ground floor with a heart that refused to settle, knowing who he was minutes from seeing.

His driver was waiting as promised, holding up a sign: *John Treadwell.*

"That's me," John said, with a smile and a nod.

"Good to meet you," said the driver, extending her hand. "I'm Amber."

Amber tried to take his luggage, but John raised his

hand, palm out. "It's okay, really. I've managed to get it all the way here from New York on my own."

"It's my job. Please." He stifled a sigh and let her take the handle. "Ms. Treadwell is waiting."

His heart skipped. Even more than a year after the divorce, Vicky hadn't reclaimed her maiden name.

"Thanks," John said, then followed Amber to a Mercedes limo parked outside the terminal.

It was hard to believe that Vicky had boarded a plane by herself. She used to have nervous breakdowns whenever they traveled together. Not just during the trip, but before and after. Awful enough to keep her from going, or bad enough in the aftermath to make them both wish she hadn't.

Would it be his job to put her back together while Amber drove them to the meeting?

He hoped not. She'd seemed to stabilize after he'd moved out, and as they'd dipped their toes into writing again, they'd found a new rhythm, even better than their old working relationship. Slow at first, then faster, until soon enough they were sharing a beautiful routine of creation.

But after they finished what John referred to as a flash trilogy, and what Vicky called "the best goddamned shit we've ever written," she requested a three-month hiatus from their partnership to work on a project of her own.

He'd hated to stop and risk losing the momentum, but what could he say?

So they took another break while Vicky wrote behind a closed door. John continued to see Dakota on weekends, but he hadn't been in the same room with his ex in a quarter-year.

Amber opened the trunk, set his luggage inside it, then opened the limo door and gestured for John to enter.

Vicky smiled as he got into the car, Amber closing the door behind him.

She looked better than John had seen her in a long time. All things considered, maybe ever.

"You look great," he said.

That was an understatement. She was glowing. Her hair was fuller, and definitely longer. Pink cheeks, eyes bright, and probably at least ten pounds gone from her body. The Vicky he'd been married to hit the gym only when dragged there under duress, but this Vicky seemed to overflow with energy

"I feel great." Vicky smiled so wide that a laugh fell out, and it didn't sound like the kind she could have throttled if she wanted to. "The last three months have been great."

"I'll admit it, I've missed writing with you, but it's clearly been great for you, and that makes me happy."

"I needed it," Vicky said. "Now I understand why you always wanted to get back to writing on your own when we were working on the Murder series. I used to take that personally, but now I get it. So thank you, and I'm sorry."

"Not necessarily better, but different, right?"

Vicky nodded. "Maybe we could say, *necessarily different.*"

Then she laughed again, an inviting little twitter. He hadn't heard her laugh like that since they'd first dated. He loved it. And hated that being married to him had made something so lighthearted and beautiful go away.

"Was it hard? You know, the subject matter."

Vicky took a moment to think, then said, "Getting the words in was actually easy, once I was deep enough to mine them, but getting there was hard. But it's not like I could write about a mother's battle with depression without wrestling a few demons myself."

"Exactly." Then after a moment he ruefully added, "Our divorce was good for you."

"I don't know that I'd say *that* exactly."

"But it was, and it's okay to say it."

Because I was bad for you.

"Well, you too then, right? *Secrets We Keep* stuck to the bestseller list for months."

He smiled, because yes it did, and yes, that had been enough to feather his family's nest and help John to change his life. "Yes, that part of this has been great."

"I owe you an apology."

She did? "For what?"

"You weren't wrong . . . sometimes I didn't take my meds."

"Because of the way they made you feel?"

"Not just that." Vicky flushed, but didn't look away. "When you were stressed, you withdrew. Emotionally, I mean. I needed you, but I didn't want to. Skipping my pills . . . I knew you'd come back if I was in trouble."

He should've nodded and told her not to worry about it but his lips quirked up before he could stop them.

"Why are you smiling?"

"Because I knew that." He took her hand in his and gave it a gentle squeeze. "I understand."

The regret in Vicky's voice kicked hard enough to crack it. "I wish I'd been more honest with you while we were married."

John shook his head. "You're not the only one with regrets in that department."

Then they were both laughing, even though it wasn't a joke.

Vicky squeezed his hand back. "I wish we could go back and do it all over."

What was he supposed to say to that? *Let's get married*

again? He'd missed her so much, but even after a reboot, what would keep them from falling back into the same miserable pattern?

She looked down and slowly withdrew her hand. "It will never be the same again, will it?"

"We'll always have Paris."

That brought back the smile he'd been missing. *Casablanca* had always been their movie — he'd taken her to see it at the rundown dollar theater near her dorms on their first date.

"We'll always have Paris," Vicky agreed. "Any idea why they had us fly into Orange County?"

"Sam said that the Shellys wanted to meet at some fancy pants restaurant in Cielo del Mar."

"Do you know much about them?"

"Only that from everything I read before getting on the plane, they seem like they're every bit as big as Sam keeps promising."

"Is Sam still pissed at me?"

John shrugged. "I'm not sure that he was ever *pissed*. He does understand."

"Do you think Sam will accept my apology if it comes with a bottle of Glenfiddich?"

"I'm sure he won't refuse a bottle of Glenfiddich."

John loved that he could still make her laugh.

Soon, their limo pulled up to a posh shopping center called The Palms Couture.

"Are we really meeting these producers at a mall restaurant?" Vicky asked. But less than a minute later she saw the place, and whispered in awe, "It's stunning."

It was. A small spot overlooking the Pacific, packed with gorgeous white flowers wherever they looked. Roses and hydrangeas, Phalaenopsis orchids, floating gardenias and Casablanca lilies, the sweet richness of their perfume hanging heavy in the air.

They were greeted by a man in a suit more expensive than any John had ever owned. Matthew, he said his name was while leading them through the empty dining room and into a back room.

Sam was already there, along with Vicky's agent, Janine. Plus Dominic and Melinda Shelly.

A round of handshakes and polite but unnecessary introductions before they sat.

Dominic was large but not giant, handsome without distraction, and dripping with a self-assurance that somehow managed to edge arrogance without ever leaving a gentleman's poise. He got right to the point.

"We're in the process of buying out a small house called Trauma Productions. My wife and I are excellent at designing win-win scenarios. It might be what we do best. That's why all of our partners are happy, and why you will be too, if you choose to work with us. We're looking for content creators that can be the best in the world at whatever they do."

"What kind of content?" John asked.

Melinda nodded like he'd asked a brilliant question rather than the obvious one. "So far, Trauma has only produced horror, but Dominic and I are watching the trends and believe that they're competing in a saturated category instead of dominating a smaller yet emerging one."

"True crime!" Sam blurted.

"Right," Dominic said. "We'd like to turn them into America's number one source for people who love true crime, by creating an intelligent lineup of scripted shows and documentaries."

"That sounds interesting." Vicky's smile was as eager as her eyes. "How do you see us being involved?"

Melinda nodded. "Transmedia is the future, not just for Shellter Productions, but for media in general. It isn't enough to have the best shows, we want games and graphic novels, fiction series and serials."

"So we're offering you and John a contract to write books based on our most popular stories or characters," Dominic finished.

"Under a pen name," Melinda added. "Avery Roth."

"Why Avery Roth?" John asked.

Melinda said, "Market testing suggests that the name will appeal to our target audience. It's just sexy enough to intrigue male readers, and sassy enough for female readers to either identify with, or want to."

They were already market testing. That was a good sign, wasn't it? But with a female pen name, it would be awkward if the burden of public appearances fell to John because Vicky relapsed. He had to ask, "What kinds of promotion will you expect us to do?"

"You won't have to do a lick of marketing. You'll write, and you'll cash your royalty checks. Trauma will design and execute every campaign."

John shot a sideways glance at Sam. It sounded too good to be true. But his agent nodded and tapped the pile of papers in front of him. His signal to let John know that what was being said had been nailed down in the contract.

So maybe it was true.

John looked at the Shellys, not quite sure where to direct his question. "I'm not saying no, at all, but this isn't really our space. We write quickly because we're writing fiction. Not as much research or fact checking, so—"

"You won't have to worry about that," Sam cut in.

"Another one of my clients, Selena Nash, is available to consult."

Selena Nash, the serial killer expert? *Impressive.*

Vicky asked, "Do you expect us to move to Los Angeles?"

John couldn't stop his smile, or even hide it. The word *us* instead of *me* warmed him to the core.

"We wouldn't dream of uprooting your daughter," Melinda answered. "This is the twenty-first century, and you should be able to work from anywhere."

"The offer is so good," Sam joked, "I triple-checked it for asterisks."

"He's right," Janine agreed.

"We think that you two are perfect for Trauma. For the kinds of stories we want to tell there, and in the style we most want to tell them." Dominic looked at his wife, as if waiting for her to take an invisible mic.

"We take care of our people," Melinda said. "You'll have whatever you need to do your best work."

It would be perfect, John thought. If Vicky was willing to commit to working with him. Not just by passing drafts back and forth, like they had been for the past year. If she couldn't stomach the thought of spending a day in the same room with him while they brainstormed . . .

"Could I have a moment alone with my co-author?"

Dominic grinned as though sure that John would say yes. "By all means."

Vicky followed him into the main dining area, still empty.

"I'm in if you are," she said the second they were out of earshot.

"Are you sure? This is going to be even more intense than writing our series. Tighter deadlines. More restrictions on how we tell the story. Collaborating with the team making the shows."

But instead of collapsing like the old Vicky would have, this one brightened with barely-repressed hope. "We weren't so good as husband and wife. But I think we'll be great as business partners. If you're willing to give it a shot?"

How many people got a second chance like this? John felt like his heart might explode, this time with happiness.

"Vicky, I think this is the beginning of a beautiful friendship."

The End

What To Read Next

SICK MINDS THINK ALIKE

Profiler Selena Nash is America's #1 expert on serial killers. No one knows it's all based on a mistake she'll never admit. But when a serial killer strikes her hometown, she knows the message is for her. Can Selena decode the killer's taunts in time to save her family?

A Quick Favor ...

If you enjoyed this book, please take a moment to write a review on your favorite bookselling site so other readers can enjoy it too. It would mean a lot to me.

Thank you,
Nolon King

About the Author

Nolon King writes fast-paced psychological thrillers set in the glitzy world of entertainment's power players with a bold, insightful voice. He's not afraid to explore the darker side of human nature through stories featuring families torn apart by secrets and lies.

Nolon loves to write about big questions and moral quandaries. How far would you go to cover up an honest mistake? Would you destroy your career to protect your family? How much of your soul would you sell to get the life of your dreams? Would you cheat on your husband to keep your children safe? Would you give in to a stalker's demands to save your marriage?

Also By Nolon King

Cold Vengeance

Cold Vengeance

Cold Reckoning

Hidden Justice

Hidden Justice

Hidden Honor

Hidden Shame

Hidden Virtue

No Justice

No Justice

No Escape

No Hope

No Return

No Stopping

No Fear

Once Upon A Crime

Once Upon A Crime

Twice Upon A Lie

Three Times a Murder

Dead For Good

Dead For Good

Left For Dead

Dead Of Night

Wake The Dead

Dead For Life

Stand Alone Novels

Pretty Killer

12

Blown

Miserable Lies

The Target

Secrets We Keep

Close To Home

Heat To Obsession

A Simple Kill

Tell Me No Lies

Red Carpet Black

Fade To Black

Victim